THE PRIME SUSPECT

Sarah sighed. Her sister was the queen of avoidance. "RahRah and I are staying out of your way so you can do your Julia Child/Rachael Ray thing." RahRah jumped up onto her shoulder and draped himself around the back of Sarah's neck. "So are you going to tell me what happened tonight?"

"I wish I knew," Emily muttered from back in the depths of the refrigerator. "Even though it's too early for him to know anything for sure, Peter said Bill apparently ate a forkful of rhubarb crisp that killed him."

"That doesn't prove Bill was murdered."

"I agree. Besides, if rhubarb crisp is what killed him, it couldn't have been mine. It would have had to be someone else's. You know as well as I do, Bill never touched my rhubarb crisp because I always use nuts in the recipe."

"Don't worry. I'll tell Peter the same thing. After all, I was married to Bill for enough years to know which of your recipes he wouldn't go near."

"Thanks. I hope you don't have to vouch for me." Emily leaned against the now-closed refrigerator and used her free hand to tuck an escaping strand of blond hair back under her towel turban.

"To tell you the truth, I have a bad feeling about this," Emily said. "The way Peter looked at me when I told him about someone else being in the Civic Center was like he wa̲ ̲ ̲ ̲ing me. I'm telling you, he believes I killed ̲ ̲ ̲

<u>BOOK YOUR PLACE ON OUR WEBSITE</u>
<u>AND MAKE THE</u>
<u>READING CONNECTION!</u>

We've created a customized website just for our very special readers, where you can get the inside scoop on everything that's going on with Zebra, Pinnacle and Kensington books.

When you come online, you'll have the exciting opportunity to:

- View covers of upcoming books
- Read sample chapters
- Learn about our future publishing schedule (listed by publication month and author)
- Find out when your favorite authors will be visiting a city near you
- Search for and order backlist books from our online catalog
- Check out author bios and background information
- Send e-mail to your favorite authors
- Meet the Kensington staff online
- Join us in weekly chats with authors, readers and other guests
- Get writing guidelines
- AND MUCH MORE!

**Visit our website at
http://www.kensingtonbooks.com**

ONE TASTE
TOO MANY

Debra H. Goldstein

𝆎

KENSINGTON BOOKS
KENSINGTON PUBLISHING CORP.
www.kensingtonbooks.com

KENSINGTON BOOKS are published by

Kensington Publishing Corp.
119 West 40th Street
New York, NY 10018

All Kensington titles, imprints, and distributed lines are available at special quantity discounts for bulk purchases for sales promotion, premiums, fund-raising, educational, or institutional use.

Special book excerpts or customized printings can also be created to fit specific needs. For details, write or phone the office of the Kensington Sales Manager: Attn.: Sales Department. Kensington Publishing Corp., 119 West 40th Street, New York, NY 10018. Phone: 1-800-221-2647.

Kensington and the K logo Reg. U.S. Pat. & TM Off.

First Printing: January 2019
ISBN-13: 978-1-4967-1947-8
ISBN-10: 1-4967-1947-6

ISBN-13: 978-1-4967-1950-8 (eBook)
ISBN-10: 1-4967-1950-6 (eBook)

10 9 8 7 6 5 4 3 2 1

Printed in the United States of America

To Joel, with love

ACKNOWLEDGMENTS

Introducing a new series to the world is fun, but frightening. The Sarah Blair series went outside my comfort zone of lawyers and judges and embraced unfamiliar concepts like using the kitchen as more than a pleasant room to walk through when going from the garage to the den. Consequently, many people helped me find my way on this journey. Their encouragement and knowledge made this series possible, but any errors are my own.

I am thankful to friends Fran and Lee Godchaux, T.K. Thorne, Susan Robinson Bauer, Judi Schulman-Miller, and Jean Felts for reading many different versions of the book, educating me on topics ranging from pace to the behavior of cats, and giving me the encouragement to bring Sarah Blair to life. Editors Barb Goffman and Lourdes Venard made me expand my thinking and the dimensions of Sarah and her friends and family. Elizabeth Hutchins, using her expertise as a trusts and estates attorney, jumped on the bandwagon to research and explain animal trusts and how Alabama law has changed in respect to them.

A special thanks to my agent, Dawn Dowdle, for her support and work on my behalf and to John Scognamiglio, my Kensington editor, who has the vision to see where the Sarah Blair mystery series and my writing career can go.

I began this book with a dedication to my husband, Joel. It is only fitting to conclude the acknowledgments with him because Joel has been my love and my cheerleader for the entire journey creating Sarah Blair.

Chapter One

"Bill's dead and, uh, I'm afraid the police think I killed him."

Sarah Blair stared at the cell phone in her hand. She could not believe the words she had just heard over it. *Bill cannot be dead.* He was her ex-husband, but like the cat he let her keep after their divorce, she always thought William Taft Blair had nine lives. And what did Emily mean that the police thought *she* had killed him? No way her twin sister could have done anything like that!

Sure, Emily wielded a cleaver with deft precision in her job as a line cook and she'd threatened Bill a few times over his treatment of Sarah during their marriage and divorce, but Sarah refused to believe Emily could or would murder anyone.

"We were at the Civic Center. I tried to save him, but I couldn't." Emily's voice cracked in a way Sarah knew tears were threatening.

"What were the two of you doing at the Civic Center after midnight?"

"The Food Expo, but that doesn't matter now. I'm at the police station. Please, come."

The call ended before Sarah could ask any of the questions still racing through her brain. The only thing she was certain of was Emily needed her.

She swung her lanky legs over the side of her bed and grabbed her jeans from the floor. It couldn't be. At thirty-four, six years older than her, Bill was too young to die. He still had so much to do and so many more people to double-cross. She doubted she would ever know how many people, besides her, he'd hurt in Wheaton.

Bill might have had a presidential name, but he lacked any presidential qualities. She poked her foot under her bed, trying to find her shoes, among the scattered college brochures. Moving her foot over a few inches, Sarah successfully hooked a shoe with her toes.

Feeling sick to her stomach, she sat down hard on her bed, disturbing her cat's carefully constructed burrow in the quilt. RahRah stretched one tan paw into the air. Sarah put her hand on his back, but he squirmed away and jumped off the bed. She was tempted to follow him for a quick comforting hug. Instead, she pulled a purple sweater from the remaining pile of clothing on the floor and yanked it over her head.

"RahRah, what could possibly possess Emily to be at the police station without a lawyer? Didn't she learn anything all those years I made her watch *Perry Mason?*"

RahRah blinked but didn't purr.

"So, you agree with me. If Em isn't a suspect, they would have taken her statement during normal business hours."

Sarah stuffed her other foot into its shoe and made up her mind. Whether Emily wanted it or not, she wasn't going to let her sit in jail without representation. She dug her phone from beneath the covers, glanced at the time on its face, and scrolled to her boss's number.

Hopefully, Harlan was home, alone, and willing to help his receptionist's sister.

Chapter Two

Sarah dug her fingernails deeper into the leather handle of Harlan's briefcase. Less than forty minutes had elapsed between Emily's call and Harlan and Sarah's arrival at the police station. Now they had been waiting almost the same amount of time to see Emily.

If she were in charge, Sarah would have already grabbed the portly officer manning the desk by his lapels and demanded he tell her where her sister was. Instead, Sarah forced herself to do what she'd promised her boss in the car—keep quiet and carry the briefcase.

"Harlan, I just relieved the desk man." The officer took a sip of his coffee. "I'm not sure who's here and who's not. Don't see anything with her name on it." He waved his hands at the papers strewn on his desk and rumpled a few.

Sarah tightened her grasp on the briefcase's handle. A ridge in the leather cut into her hand but she ignored it. Offices and other unguarded rooms were on this floor. Unless her sister was arrested, she couldn't be too far away.

Harlan leaned forward and placed one manicured hand on the desk man's computer screen and the other near the telephone on the desk. "Using one of these probably would be faster."

The officer grunted but picked up his phone. He punched in a few numbers. "Emily? Emily Johnson?" He glanced at Harlan, who nodded. The officer cocked his thumb over his left shoulder. "Second door to the right."

Harlan started down the beige hall, with Sarah behind him.

"Hey," the desk man's voice followed them, "where do you think she's going?"

Sarah froze, but Harlan reached back for her elbow and tugged her forward. "She's part of my legal team."

He kept walking.

Keeping up with his brisk pace, Sarah hoped the desk officer didn't see her smile. Harlan's instant promotion from his law firm receptionist to a member of his legal team amused her, despite the situation. Not bad for someone whose education ended when she got married a week out of high school.

When Harlan stopped in front of a wooden door, Sarah stared from her higher vantage point at the balding spot atop Harlan's head. She was surprised, as usual, to see it. Unless she was standing beside him, he always seemed taller than her and far younger than thirty-eight. She stood back as he rapped on the door and opened it without waiting for an answer.

From the doorway, Sarah saw Emily seated at a gunmetal-gray table. A pad, pen, Diet Coke can, and a cup of coffee were the only things in front of her.

Peter Mueller, the Wheaton police chief, sat across from Emily.

Sarah realized that, except for campaign advertisements on television or in the newspaper, she hadn't seen him since he graduated from their Birmingham high school a couple of years ahead of her. Obviously, moving to nearby Wheaton, Alabama, had been a good career move.

The rising level of Emily's voice brought Sarah's focus back to Emily. "There was somebody else in the Civic Center."

"Who?" Peter asked.

"I don't know. I was giving Bill CPR when I heard someone and called out for help."

Sarah stared at Emily's hands unconsciously pantomiming administering CPR. They were, like the top of Emily's blouse, visible above the table and stained with red splotches. "Em, you're bleeding!"

"Relax. It's rhubarb," Peter said.

"Rhubarb?"

Emily glanced at her blouse and hands. Spreading her red-stained fingers, she giggled. "Peter thinks it's rhubarb from one of my rhubarb crisps. He doesn't believe Bill wouldn't have touched, let alone eaten, one of mine. I keep telling him . . ."

Sarah raised her hand. "Em, don't say another word. I brought Harlan with me."

She opened her mouth, but before she could say anything more, something sharp jammed into Sarah's side, shoving her into Harlan. He grabbed Sarah's arm and steadied her as a bottle-tinted redhead, the desk officer on her heels, barreled past them, straight toward Emily. Sarah recognized the iron-hipped woman as Jane Clark, a line cook Emily worked with and Bill's latest bimbo.

"You, you killed him!" Jane yelled. "You killed Bill so he wouldn't throw you out of the restaurant."

The desk man grabbed for Jane, catching her arm, but the dynamo twisted free. She lunged at Emily, nails extended to scratch her face.

"Jane, stop it!" Emily sidestepped.

Peter and the other officer wrestled the angry woman into the chair where Emily had sat.

Sarah rushed to her sister's side and gingerly touched her twin's cheek, relieved the skin appeared to be intact.

"Jane," Emily said, "are you crazy?"

The redhead glared at Emily and Sarah, tears in her eyes, as the police officers slowly released their grasp of her arms. Neither moved from her side.

"What's going on here?" Peter said.

Jane pointed to Emily. "I caught her rifling through Southwind's business records last week and told Bill what she'd been doing. He was furious and assured me he'd have her kicked out of the Food Expo. Bill swore she'd never work at Southwind or any other upscale restaurant again."

Emily hesitated. "You don't know what you're talking about, Jane."

Sarah stared at Emily. The idea of Em searching through private business records didn't make sense. Besides, even if she went through some Southwind files, why would Bill care? As chairman of the Civic Center, Bill would justifiably have exploded if Emily or anyone messed with his pet project, the Food Expo, but there was no personal connection between Bill and the restaurant where Emily worked, at least that Sarah knew about. Certainly, the rat wouldn't deliberately hurt his former sister-in-law simply to appease his girlfriend of the week. Could Bill possibly have sunk that low?

Peter nodded at the officer and the door. "Please escort Ms. Clark to room three." He turned his attention to the furious redhead. "Jane, go with him. I'll be there in a few minutes to discuss this with you."

Jane scowled at him but stood and started toward the door. The desk officer trailed, his hand firmly on her arm. Passing Sarah, Jane stopped so abruptly the officer almost tripped over her heels.

"Cat thief," she hissed.

Jane's spittle sprayed across Sarah's cheek. She forced herself not to touch her face until after the officer had guided Jane from the room. Cat thief? What in the world was Jane talking about?

When the metal door closed, Sarah put her arms around her trembling sister and held her tightly, their long, dark and light hair entwined.

"Bill's really dead?" Sarah asked.

Emily nodded.

Sarah wanted to quiz her twin about what was going on but thought it best to wait. She couldn't read the line over her sister's brow but knew Emily's usually buoyant energy had leaked out like a deflated balloon at Jane's mention of the Food Expo and Southwind.

Jane's accusation couldn't be true. Yes, Emily had thought and said unkind things about Bill during the divorce proceedings—as any loyal sister would—but Emily could never kill anyone, even Bill. She was too much of a straight arrow. Besides, when it came to the restaurant business, Emily was a true professional. She'd never do anything to risk her career.

From her first baby steps, Emily had been their mother's shadow in the kitchen. She'd continued her singular focus, skipping college to attend the culinary institute and work her way up the chef ladder at restaurants in Birmingham, San Francisco, and now, Wheaton. Sarah knew how important working under Southwind's Chef Marcus was to Emily. If it wasn't, Emily would never have come back to Wheaton. No, there was absolutely no way Emily would have done anything to undermine her upcoming chance to be promoted from line cook to sous chef.

"Let's get back to talking about what happened." Peter's voice made it clear his role was more police chief than old friend.

Sarah looked at him more closely. He'd only gained a few pounds and his hair and eyes were still dark, but deep lines were etched into his forehead.

Harlan retrieved his briefcase from the floor, where Sarah had dropped it, and placed it precisely on the table. "I'm representing Emily. I'm advising her not to say anything more until we have a chance to talk."

Peter frowned. "Harlan, you know it's proper protocol for me to get a statement from anyone who witnessed a crime or its aftermath."

"What makes you think this was a crime? People have heart attacks, seizures, and strokes all the time."

Sarah listened to the two volley back and forth, with Emily in the middle. She glanced at Peter.

"You're probably right," Peter said, "but I won't know until I get the autopsy and tox reports back. In the meantime, this late at night, when I find a body covered in rhubarb, clutching a fork and not breathing, I tend to think in terms of a crime scene."

"I've got nothing to hide. Bill was already—" Emily began.

Harlan rested his hand on her arm, stopping her, and said in his neatly clipped voice, "I need to speak with my client. Besides, you don't even know if there is a crime."

Sarah nodded in agreement, but her stomach sank at Peter's expression. Somehow, he knew.

She'd gotten to know Peter during high school when he came around to visit Emily, who usually was either at cheerleading practice or out with the more popular boys. He never acted without considering things from all angles. If Peter didn't think Bill died from a heart attack or a stroke, there must be some sign of poisoning or a wound that convinced him Bill was murdered. Unfortunately, from what she'd overheard Emily telling Peter, if this was his conclusion, the only person he'd found in the locked Civic Center with Bill was rhubarb-covered Emily.

Chapter Three

"There's nothing I couldn't have said while Peter was in here. I didn't do anything."

"Emily, humor me. I can't do a good job representing you if I don't have the facts." Harlan pulled two pads from his briefcase and gestured toward a chair with the one he handed Sarah. "Take notes. You're part of my team today."

Sarah slid into the chair, staring, as was Harlan, at her twin.

"Now, Emily," Harlan said. "Why don't you tell us how you got covered in rhubarb?"

Emily looked at her blouse and then at her hands. Staring at them, she began to laugh uncontrollably. She held her hands up and waved her fingers, then grew more serious as she began to talk. "I guess I got it all over me when I gave Bill CPR."

"CPR?" Harlan sat beside Sarah and made a note on his legal pad. "Why don't you start at the beginning?"

"Bill called me to come to the Civic Center."

"You? In the middle of the night? Why?" Sarah asked.

Emily gazed at her hands. "I was getting ready for bed, so it was just before midnight when he called and told me there was a problem at the Civic Center. He wanted me to come immediately."

"And you went?" Harlan waited, pen posed in the air.

"Of course. What choice did I have? He was head of the Expo and part owner of Southwind."

"What?" Sarah stared at her sister.

Emily avoided making eye contact with her.

"You two can discuss that later." Harlan seemed to ignore the exchange between the sisters. "Right now, I need to know exactly what happened tonight. Emily?"

"I told you, Bill called and I went to the Civic Center. His car was the only one in the front parking lot. I parked mine next to his and went up to the main entrance. The glass doors were locked, so I used my passkey to get in."

"Could you see him or anything through the glass doors?"

"No. The main lights were off. Once I let myself in, the Civic Center's emergency lights shone enough for me to make my way through the aisles in the main exhibition room to look for Bill."

"Aisles?"

"Right. The booths for the Food Expo were set up yesterday so the room is now divided into four rows of stalls. Each row has a central walking aisle, except for the booths in the middle of the room. Those face an eating area and open space in front of a stage. When I neared the second aisle, I called out to Bill again, but there was no answer."

Sarah stared at her sister. "Why didn't you just leave?"

"I couldn't. I didn't want to make Bill mad. So I worked my way toward the center of the room, where the Southwind booth is adjacent to the food court area." Emily put her head into her hands.

When she raised her head, tears escaped the corners of her eyes. "He was lying in front of the Southwind booth. I yelled his name and ran to him. He didn't move. He just lay there, holding a fork, sprawled on his back next to a smashed rhubarb pie."

"Did you touch him?" Harlan asked.

"Yes. He was so still. I felt his neck to see if he was dead or alive."

"And?"

"I wasn't sure, so I called nine-one-one and started giving him CPR, like they taught us in Girl Scouts." Emily glanced at Sarah. "Or at least taught most of us."

Sarah leaned forward. This wasn't the time to remember their respective Girl Scout experiences. "You mentioned someone else was in the Civic Center with you?"

"Yes. I didn't realize it then, though. I was too busy trying to help Bill."

Seeing the color drain from her sister's face, Sarah put her hand on her sister's. "Tell me."

"Except for where there were emergency lights, it was dark and quiet. I cupped my hands over his chest and pushed, counting the compressions in my head. When I got to one hundred, I felt his neck again and checked if his chest was moving. Nothing. I put my face over his to see if I could feel any breath on my cheek. I couldn't."

Emily's gaze was still directed at her, but Sarah got the feeling she wasn't what Emily was seeing.

"Remember how we used to kid that the line of his jaw was always stiff? Well, when I rocked back on my knees, I noticed it was more set than usual. I looked at my hands and realized the rhubarb from his shirt was on me, too."

"How did you know it was rhubarb, not blood?" Harlan said.

"I guess by smell and feel and seeing rhubarb crisp all over the place." She shook her head. "Harlan, I honestly never thought about blood. What passed through my mind for a moment was wondering if the dry cleaner would be able to get the stains out of his shirt. It was one of those white, starched, monogrammed ones. Considering the situation, I threw that idea out of my mind and began pressing and counting again. I stopped when I heard someone else."

Harlan raised his hand. "Could it have been one of the emergency responders? Surely they must have gotten there by then?"

"Absolutely not. They didn't get there until later. When they did, I had to let them in through the front door. From the sound, this person stumbled into something in one of the aisles behind me."

"If you heard someone, why didn't you go find the person?" Sarah asked.

"I couldn't leave Bill, but I shouted 'Help! Please help us!' The *click* of the Civic Center's back door was the only answer to my plea."

Chapter Four

Sarah sat Indian-style on the floor of her apartment. At three thirty in the morning, she was happy to let Emily, in a borrowed oxford cloth shirt and rolled-up jeans, check out her refrigerator while she stroked her Siamese cat's soft fur. Although RahRah's purr wasn't audible, contentment vibrated through his body.

Emily tightened the towel wrapped around her wet hair. "It was great Harlan convinced Peter to deal with Jane tonight, or should I say this morning, and let me come back at ten to give my statement." She peered into the refrigerator. "Spaghetti, nail polish, eggs . . . don't you ever go grocery shopping?"

"I've been meaning to make a run."

"Well, I'm starved. Let's see what I can do with what you have." Emily pulled a carton of eggs from the refrigerator and checked its date stamp. "Great. By the way, these passed their last day to be sold two weeks ago." She rummaged farther in the refrigerator. "Do you have any kale or spinach?"

Sarah couldn't believe Emily was more worried about food dates and healthy eating than the fact Bill was dead. Maybe she was traumatized? Perhaps she was avoiding talking about Bill's death for another reason? After all, Emily was the one who found Bill, and she'd never shied away from voicing her opinion of him during Sarah's divorce. Perhaps she was afraid of being Peter's prime suspect.

"Em," Sarah said, "we've got to talk about tonight. Why were you at the Civic Center so late?"

"To meet Bill. He is . . . was chairman of the Civic Center."

Sarah fought not to roll her eyes. She might have divorced Bill, but she hadn't lost track of his roles with the Economic Development Council and Civic Center. "That doesn't explain why you were there so late to meet him."

Emily opened another drawer in the refrigerator. "Do you have any vegetables?"

"They're on my list." Sarah watched her sister examine the milk and cheese packaging for their expiration dates. She wondered how long Emily would delay addressing her question. Sarah's efficiency apartment didn't have much room beyond the refrigerator for Emily to hide.

"Is my food safe?"

"Barely, but I think we have enough for me to whip up an omelet."

"You should be thrilled you found more than spaghetti and nail polish in there. Besides, you got a shower *and* you didn't have to go home and explain to Mom what you've been doing tonight. You know she would demand every last detail."

"Point taken, except your last argument is moot. Mom left yesterday for that Mexican spa. Can you imagine spending a week in a place without Internet, news, or telephones?"

Sarah instinctively glanced at her cell phone on the floor next to RahRah. "No, I can't." She pulled RahRah closer. "Then again, I'm not sure I want to see the local news."

"Me either." Emily hesitated. "Nothing about tonight seems real."

She began bustling around the kitchen. "Why are you still sitting there? I thought you said you were hungry, too." She went back to the refrigerator searching for another ingredient.

Sarah sighed. Her sister was the queen of avoidance. "RahRah and I are staying out of your way so you can do your Julia Child/Rachael Ray thing." RahRah jumped up onto her shoulder and draped himself around the back of Sarah's neck. "So are you going to tell me what happened tonight?"

"I wish I knew," Emily muttered from back in the depths of the refrigerator. "Even though it's too early for him to know anything for sure, Peter said Bill apparently ate a forkful of rhubarb crisp that killed him."

"That doesn't prove Bill was murdered."

"I agree. Besides, if rhubarb crisp is what killed him, it couldn't have been mine. It would have had to be someone else's. You know as well as I do, Bill never touched my rhubarb crisp because I always use nuts in the recipe."

"Don't worry. I'll tell Peter the same thing. After all, I was married to Bill for enough years to know which of your recipes he wouldn't go near."

"Thanks. I hope you don't have to vouch for me." Emily leaned against the now-closed refrigerator and used her free hand to tuck an escaping strand of blond hair back under her towel turban.

"To tell you the truth, I have a bad feeling about

this," Emily said. "The way Peter looked at me when I told him about someone else being in the Civic Center was like he was humoring me. I'm telling you, he believes I killed Bill."

"Aw, come on. That's not like Peter. He's always been a fair guy." She yawned and stared at her twin. "Is there some reason for Peter to suspect you?"

"Absolutely not."

"What about what Jane was accusing you of? Rifling through records? Bill being able to somehow get you kicked out of the Expo and fired from Southwind?"

Emily frowned. "Sarah, Southwind and this expo are important to my career. You know how much I've been looking forward to the next four days. It's more important than ever because if I don't make a good impression with my food, Jane or one of the other Southwind cooks has a chance to slip past me for the sous chef spot that recently opened."

Sarah watched her sister put a frying pan on the burner. If winning the competition and showing well was so important to selecting the next sous chef, who could say the rat wouldn't have tried to interfere on behalf of his bimbo. "You know, if Peter thinks you felt Bill somehow stood in the way of you advancing your career, he might view that as a motive for murder."

"Surely Peter knows I'd never kill over a job."

Sarah flipped her left palm up in an "I don't know" gesture.

"Crap." Emily opened the partially filled egg carton. "If Peter suspects me, he'll probably want to question me for more than a few minutes today. With the Expo opening Friday night, today, I need to get things ready at the Civic Center and at the restaurant instead of being stuck at the police station."

She took an egg from the carton. "We have to find him someone else to investigate."

"And how do you propose we do that? I don't think I've seen this scenario on any of the TV shows I've watched recently."

Using one hand, Emily cracked the first egg into a bowl. She tossed the shell back into the egg container and started to reach for another egg but stopped. "The Civic Center is the most logical place for us to start looking for another suspect."

Sarah didn't quite follow Emily's reasoning, but she waited for her sister to explain.

"Bill died there, so that's the first place for us to look for answers. Between giving my statement to Peter and prepping for the Food Expo, I won't have much time to snoop around, but you could."

Sarah started to protest, but Emily kept talking.

From experience, Sarah knew Emily's flushed face and rushed words were dead giveaways the wheels of her brain were whirling. "It's simple. I know you must work today and tomorrow, but after work Friday and for the rest of the weekend, you can pretend to be my assistant. That way, no one will question you being anywhere in the Expo area."

Emily's assistant? Was she kidding? "Em, I'm a true believer in being a supportive sister, but you know me when it comes to the kitchen. Don't you remember my wedding shower? My friends subtitled it 'Can She Identify What's in the Box?' When I opened the beautiful floral print paper plates and napkins and held them up, you were the one who quipped, 'Oh, look. She got her good china.'"

"Don't worry. You won't be cooking. Much. Just pretending to help. It will be easy. All you have to do is fake a few things."

A feeling of doom joined the hunger pains in Sarah's stomach. She extricated herself from RahRah and washed her hands, hoping whatever Emily was concocting for the demonstration really didn't require much time in the Expo kitchen but, in case, Sarah said a prayer she wouldn't accidently blow the Civic Center up with her culinary skills. "Perhaps we should rethink this. I could probably snoop better in a trench coat than an apron."

"No, it's foolproof. Everyone knows the Southwind staff is stretched thin between the restaurant and the Expo, so nobody will be suspicious I asked you to help out in our booth."

"Maybe not, but they're going to question your sanity level when they see how I function in the kitchen. Have you forgotten that while Mom was teaching you to cook, I was watching *Perry Mason*? I only visited the kitchen to empty the dishwasher during the first commercial, set the table during the second, and eat dinner right after the confession."

"Not a problem." Emily held an egg out toward Sarah. "I'll tell them you need a little extra cash and this is my way of helping you out."

"How saintly." Sarah didn't take the egg. She didn't want to admit the truth behind Emily's statement. If she hoped to go back to school, even part-time, anything she could squirrel away would help.

"Really, it's a perfect cover. You'll be able to move around freely during the Expo."

"Why don't I just wear a sign: 'I'll Work for Food or Money'?"

"Don't be silly." Emily proffered the egg again. "Folks know things have been tight for you since your divorce, so they won't be surprised I'm giving you a part-time job. They'll be too busy whispering behind your back to consider you're snooping. Now, take this egg. You need to learn how to break it with one hand."

"Huh? Two has always worked for me."

"Two isn't as fast and doesn't look professional." Emily gave the egg in her hand to Sarah and selected another one from the box. "First, grasp it with all of your fingers. No, look at how I'm putting my fingers. My thumb and first finger are holding one end while my second and third fingers press the other end into the heel of my palm."

She held her egg so Sarah could mimic her motions but jumped back as Sarah squeezed her egg so tightly it burst across the counter. "Em, if I can't even break an egg, how will I convince anyone I'm a cook? Maybe I need another cover?"

Emily tore off a piece of paper towel and cleaned up Sarah's mess. "Don't worry. We have enough eggs for you to learn this."

Sarah carefully hit another egg against the edge of the frying pan. A broken line appeared in it.

"That's good," Emily said. "Now, without moving your thumb and index finger ease the egg apart on both sides of the crack and let the yolk drop into this bowl."

Sarah pressed her lips together. She released them into a smile as her yolk fell perfectly into the bowl. "That wasn't as bad as I thought it would be."

"Of course it wasn't. Now try again."

Sarah made a face but picked up another egg.

Emily turned a chair from the table so she could sit astride it and watch Sarah work.

"Why did Bill ask you to meet him so late? Why not Chef Marcus?"

Emily got up and turned her back toward Sarah as she filled a measuring cup with water from the sink.

"Em?"

"Southwind has the Civic Center contract, but Chef Marcus made me the liaison between the restaurant and the Civic Center. Tonight, when Bill phoned and told me there was a problem at the Civic Center, it was my job to respond."

Emily put the measuring cup near Sarah's bowl of eggs. She looked down and ran her finger around the cup's rim. She finally raised her eyes to meet Sarah's gaze. "Like I told Harlan at the police station, Chef Marcus ran into financial difficulties and Bill bailed him out in exchange for a partnership interest. He also pulled the strings for Southwind to receive the Civic Center's catering contract."

Sarah stopped, letting the white drip from the egg she'd just cracked. "I don't understand. Why didn't you tell me? Did it slip your mind?" She dropped the egg in her hand into the trash and wiped her hand on her jeans.

"I didn't know Bill was involved with Southwind when I first came back." Emily poured a drop of water from the measuring cup into the bowl with the eggs. "By the way, always add a dash of water. The steam of the water will rise when it cooks, making the eggs light and airy."

Sarah stared at her twin. She could feel steam rising somewhere besides the frying pan. "You may not have known when you took the job, but you obviously found out a while ago."

Emily didn't say or do anything to deny Sarah's accusation.

"Once you knew, how could you work at a restaurant

funded by Bill? I thought, after my divorce, your loyalty was to me."

"It was and still is. Honestly, by the time I knew, it didn't seem important." She busied herself pouring the egg mixture into the pan, adding cheese and finishing their omelet. Dividing the finished omelet in two, Emily placed the portions on two plates. "Salt and pepper to your taste."

As Emily swallowed a forkful of her omelet, Sarah put her plate back on the counter. Not important? How could Emily act so casually when Sarah felt so betrayed? "I still don't understand why you never told me."

"For just this reason. I didn't want to upset you. Plus, I was afraid if you knew Chef Marcus sold Bill a piece of the action to pay off his debts and they planned to move Southwind from the shopping center into one of the old houses on Main Street, you'd ask me to quit. By that point, I loved Southwind and didn't want to leave."

A tear slipped down Emily's cheek. "Honestly, if I'd known Bill was part of the operation when I was offered the job, I wouldn't have touched it with a ten-foot pole."

Emily pointed at Sarah's plate. "Your eggs are going to get cold."

Sarah picked up her fork and swallowed a forkful of omelet. She understood her sister's motivation, but something bothered her. She thought for a minute and then realized it was the repeated use of the word *honestly*. If someone told you his actions were honest, her father taught her, you could bet something wasn't on the up-and-up.

Chapter Five

Barely four hours later, RahRah rolled onto his side on the blanket next to Sarah. Sometime during the few hours she'd slept, he'd jumped onto the double bed and pressed himself between Sarah and a still softly snoring Emily. He licked a paw. His fifteen pounds felt good to Sarah, offsetting the chill that had settled between the twins.

Their disagreement replayed itself in Sarah's mind. She was guilty of harping on Bill's involvement with Southwind. Because it had been so late and there was no way to get away from each other in the apartment's cramped space, they'd called a silent truce and gone to bed. Emily's breathing quickly became a steady in-and-out rhythm, while Sarah slept fitfully. She woke at one point from a dream in which she was running down a hall carrying her tan cat, with Jane chasing behind them wielding a meat cleaver.

Sarah shuddered. "I won't let that wicked Jane get you." She reached for RahRah, who picked that moment to strut over her legs to a place on the bed, just beyond her reach, where the early-morning sunshine came through a crack in the closed curtains.

Before Sarah could lie back on her pillows again, her phone rang. She grabbed it from her nightstand charger. The number flashing on the screen was unfamiliar, but because it was local, she pushed the green button. "Hello," she said, her voice hushed.

"Morning, Sarah. Peter here. How are you?"

"Fine. And you?" She didn't wait for him to answer. "Emily's not up yet, but she'll be in your office with Harlan around ten."

This time, she gave him an opportunity to talk. Instead, he coughed or cleared his throat. She wasn't sure which.

"It isn't Emily I'm calling about. It's you. I need you to come to the station this morning, too."

"Why? I don't have anything to add to your investigation. Besides, with Harlan being with Emily, I need to stay in the office manning the phone and reception desk."

Whether it was hearing her name or the rising tone of Sarah's voice, Emily opened her eyes. She tucked the blanket more tightly around her but said nothing.

"Sarah, a few things have come up. I think it would be better if we could discuss them in person."

"But—"

"I'd really appreciate it if you'd come in after Emily gives her statement."

Sarah didn't answer.

"Please. You've got a situation we need to address about your cat."

"RahRah?" She looked across the bed, where RahRah preened himself in the sunlight. "My cat is a police matter?"

"Seems there's a question whether she's your cat."

"Him. RahRah's a boy."

Next to her, Emily propped herself up on one elbow.

Sarah motioned her to keep quiet. "Peter, exactly what are you talking about?"

"I'll explain when you get here. Tell you what, if you'd be more comfortable having Harlan with you, why don't you either have him turn on his answering machine for an hour or get someone else to cover his office?" He hung up.

She stared at the disconnected phone for a moment before throwing it on the bed.

Chapter Six

"I don't know what you're implying. RahRah belongs to me. I don't see how Jane could have gotten any kind of court order to take my cat without me being present."

"She hasn't, yet," Peter said.

Sarah jumped up from one of Peter's two guest chairs. Her elbow knocked against a two-shelf plastic organizer filled with file folders on the corner of Peter's desk. He grabbed for it, losing only one folder.

"Harlan"—Sarah ignored Peter and the fallen file, and turned to the man seated in the second guest chair—"tell Peter how ludicrous this is."

"It's ludicrous." Harlan didn't bother to raise his head from where he was busy scribbling on a yellow legal pad.

Relieved that Harlan had stayed after Emily gave her statement, Sarah couldn't believe how Peter seemed to be linking Bill, Jane, and RahRah together. It was insane. Maybe Harlan could resolve all of this quickly.

His only quid pro quo demand for staying had been

that Emily cover the office phones until Sarah returned. To Sarah's surprise, considering Emily's past fretting about how much time being at the police station was taking from her duties at the Expo and Southwind, Emily agreed to his request immediately. The way things were going, Sarah was grateful to her sister, too.

Sarah placed her hands on the edge of Peter's desk and bent toward where he waited, now leaning back, fingers pressed together tent-style.

"Peter," she said, glaring at his upturned face. "RahRah has been with me since Bill's mother died. In fact, he's the only thing Bill and I didn't fight over during our divorce."

Peter didn't move. "Why do you think that was?"

"Because he hated RahRah." She sat down again. Her charcoal gaze met Peter's. "That's not quite true. Bill was allergic to so many things. Nuts, mold, rag-weed, and cats, to name a few. If he got near a cat or cat hair, his eyes teared and he got stuffed up like he had a bad cold."

Harlan stopped writing. He rested the back of his pen just over his left ear. "If Bill was so allergic to cats, why did the two of you let Bill's mother keep RahRah when she moved to Wheaton?"

"They came as a pair. During Hurricane Katrina, Mother Blair literally plucked RahRah from the water when she was evacuated from her house to Baton Rouge. She lost everything else to New Orleans's swirling floodwaters, so she was adamant she wasn't ever going to abandon her adopted, scrawny fur ball, Katrina the Kat."

"Katrina? I thought the cat's name is RahRah," Peter said.

Sarah relaxed her tightened lips into a smile.

"Mother Blair christened the kitten Katrina the Kat before she realized she was a he. Being in the South, she didn't think shortening his name to KK would be politically correct, so she decided to butcher the word *rah-rah* into a name because he was so enthusiastic."

Harlan pulled the pen from his ear. "I still don't understand why you let her keep RahRah when she moved in with you if Bill was so allergic to him."

Sarah laughed. "You didn't know Mother Blair when she had a bee in her bonnet. Besides, technically, Mother Blair and RahRah never moved in with us."

"But I thought she lived with Bill and you after she was evacuated," Peter said.

"No. She originally was evacuated to a shelter and then an apartment in Baton Rouge. She lived there for almost a year before Bill found the house on Main Street with its separate carriage house. He thought it would be a good investment and provide a great way for his mother to live closer to us without interfering with our privacy."

Sarah grimaced and shook her head. "I was eighteen, married two months, and so madly in love with my husband, I never thought to question his plan. Within a few weeks, we moved into our respective homes, with RahRah having free run of Mother Blair's place."

"Sounds like Bill thought everything out," Harlan said.

"He always did."

"Wasn't it a little unusual for you to stay in contact with your mother-in-law after your divorce?" Peter asked.

"Probably," Sarah said. "But Mother Blair was a very

special woman. From day one, she treated me like a daughter. She was diagnosed with cancer right about the time Bill left me. Bill and I may not have worked out, but that didn't seem like a good reason for me to abandon his mother and RahRah. She died before the business side of our divorce was finalized."

Quickly wiping her hand under her eye to prevent a tear from escaping, Sarah averted her face from Peter.

He tapped his hand on his desk. "When Mrs. Blair died, what happened to RahRah?"

Sarah turned her head back in his direction. "I don't know what Bill did with RahRah for the few days after her death. At the end of Mother Blair's funeral, Bill took me aside and told me because of his allergies, he couldn't keep RahRah, but he was sure his mother would want me, instead of a stranger, to take care of him."

"You agreed?" Peter said.

"Of course. I've volunteered at the animal shelter for years. I know what happens to cats without a place to go. Besides, I love RahRah." She stared at Peter and Harlan. "You may only think of him as a cat, but he has a definite personality. I jumped at the chance to keep him from losing Mother Blair and me at the same time."

Peter said nothing. He opened a folder and picked up the single sheet in it. Slowly he scanned it. Sarah tried to read the paper from upside down but couldn't see the words. To distract herself from the silence filling the room, she concentrated on the rest of Peter's office.

Behind him was a wooden credenza. A picture of a younger Peter and two boys sat on it. The older child was a miniature version of Peter. Other than the one picture, the credenza was bare. She looked around the office for other family snapshots or children's drawings, but there were none. She wondered about his family. His campaign ads included a wife.

Two locking metal filing cabinets flanked the credenza. The guest chairs, his pressed-wood desk, a computer, and a phone were the rest of his formal decor. File folders and white-lined mini legal pads, many with writing scrawled on them, were spread across his desk. They were the only things that appeared out of place in his office, but she felt certain Peter knew the exact location of each piece of paper or file.

Peter closed the folder without showing Sarah or Harlan the piece of paper. He rose, came around his desk, and perched on its edge in front of Sarah. Rather than immediately speaking, he ran his thumb up and down one of his belt loops before anchoring his hand in it. "Did Bill or Mrs. Blair's estate provide you with a stipend to care for RahRah?"

Sarah glanced from Peter to Harlan, who studied his legal pad but didn't stop her from answering. "Peter, if Harlan hadn't given me a job as his receptionist, I couldn't afford my apartment or keep RahRah in cat food. Bill gave me RahRah, but he fought me over our other assets."

Sarah couldn't hold back the tears this time. She reached into her pocket for a nonexistent tissue. Before she could dry her eyes with the back of her hand, Harlan pressed his soft white handkerchief into her hand. She took it gratefully.

Delicately she wiped her eyes and blew her nose into the monogrammed hankie. Uncertain of the proper protocol for returning a used handkerchief, she slipped it into her pocket until she could launder it.

"Did Mrs. Blair ever give you or did you perhaps take some jewelry before or after your divorce?"

"Peter," Harlan said, "what are you getting at?"

"I'm just trying to find out if Sarah has any of Mrs. Blair's jewelry."

Harlan raised a hand to signal Sarah not to say anything. "Are you trying to find a particular piece?"

"A diamond-and-pearl bracelet."

"Peter Mueller, the only piece of jewelry I have from Mother Blair is this bracelet." She held up her arm to show a slim gold bracelet. "She gave me this when Bill and I got engaged. The one I think you're talking about belonged to her mother. She let me wear it as something borrowed on our wedding day. On our first anniversary, she gave it to me in the hope I would have a daughter who would eventually wear it to her own wedding."

"So you do have it?" Peter said.

Sarah shook her head. "No. I insisted on giving it back to her when Bill and I separated."

Harlan leaned forward in his chair. "And she took it back from you?"

"Finally," Sarah said. "She wanted me to keep it because she still felt like I was a daughter, but, under the circumstances, I couldn't keep one of her favorite pieces. I wanted her to have it back in case Bill ever had a daughter."

"Do you know where it is today?"

"I have no idea, but as her only child, Bill must have inherited all of her jewelry, so I assume it's with the rest of her things, unless he gave it to one of his bimbos. Have you checked with Jane?"

"She's the one accusing you of having it."

"And you believe her? Harlan, can we do something about all these lies she's telling about me?"

He twisted his mouth somewhere between a smile and a frown. "Peter, is that all you have to ask Sarah?"

"One more question," Peter said.

Sarah trembled, but she didn't know if it was from anger or indignation. She tightly grasped the sides of her chair, hoping to keep her emotions in check but her cheeks heated. "I already told you, I never lived or even stayed in the carriage house. It was Bill's mother's home until her death. I don't know what Bill did with RahRah for the few days before the funeral, but Bill brought him to me shortly after the service and other than this one bracelet, I have no jewelry that belonged to Mother Blair."

Harlan interrupted her. "Bill and Sarah didn't end their marriage on the best of terms, but I think it's pretty well known in the business community the carriage house sat empty for a long time because Bill hoped his property would be part of the new entertainment district the economic council is promoting."

"I knew several houses on that block have been converted to multifamily usage and there has been talk of making some of the big houses restaurants or hotels, but I didn't realize Bill's property was one being considered." Peter rubbed his hand against the stubble on his cheek. "Harlan, did you ever do any work on the Downtown District for Bill?"

"No. When I was on the Economic Development Council, the idea of an entertainment district, or Downtown District, hadn't been developed yet. He did ask me, as a council member, what owners in that area could and couldn't do with their property from a zoning perspective."

"In that case, having served on committees and councils with him and answering economic development questions, don't you have a conflict of interest representing Emily and Sarah?"

"I don't think so. I never answered anything for him personally and once I resigned from the council, which predated any entertainment district discussions or any dealings with his properties, he never engaged my services privately or for the council. Why do you ask?"

"We're still looking into the details," Peter said, drumming his fingers on the folder on his desk, "but it appears Mrs. Blair actually owned the property and houses and that when she died, she only bequeathed Bill the house Sarah shared with him."

"She owned the property?" Sarah asked.

"Apparently, Bill didn't have the money to buy the two houses but his mother did. That's why he brought her to Wheaton from Baton Rouge."

"I had no idea," Sarah said. "Bill took care of everything financial."

"Well, it seems while she put up the money for the property purchase and bequeathed all rights in the big house to Bill, Mrs. Blair left an animal trust that explicitly provided for RahRah to receive full-time care in the carriage house during her, I mean his, lifetime. His caretaker is authorized to receive a stipend."

"Are you saying there's an animal trust for Sarah to take care of RahRah in the carriage house?"

"Not exactly, Harlan." Peter came around his desk and perched on the edge in front of Harlan and Sarah. "Although there might be some dispute as to whether Bill should have compensated Sarah for RahRah's care during the past few years, there is an allegation that Bill, as trustee of his mother's estate, named a different caretaker."

Harlan rested his pen on his pad. "Allegation? Is there any basis for you to believe there is some credibility to it?"

Sarah glanced from Harlan to Peter. "I've never heard of this before. Who is making this so-called allegation?"

"Jane," Peter said. "She has documents she contends substantiate Bill was the named trustee and that the reason she recently moved into the carriage house was he asked her to live there and be RahRah's designated caretaker. Jane claims that, despite Bill's repeated demands, you've refused to return the cat without receiving compensation."

"That's a lie!" Sarah stood. Her shoulder just missed Peter's face. "This is insulting. I adopted RahRah because he was Mother Blair's cat. Not for some stipend I've never seen or heard anything about."

"Jane seems to think otherwise," Peter said. "She wants RahRah brought back to the carriage house immediately."

"What?"

"I've got a little more investigating to do, but right now, it looks like she might have a valid claim if she goes to court."

"Peter," Harlan said, "on what grounds are you making this legal determination?"

"I'm not determining anything. That's for a court of law, but if we can work it out now based on the documents Bill signed, it probably would be easier on everyone."

Harlan snorted. "And these documents just appeared?

Are you sure they're real? Want to tell me where they were during the past three years while Sarah was caring for RahRah without benefit of a stipend or the carriage house? Was this trust dormant during those years?"

"Well . . ."

"Well, it seems to me, that when Bill probated his mother's will, the trust would have appeared."

Peter cleared his throat and ran his fingers through his hair. "There seems to be some question whether Bill ever probated his mother's will."

"Sounds to me like you have a lot more important things to investigate relating to Bill's death than Jane's allegations about RahRah's cat trust."

"The cat trust wasn't high on our list until Jane brought to my attention that Bill, as trustee, kept the stipend amount each month. Under the circumstances, I can't rule out whether finding out Sarah was cheated out of the stipend and the carriage house by Bill, plus the other things he took in their divorce, might not be enough motivation for Emily or her sister to have killed him."

In as tightly controlled a voice as she could muster, Sarah said, "There is no way I'm going to listen to any more of this nonsense. Neither my sister nor I had anything to do with Bill's death." She took a breath and let out a sigh before adding, in a low voice that Peter bent forward to hear, "I didn't kill anyone, steal RahRah, or take any jewelry. I'm not sure what Jane's game is, but I know she's a liar. Instead of wasting time worrying about my cat and annoying me, shouldn't you be figuring out who, other than my sister, or, I guess, now me, murdered Bill? That is, if he actually was killed."

Chapter Seven

Furious, Sarah stomped out of the station. She didn't know which of Peter's allegations or conclusions was the craziest. The only amusing thing, if one could call it that, was she could tell her sister Peter's narrow-mindedness had fueled her motivation to help Emily develop a wider suspect base.

Sarah stopped in front of the building that co-housed the fire and police departments. Neither Harlan nor Peter had followed her. She clutched and unclutched her hands, willing herself to calm down.

Hearing the bells of the carillon on the far side of the square ringing, Sarah realized it was noon. Harlan's office was one street over to the left, diagonally across from the strip center that housed Southwind, while her apartment, which was closer to the Civic Center, was two blocks to the right. Back to work seemed obvious, but the devil on her shoulder hissed it was lunchtime and she needed a few minutes to pull herself together and sort through Jane's various allegations. The longer she waited to do it, the more Peter might believe them.

Knowing Harlan had Emily there, Sarah didn't feel

pressed to go directly back to work. Instead, she took a deep breath and looked around the bricked city square. The city buildings on the remaining sides of the square were each built from the white crystalline marble Alabama claimed as its own.

If today was Saturday, she'd head straight for the public library. Libraries were her home away from home as long as she could remember. That was where she'd first found an Erle Stanley Gardner book and fallen in love with the idea of becoming a lawyer or private detective. Things changed when she met Bill.

"I don't want to wait for you. Delaying school a year won't be a big deal," he'd said when they were dating.

She'd believed him then and when he'd done things like upending her ironing board with the hot iron sitting on it. "Honey, private eyes and lawyers figure things out. You can't even iron a shirt without scorching it. Before we waste money on school, why don't you get my mother to show you how to do a few things around here?"

While Sarah learned plenty from Bill's mother, it apparently wasn't enough to keep Bill from wandering elsewhere to find women with more expertise. Considering everything, she couldn't believe Peter thought Emily or she killed Bill or she took a piece of Mother Blair's jewelry. It was even harder for her to get her head around what Peter had said about RahRah.

Sarah had read about people making provisions for their pets in their wills, but she thought only movie stars or people with too much money did that. Mother Blair definitely didn't fit the image of a movie star or a kook. Surely, if Bill's mother could see things now, she wouldn't want RahRah taken from his loving home to live out his remaining eight lives with a gold digger.

Thinking of RahRah made the decision to give in

to the devil easier. If Harlan was annoyed, she would always argue this lunch hour was business development for him. After all, there could come a day when RahRah, having the run of a better house and a higher income than Sarah's, might hire Harlan as his kitty lawyer.

Unlocking her door, Sarah surveyed the condition of her apartment. One of the problems with an efficiency unit was that if anything was out of place, it stuck out like a sore finger. She and Emily had been in such a rush to leave this morning that the place looked like it had been hit by a whirlwind. RahRah was nowhere to be seen. She called his name, but he didn't appear. He probably shared her feelings about the disarray and had gone into hiding until Sarah straightened up a bit.

RahRah didn't poke his nose out from under the bed until she loaded the dishwasher, made the bed, and sat at the butcher-block kitchen table with a peanut butter and banana sandwich. He strolled right by her to his empty bowl. A low gurgle came from his throat.

"Well, la di dah. You already finished your food. Let me eat my lunch and I'll get an extra treat for you."

A few bites into her sandwich, a noise from the closet area made Sarah look in that direction. RahRah was nudging the partially open closet door a little farther each time, until he saw his reflected image. At that point, he jumped away. Laughing, Sarah picked him up. She hugged the squirming cat while kicking the door closed.

"You are one fifteen-pound scaredy-cat and I love you." Still holding him firmly, she sat at her two-person kitchen table.

RahRah pushed against her, stretching out in her

lap to be stroked. Forgetting about her sandwich, she concentrated on meeting his demand until he swatted her hand away with his paw. Before he could escape from her lap, she engulfed him in her arms and buried her face in his fur. This time, Sarah couldn't stop the tears from flowing and she didn't try.

Chapter Eight

Sarah waited for Emily to find the button on the reception desk and buzz her into Harlan's office. She hoped the little bit of makeup she'd thrown on was enough to prevent Harlan and Emily from noticing she'd been crying.

"Where have you been? Harlan's been back for almost an hour."

"I'm sorry," Sarah said. "I stopped home to feed RahRah and grab a sandwich. I didn't realize you were in a rush. How did your statement go?"

"Better than I expected. I told Peter what happened and that was that." Emily pointed at the wall clock. "I hoped to get to Southwind in time to help with lunch service and prep dinner. Lunch is over now."

"I'm sorry." Sarah came around the desk to relieve her sister. "I didn't realize you were working at the Expo opening tonight and planning to do a day shift at the restaurant, too."

Emily sighed as she grabbed her jacket from the back of her chair and draped it over her arm. "Everyone from Southwind is setting up and working scheduled shifts at the Expo this weekend, but the restaurant is open for business as usual. We'll all be working overtime, going back and forth between the Expo and the restaurant."

"I hadn't thought about that. Sounds exhausting."

Emily began to respond but stopped midsentence when Harlan stuck his head out of his office and said, "Thought about what?"

"That Southwind doesn't close simply because we're also staffing the Civic Center for the next few days." Emily looked at Sarah. "In fact, not only are we all balancing our time between the Expo and Southwind's regular dining crowd, but Chef Marcus took on a small catering job for tonight, too." She turned to leave, but Harlan stepped into her path to the door.

"Sounds like Chef Marcus is a bit ambitious."

Emily stiffened. "I'd say industrious." She tried passing Harlan. "Excuse me, please."

He didn't budge.

"Harlan," Emily said, "Sarah's here so you don't need me anymore. I've got to get back."

Sarah could swear Harlan's eyes twinkled as, still holding his ground, he held up his glasses and examined them, as if checking for a dirt spot. Finally, resting them on his face again, he extended his hand toward his private office. "I hate to delay you any longer, but I really need a few minutes for the three of us to sit down together. It's important."

In his office, Harlan selected the leather wingback chair next to the couch, where Sarah chose to sit.

As he settled himself into its deep seat, Emily, who had remained standing by his door, interrupted any moment he might have taken to gather his thoughts. "Harlan, is there some news on what killed Bill?"

He shook his head. "No, but after Sarah left Peter's office, I stayed and talked with him. There are still a few things that concern him. I think Peter will want to talk with you again."

Emily glanced at her watch and frowned. "I don't have time for that. Look, I'm really sorry about Bill, but I don't have anything to add to the statement I gave Peter today or what I told him last night."

"Maybe not, but Peter's stuck in one of those 'just the facts' modes."

"You're concerned he's trying to fit things into his version of the facts, aren't you?" Emily asked.

Harlan nodded, but Sarah furrowed her brow. "What are you talking about?"

Emily planted her hands on her hips. "This morning was all for show, wasn't it, Harlan? Peter isn't waiting for the tox reports or searching for the real killer. He's zeroed in on me."

"You're jumping to conclusions. It's way too early to think like that. Peter still is investigating other suspects," Harlan said.

Emily moved closer to the edge of Harlan's desk. "I'm sorry. I just don't share your confidence in Peter. I think he already can see the DA's opening statement: 'Ladies and gentlemen of the jury, although Bill Blair hated rhubarb and allegedly would never have eaten Emily Johnson's rhubarb crisp because he was aware she used nuts in her topping and he was deathly allergic to nuts, we are hard-pressed to get around the circumstantial evidence. A locked Civic Center, rhubarb covering the victim, and one of her forks grasped in his fist might not be enough to lead you to believe she is the murderer, but—'"

Harlan gestured a stop motion with his left hand. "Your fork? Peter never said . . ."

"We're using novelty plastic forks with the restaurant's name on them in our booth. Chef Marcus thought they would be a walking advertisement for Southwind. When I was giving Bill CPR, I recognized the logo on the fork in his hand."

"That doesn't necessarily tie the fork to you," Sarah said. "You aren't the only one in the booth and if the forks were lying out when everyone was setting up, anyone in the Civic Center could have handed one to Bill." She turned to face Harlan. "Surely you can convince Peter and a jury that Bill or anyone could have picked up one of the forks."

Emily waved her hand dismissively. "Not if there isn't any evidence to the contrary. Right, Harlan?"

"Even if the evidence is circumstantial, I can assure you Peter doesn't consider you his only suspect. Besides, if we ever end up in a hearing, there are plenty of ways I can create reasonable doubt in the minds of a jury. You aren't the only one who might have a motive for killing Bill."

"Yeah," Sarah said. "Guess who else is in the club." She filled her sister in on what had transpired during her meeting with Peter. "I was already committed to helping clear your name, but this only adds to my motivation to help you find more suspects."

"Whoa." Harlan raised his hands in a "hold it" fashion. "You two need to stay out of the investigation. No sleuthing, snooping, or anything of that nature. Leave it to the professionals. I assure you, Peter's a good guy. He'll come up with the right suspect eventually."

"Not soon enough for me," Emily said.

"I understand, but no amateur sleuthing." Harlan looked at his watch. "It's getting late. Sarah, I doubt either of us will be very productive this afternoon. Why don't you go to the Civic Center with Emily and see if you can help her make up the time she couldn't work while you took your extended lunch."

Before Sarah could get any words out, Emily clapped her hands. "You're a sweetie!"

Seeing Harlan blush, Sarah muttered her thanks and quickly retrieved her purse from her desk. With a final good-bye to Harlan, the twins left the office.

"If you think it will be a late evening," Sarah said, "we should take another minute and get my car and make sure RahRah has enough food. I can meet you at the Civic Center."

Emily checked her watch. "At this point, I can take another minute. After all, I'm going to have a top-notch helper tonight."

On the sidewalk in front of her house, Sarah handed her key fob to Emily. "Back my car down the driveway while I run inside and check on RahRah. It will only take a moment." Without waiting for an answer, she dashed into the house and quickly tended to RahRah's needs.

"He's set." She slid into the passenger seat beside Emily. Considering that Emily already thought she was obsessed with RahRah, she didn't think she needed to go into a recitation of how cute he'd looked lying in his special place in the kitchen. Instead, she peered out the window as Emily eased the car into traffic and drove the few blocks to the Civic Center. She parked but didn't turn off the ignition or get out of the car. Surprised Emily was delaying, Sarah stared at her.

"Before we go in," Emily said, "we probably should consider who, besides the two of us, might have had a motive for killing Bill."

"I'm not sure about motive, but whoever killed Bill

had access to the Civic Center. And because Bill was holding a fork marked with the Southwind name, we can't rule out that it was a member of the Southwind group."

Emily shook her head vehemently. "No way. Except Jane and, I guess, Bill, everyone else is good folks."

"You never know. Besides, what about the fork? That's a tie-in."

"Those forks are on all the counters of our booth. A chef from next door, someone from three rows over, or even Bill could have picked it up. The fork doesn't necessarily tie it to me or someone else from Southwind."

"Well, whether the person worked for Southwind or not, it has to be someone who could easily go in and out of the exhibition area at any time without anyone thinking they're in the wrong place."

"That's just about everyone in town." Emily got out of the car and slammed the door behind her.

Chapter Nine

Sarah watched her sister in awe. Instead of the angry person she'd been in the car, Expo Emily was in full charge—cool, detached, and giving orders. It was Chef Marcus who was falling apart. He sat in a chair someone had stuck across from a wide-open refrigerator and freezer in the back room of the exhibition hall, running his hands through his dark, curly hair. Although there were stand-alone booths at the front of this room, the space by the refrigerator looked more like a stock area for the different exhibitors.

Chef Marcus's mumbled mutterings of "I'm ruined" and "Who would do this to us?" were overshadowed for Sarah by the fact that the red-haired vixen, who attacked Emily the night before and was demanding she surrender RahRah, had an arm wrapped around his broad shoulders and her head bent close to his. Apparently, Jane was well on the road to recovery from losing Bill.

"It's going to be all right. No one can blame you for what happened," Jane said to Marcus. She looked up and glared at Emily, but Emily ignored her.

Emily seemed focused on the three other people

wearing Southwind shirts. The two men appeared about Emily and Sarah's age, while Sarah pegged the third Southwind employee, a woman, as several years younger than the rest of the group. The four stood just beyond a puddle of water that surrounded the bottom of the stainless-steel refrigeration unit. Sarah moved closer to the group.

"Jacob," Emily said to the beardless man standing near her, "what's going on?"

Jacob paused to peek at his watch, which Sarah couldn't help but notice looked a lot like the Rolex Harlan wore. "I met Richard in the other room, by the Southwind booth, about three hours ago."

Sarah wished he would talk faster before she was overcome by the sick fishy smell coming from the refrigerator. She doubted anything in there wasn't spoiled. She certainly didn't want to find out.

"We spent a good amount of time pulling booth stuff like tablecloths, plastic forks, and cups together," Jacob said. "About an hour or so ago, we decided we needed to start on the food for tonight's catering job. When we came in here to do that, we saw the puddle. The refrigerator door was ajar. I started to stick my hand in to see if things were still cold, but that's when Richard noticed the power cord was cut. We immediately called Chef Marcus at the restaurant."

Emily shook her head and then brushed her hair back out of her eyes. "Marcus, I didn't realize you were planning to prep the Holt dinner here, rather than at the restaurant."

The folding chair creaked as he shifted his weight, forcing Jane to quickly step away from him. She puffed out her chest as she faced Emily.

"After Chief Mueller gave us permission to come back into the Civic Center this afternoon, nobody knew where you were. Marcus and I decided I should set up my Expo station and whip up the Holts' dinner, while he focused on Southwind's lunch and dinner service."

From the still way Emily held herself, Sarah couldn't tell if her sister was shooting daggers at Chef Marcus and Jane, but there was no question he turned his face to avoid meeting Emily's gaze.

"I guess we'll simply have to explain what happened when we apologize to Mrs. Holt for not being able to complete the job," Jane said.

Emily glared at her. "Canceling isn't part of the Southwind style of doing business. We have to make this work. Of course, we can't take a chance of using anything from this refrigerator or freezer. We're simply going to have to start over for the dinner we're catering for the Holts tonight."

"But we don't have time," the much younger woman chef said as she stepped away from Jacob and Richard. She waved a tattoo-sleeved arm in the direction of the refrigeration unit. "The Holt party is at eight and it's after three."

Sarah thought she heard an audible sob or sigh from Chef Marcus, but it was overshadowed by Emily's firm voice.

"We can't back out of a private dinner Chef Marcus agreed to have Southwind cater," Emily said. "That's not the kind of reputation any of us wants our restaurant to get, is it?"

The two men and the woman, who towered over them, shook their heads.

"Luckily," Emily said, "the Holts are only having ten dinner guests. Has anyone checked the other refrigerator?"

"Yes," the tattooed woman replied. "It doesn't appear that it was tampered with."

"Good," Emily said. "That means our salad and vegetables are okay. We can serve a partially cold buffet dinner."

"I can make a vegetable appetizer tray if you do a grocery run for the main dish," Richard volunteered. "When you get back from the store, I can help with something else."

"Perfect," Emily said. "Richard, there are extra cutting boards you can use under one of my tables in the Southwind booth area. Prep for a tray for twelve. In the meantime, Jacob and I will do a quick food run."

Emily looked at Jane, who still had a hand resting on Marcus's shoulder. "Jane, please help Richard. The two of you can wash, tear, slice, and separately bag enough lettuce, radishes, tomatoes, mushrooms, and peppers for a big salad. We'll put it together at the house."

"But . . ." Jane said.

The man, who Sarah remembered was Richard, ignored Jane and began walking to the next room. Sarah couldn't take her eyes off him. Unlike the copper-skinned woman who had one obvious tattoo, every inch of his skin appeared to be inked. He even had tattoos on his hands and across his knuckles.

Jane's loud objections to Emily's instructions drew Sarah's attention away from trying to decipher his artwork.

Emily cut Jane off. "Either go help Richard or leave."

Jane bristled but hushed after Chef Marcus took her hand and held it, saying something quietly to her. Whatever he said, Jane smiled. She let her hand linger in his for another moment before she went off in the same direction as Richard.

Despite his pep talk to Jane, Chef Marcus remained seated, his face now back in his hands. Sarah tried to figure out why. It wasn't like he was a new chef. Surely, even if his young staff hadn't been through a time-crunch crisis before, he had.

"Grace," Emily said to the woman chef, "until Jacob and I get back with more food, you and my sister can throw out everything in this refrigerator and freezer."

Chef Marcus softly moaned again.

"Chef Marcus, why don't you help Richard and Jane until Jacob and I get back?"

With effort, Chef Marcus rose and ambled in the direction Jane had gone.

Turning back to Grace and Sarah, Emily said, "Grace, this is my sister, Sarah Blair. Sarah, this is Grace Winston, my right hand. Besides the two of you throwing things out, would one of you grab a sheet of paper and list what the two of you are tossing? Oh, and, Sarah, use your phone to take pictures of this area and what ends up in the garbage. I'm sure the insurance company will want us to document as much as possible."

"Em, don't you think you should call the police first?"

"The police?" Grace asked.

Sarah pointed to where the plug was in the wall but the cord lay frayed on the floor. "This looks deliberate. It seems to me we should leave this area untouched until the police see it."

Grace stepped away from the refrigerator, but Emily motioned her back.

She faced off against her sister. "We simply don't have the time. We need to clean up before we can cook. There can't be the slightest possibility of cross-contamination from the rotten shrimp, scallops, chicken, and other proteins. If we get rid of them and clean our surfaces, we should be able to pull off tonight's dinner safely, but it's going to take all of us working at full force starting now."

"Peter won't be happy with you mucking up his crime site."

"If I wasn't a bit spooked that Bill's death and this cord being cut might be related because someone is out to get Southwind or Marcus, I wouldn't call the police." She pulled her cell phone from her pocket. "We don't have the time to wait for the police to come or chance them closing our booth down as a crime scene, so while I'm calling Peter's office, you two snap some photos and start cleaning the refrigerator out."

While Emily placed the call and wandered into the next room, Grace began pulling a large drum trash can across the room. Sarah rushed to help her, but Grace waved her off. "I've got this."

She pointed toward a chest of drawers. Its top was being used as a workstation. "There's paper and a pen in the second drawer and, while you're over there, grab us each a pair of rubber gloves from one of the boxes on top."

Sarah did as she was told.

With their gloves on and the can positioned, Grace opened the refrigerator all the way. The odor intensified. Grace stepped up to the refrigerator as Sarah silently debated whether it would be immature to hold her nose while they worked.

Chapter Ten

Sarah couldn't believe it. Six twenty-five and the Southwind van was loaded and ready for everything to be delivered to the Holts.

"Thank you, everyone. We did it," Emily declared.

Sarah and Emily stood in the middle of the parking lot as Grace squeezed into the front seat with Chef Marcus and Jacob. They waved as the van pulled away.

"I should have gone with Marcus, too." Jane stomped away from them toward the Civic Center.

From mid-parking lot, Sarah watched Jane yank the building's door open. For someone who was so broken up last night, Jane's cozy behavior around Chef Marcus made Sarah wonder exactly how close they were.

Maybe Sarah's investigation would reveal a secret involvement between them so Jane could become the prime suspect. After all, if Chef Marcus and Jane were super-chummy and Bill had found out, Jane, rather than Emily, might have been the one in danger of being fired. Taking it one step further, Jane, being Bill's girlfriend, would have been just as familiar as Emily with Bill's allergies. It wouldn't have been that difficult for her to feed him Emily's rhubarb crisp, telling him it was hers.

Sarah made a mental note to find a way to ask the other line cooks if they'd noticed anything going on between Chef Marcus and Jane. It was too bad Emily hadn't sent Jane in the van with the food.

"Em, why didn't you let Jane go with Chef Marcus? It would have gotten her out of your hair for a few hours."

"If we were staying to serve, Jane would have been the first in the truck. She's good at that."

"So?"

"Mrs. Holt requires caterers to be gone before her guests arrive. She likes things to look like she whipped dinner up herself."

"Under those conditions, I understand you sending Grace and Jacob to set everything up, but Chef Marcus?"

"He didn't go along to help with food preparation."

Sarah wrinkled her brow, trying to figure out why he was along for the ride if he wasn't working.

"Chef Marcus is the master of charm," Emily said. "His job is to make nice to Deborah Holt so that down the road the first catering company she calls or tells her friends about is Southwind."

Sarah nodded. Even as Harlan's receptionist, she understood the importance of always making Harlan's clients feel welcome and appreciated. Sending Chef Marcus was clearly good business. The question was whether the idea was his or Emily's. If she had to bet from what she'd seen during the past day, not only was Emily a competent chef and dynamo kitchen manager, but she had business brains, too. If she was this good working for other people at twenty-eight, Sarah could only imagine how far Emily might go in the culinary world. That was, if she didn't end up spending the best years of her life behind bars.

Sarah wished she had a talent like Emily's or enough money to go back to school. So far, Sarah had scratched several options off her list of possibilities. For years she'd dreamed of a law-related career, but marrying Bill changed all that. Cooking also was a definite failure. Considering her limited computer skills and so-so filing, her outlook as a top-notch receptionist probably was about level with her cooking. She was lucky Harlan was such an easygoing boss.

At one time she had added wife to her failure list, but after some reflection and a little counseling, Sarah concluded her problem in the marriage area was in her choosing ability rather than from any deficit in her performance.

The arrival of a police cruiser interrupted Sarah's pity party. Chief Mueller was driving.

Peter zeroed in on Sarah and Emily as he got out of his car. "Hi! What's going on?"

"It's about time you got here," Emily said.

"What are you talking about?"

"Aren't you here about the sabotaged refrigerator?"

"Sabotage? First I've heard of that."

"Our police force at work again. Don't your people ever communicate?"

Peter's neck flushed, but other than looping his thumb through one of the belt loops negated by his choice of suspenders, he didn't move.

Emily stood her ground, toe-to-toe to him. "This afternoon, our staff found the main refrigeration unit's power cord cut. I reported the crime to your office."

Seeing Peter's jaw muscles twitch, Sarah interjected herself into the conversation. "The power source to the unit appears to have been intentionally severed. Would you like to see it?"

She led Peter into the building and the room with the sabotaged refrigerator. He bent to examine the cut power cord.

"We left it exactly as we found it," Sarah assured him.

"But"—he glanced from his kneeling position around the now spotless room—"you destroyed any other evidence." He stood. "I should put all of you in jail for tampering with the scene of a crime."

Sarah bristled. This wasn't the calm, steady Peter she remembered. She moved into his personal space. Peter flinched ever so slightly as he took a step backward.

"The Southwind folks didn't have time to lollygag around until someone from your shop responded. Obviously, from what you just said, it's a good thing we went ahead with what we had to do."

"I'll follow up on the communication failure and get some techs to check out that cord."

Emily, who now stood beside Sarah, pointed to the big clock hanging on the wall. "Please make sure they don't make as big a mess as last night. We won't have time to clean up a second time before we start serving customers. Now, if you'll excuse us, we've got more setup work to do."

"I think they'll need to do it without you tonight," Peter said. "We got the fingerprint report back and, other than Bill's, yours are the only prints on the fork. I think you've got some explaining to do."

The line of Emily's jaw stiffened. Sarah reached for Emily's hand, but an angry Emily shook her off.

"I've told you everything I know. I don't have any more time to waste on this tonight. Besides, how did you get my fingerprints? Off my soda can?"

"We didn't have to resort to the soda can trick. Your

prints are on file from when you applied for your security clearance to have a pass to the Civic Center."

He placed his left hand on the handcuffs hanging from his belt. With a flip of his other wrist, he gestured for Emily to walk out in front of him. "I don't think you understand. You now are a person of interest, and I'd really appreciate it if you'd voluntarily come down to the station and answer a few more questions."

Sarah and Emily exchanged glances. Emily started in the direction Peter pointed but then stopped. She took off her chef's jacket and carefully handed it to Sarah.

Sarah reached beyond the jacket and rested her fingers on her sister's hand. "It's going to be all right. I'll call Harlan for you."

Emily nodded. "Just in case, though, you better practice breaking eggs with one hand." She forced a grin. "And I know, don't say anything until Harlan gets there."

Chapter Eleven

Sarah picked up her sister's jacket from the box where she had left it when she called Harlan. She tried to wipe a smudge off its sleeve with her hand.

"That's not going to come off without bleach."

Sarah jerked around to see who the speaker was. The young chef with the tattooed right arm stood there. Grace. Apparently, the dinner had successfully been delivered and set up at the Holts'.

Close up, Sarah could see the ink on the arm exposed below Grace's T-shirt was comprised of several interwoven food and vegetable designs worked around what appeared to be Japanese or Chinese letters.

Following Sarah's gaze, Grace said, "My way of advocating farm to table."

"Oh." Sarah fumbled for what to say next. It wouldn't be polite to note that the artwork didn't convey that idea. She imagined anything she said, besides coming across as an insult, would highlight the few years' difference in their ages was a gaping crevice.

Grace apparently saw no problem with tattoos and piercings while Sarah had been brought up to think of them as something people in business hid. Although some of her contemporaries had little butterflies or miniature symbols tucked where the sun didn't shine, Sarah knew none would fathom the idea of getting a full-arm sleeve.

The idea of getting even a small tattoo scared Sarah. She worried too much about the cleanliness of the needle, what it would look like if her skin shriveled with age and the wings sagged, or if she simply woke up one day and hated it.

Grace saved the moment. "Where's Emily?"

"She had to leave for a little while, but she left me here to help. What's left to do?" Sarah began to unbutton and roll up her sleeves.

"Plenty, but we need to go to a meeting first."

Grace whistled to catch Jacob's attention. When he looked up, she yelled, "Chef Marcus wants us all in the other room for a moment."

He obediently trotted toward them.

"If you're going to sub for Emily, you better come along, too."

Take Emily's place? No way. Hopefully, Chef Marcus had some tasks to be done, like setting a table or sweeping a floor. She couldn't be expected to display Emily's food or be part of the food competitions or exhibitions without any preparation. It wasn't part of the bargain of being a twin or a quasi-detective. Besides, having Sarah cook would do little to preserve Emily's career. It might even permanently finish it.

Everyone already in the Civic Center's back room encircled Chef Marcus, who stood in the open area near the refrigerators and ovens. Although still looking paler than Sarah remembered him from past days, he seemed to be back in control. He acknowledged the arrival of the last three with a nod of his head but continued addressing the group.

"First, let me tell you how very pleased with our service Mrs. Holt was. I appreciate everyone's help pulling the dinner off, but we're not done yet. Our setup for the Expo is behind. We've got a lot to do here and at the restaurant before the Expo begins, but I know we can pull it off working together."

Chef Marcus cleared his throat. "The fact is, Mr. Blair was our champion. With him gone, our role at the Civic Center and as a premier restaurant in this community rests on our next dinner services at Southwind and our Expo performance throughout the weekend. To say it more plainly, our jobs depend on making sure the Food Expo is a success and keeping the Civic Center powers happy."

"How do those two differ?" Sarah whispered to Grace.

Chef Marcus's next sentence made it seem like he had overheard her. "Southwind's Civic Center contract was only for a year. With new leadership coming in, the board is bound to rebid the contract. Even if we don't win it again, we want people to associate Southwind and our catering efforts with quality. That's why it's important the Southwind booth, displays, and samplings tied to the Food Expo go well, but we also have to keep the workers and board members satisfied behind the scenes."

Jane nodded fiercely beside Chef Marcus.

He ignored her. "Unfortunately, I got a text from Emily that she's tied up at the police station. Because we don't know how long she'll be, we're going to have to divide up her responsibilities, too."

Jane immediately stepped in front of Chef Marcus. "I can supervise the Civic Center staff table and take over supervision of the exhibition area."

"Oh, no," Grace said so softly only Sarah heard her.

From the corner of her eye, Sarah saw Grace relax when Marcus responded. "Thank you, but that's too much to ask of one person. If you stick to making people happy at your Southwind exhibition table and doing a bang-up job during your food presentation and the contest, that will be more than enough."

He consulted a piece of paper he was holding. "I've made a list of assignments for each of you in addition to the shifts you'll be putting in at the booth and restaurant. Grace, I'd like you to oversee the back-room staff table. Jacob and Richard, I need you to keep track of the exhibitor and volunteer boxed lunches and make sure we have enough ice and drinks on hand. I'm going to meet and greet and try to massage a few egos. Okay, all?"

"What about me?" Sarah asked. "Hopefully, Emily will be back soon, but what can I do in her place in the meantime?"

"Thank you. It's kind of you to offer to pitch in for her, Sarah. Normally, your sister would have overseen everything to do with the Civic Center food contract."

Involuntarily, Sarah shrank into herself as her hand went to her neck.

For the first time, Chef Marcus smiled. She couldn't help but note he had an engaging grin that made him appear downright boyish.

"Don't worry, I'll take care of her stuff. Hopefully, she'll be back by the time the Expo opens, so why don't you just help Grace get Emily's display area set up."

Sarah wished Chef Marcus's list could tell her how to help her sister. Now that Peter had matched Emily's fingerprints to those on the fork, it was going to be harder than ever to make him look for another suspect. Her stomach was flip-flopping at the thought of investigating without her twin's help, but she knew she had no other choice.

She missed the next direction Chef Marcus gave, but he caught her attention when he turned back to her. "It also would be great if you'd try to contact Emily and find out if there is any specific prep or shopping she needs done for her personal demonstration and contest entry."

"Sure, but we might need a plan B." Sarah carefully avoided hinting at Emily being arrested and unable to return, but it didn't matter.

Chef Marcus had moved on to something else.

"Don't worry about plan B yet," Grace whispered. "You called Harlan. He'll have her back in plenty of time for the exhibition. He's fantastic. In the meantime, let's see if we can figure out what's still needed for Emily's booth."

Sarah nodded, but she didn't feel Grace's confidence.

Chapter Twelve

Standing with Grace in front of the Southwind booth, Sarah couldn't believe the shambles it was in. It was a direct contrast to the back room where Marcus had held his meeting and to the two rows of booths in the exhibition hall that sat behind the Southwind row. In those areas, almost everyone had gone home for the night.

Sarah stepped back to get a better view of the three companies sharing the first row. People still were working in the single stalls housing the Vino Shoppe and Kathy's Cookies, which adjoined either side of Southwind's three-section booth. Both booths appeared well on the way to being ready in time for the opening of the Expo.

The same thing couldn't be said about the space under the Southwind banner. A good dent had been made in cleaning and setting up the two outer sections, but the center area was a disaster. Torn crime-scene tape flapped and a mound of obviously soiled tablecloths had been dumped on the booth's center table.

"This is Emily's part of the booth." Grace pointed

toward the untouched middle. "Between being gone today and concentrating on the Holt dinner, she didn't get much done. And when she was here, I don't think she was eager to be in this room."

"I can understand why," Sarah said. "Doesn't it creep you out to be standing near the place Emily tried to resuscitate Bill?"

Grace shook her head and started toward the end of the row. Staying put, Sarah shuddered and averted her gaze from what she imagined was a stain on the carpet. Instead, she focused on the long tables used to divide the Southwind booth into three distinct stations.

The back of each of the three squared-off sections was set up with a microwave, large convection toaster oven, mini-refrigerator, and two-burner cooktop. Although she thought the tables made three separate squares, she realized, as she followed Grace through an entrance at the far end of the booth, that a slight opening had been left between the appliances and ends of the side tables so one could easily get from section to section of the booth without having to leave Southwind's designated area.

Sarah stopped in the middle of Emily's tables and surveyed the situation. Emily or someone apparently had wiped most of the fingerprint powder off her microwave, large convection toaster oven, and two-burner mini-stove, but the rest of Emily's area made Sarah want to turn and run. She looked at Grace. "Where do we start?"

"Right here." Grace pulled a box from under one of Emily's side tables. Grace opened the box and removed a stack of clean tablecloths. She handed them to Sarah. "After I wipe the tables, you can put these on them."

Her hands emptied, Grace scooped up the pile of dirty linens and tossed them on the floor outside the booth. She threw the other trash cluttering Emily's tables into a nearby garbage can and reached under one of the tables for a roll of paper towels she used to wipe the tables off. Once she finished, she nodded toward the tables. "They're ready for you."

Sarah immediately unfolded and placed the clean tablecloths on Emily's three tables. She smoothed the creases out of the cloths. "What else do we need to do?"

"Stockpile the serving areas and put the extra stuff out of sight under Emily's tables." When Sarah froze in place, Grace added, "Things like extra plastic cups and utensils. Once people start taking samples, you'll be amazed how fast everything you put on the front table disappears."

Sarah nodded. She'd been to enough of Emily's food fair tables to know how people devoured free samples.

"How many forks and cups do I need to put out?"

"Cover the entire front table with those mini plastic cups. Emily plans to fill each one with a taste of crisp or spinach pie, assembly-line style, just before the guests arrive. That way, her food will taste fresh."

"That makes sense, but what if she doesn't get back in time? I'm not sure what to do."

"Don't worry. Harlan will get her back."

"You sound like you know Harlan fairly well?"

"Well enough to trust him to spring Emily with time to spare before the Expo, but if he doesn't, Emily and

I started making her spinach pies and rhubarb crisps yesterday afternoon. We have enough spinach pies to start with, but the rest we'll have to make from scratch. I have Emily's recipes, but I'm going to need your help."

"But I'm not a cook."

"No, but you have two hands. In a kitchen, that can be important. While I'm running around doing my other duties as assigned, you can help me heat and serve. I promise, if we have to, we'll pull it off."

Grace was ahead of her. She'd already thought through the scenario of Emily not being back for the Expo. Apparently, she wasn't as confident about Emily's immediate release as she seemed. Either her earlier bravado was an act for Sarah's benefit or to ease both of their fears. Grace's physical appearance might have been off-putting at first, but now Sarah found she liked this woman.

"Grace," Sarah said, "I was wondering, is there something going on between Chef Marcus and Jane? She certainly seemed willing to do anything for him."

"We all are. He's a good guy."

"He seemed pretty upset this afternoon."

"Chef Marcus had a right to be. He's worked hard to make Southwind a great restaurant."

"Well, they seemed pretty friendly."

Grace shot Sarah a look she interpreted as either quizzical or a message to back off. "I don't know what you're getting at. Chef Marcus is super-friendly, a real charmer and something of a flirt, but he never got between Jane and Mr. Blair."

Sarah concentrated on smoothing a wrinkle out of the tablecloth. "Oh, I didn't mean that. I just wondered, seeing them together earlier, if they are good friends like Emily and you seem to be."

"I guess." Grace picked up an empty box marked NAPKINS.

Before Grace could move away from her, Sarah hurried to ask another question. "What about Richard and Jacob? Do you think either one of them might have cut the cord on the refrigerator?"

Grace leaned closer to Sarah and dropped her voice. "I can't think of why they would. Jacob is too goody-goody and it wouldn't be in Richard's best interest, but it might have been one of Richard's friends."

Sarah waited, hoping Grace would continue.

"Richard got in with a rough crowd in high school. After a few of them were arrested, he settled down and ended up in culinary school. He's willing to work, but I can't say that for all of his friends."

Her interest piqued, Sarah started to follow up with her line of questioning, but Grace cut her off with a wave of her hand. "Speaking of working, why don't you clean the fingerprint powder off the display holder and set it up on the corner between the front and side tables while I go get the samples of Emily's rhubarb crisp and spinach pie I was able to save last night."

Sarah followed the direction of Grace's finger to where a dusty fixture with shelves lay partially hidden under a table. "What? I thought the police took all of Emily's rhubarb crisps. Did you hide some?"

Grace laughed. "They took the real rhubarb crisps. That's why either she or the two of us are going to have to remake them for the Expo. What I'm talking about is a plastic mock-up Emily made and painted.

It looks real but, believe me, if Mr. Blair got a mouthful of it, he might have puked, but it wouldn't have killed him. Don't worry. By the time you finish helping Emily or me, you'll be a kitchen pro."

Sarah doubted that, but as she dutifully set up the display while Grace went to get the mock-ups, she stared at the sign's printed words promising spinach pie and rhubarb crisp. She didn't know if she should laugh or cry. Instead, she prayed for Emily to be back soon.

Chapter Thirteen

At eight a.m. on Friday, Sarah unlocked the front door to Harlan's office and punched in the alarm code. She worked her way from the front door through the first floor of the old house, flipping the light switches on as she went. In his private office, she dropped the cheese and apple pastries she'd picked up on her way to work and the newspaper she'd retrieved from the lawn onto his desk.

Next, she brewed a fresh pot of coffee. Eight thirty still was too early for Harlan to be in, but she wanted everything purring smoothly when he arrived at nine. Not many bosses were as kind, understanding, and generous as Harlan had been since Wednesday night. Between rescheduled appointments and a motion docket at the courthouse, today was going to be busy.

She felt guilty over how much time Emily and she had taken away from Harlan's paying law practice and his sleep. From when she woke him two nights ago to meet Emily at the station, Harlan had been a prince. Most lawyers working pro bono would have run as fast as they could in the opposite direction once their client was released. Instead, Harlan went back to the police station with Emily for her statement, sat with Sarah to hear Jane's RahRah and jewelry accusations, and stayed with Emily while Peter questioned her most of last night.

If Sarah got anywhere near the stack of spinach pies and rhubarb crisp casseroles she bet Emily was madly making since she left the station house, she gladly would put her hand on one to swear she'd never again tell a lawyer joke. Coming to the office early today was the least Sarah believed she could do in exchange for getting a reprieve from having to cook or be involved in a food presentation.

Sarah had finished typing the last of the backlog of letters Harlan had dictated when she heard his key in the back door. A moment later, his footsteps echoed in the back hall that led to his office.

She waited to speak until he came out of his office. "Good morning."

"Morning." He zeroed in on the coffeepot. "Coffee from today?"

"Absolutely. Plus, I ran by the bakeshop. On your desk is your choice of an apple or cheese pastry."

"Thanks, but I'll pass. I stopped for breakfast at The Grill on my way in." He stood in front of her desk without saying anything.

She tried not to squirm under his silent gaze. "I've typed and printed all of the letters you left me. I'm sorry I got behind with these." She pushed a manila folder across her desk toward him. "Here are the ones ready for signature. I'll print the last one and bring it to you in a moment. I also typed the e-mails and sent them to your draft folder . . ." Her voice trailed off as she realized she was rambling. "Harlan, is there something wrong?"

"Come into my office, please."

She picked up a pen and notebook and followed him into his office, racking her brain to figure out an argument she could use to keep her job if he said her services were no longer needed. If she were in his position, between her having been behind on his correspondence, taking the long lunch hour yesterday, and bringing her personal problems to the office, she'd be inclined to let herself go. She wished she could point to her otherwise stellar performance as his secretary/receptionist, but she knew that wasn't the case. Perhaps there was another argument? Other than the fact that she was nice to his clients and they both volunteered at the animal shelter, none came to mind. Considering Harlan managed with only a part-time typist before he hired her, she was thankful he'd tolerated her various gaffes up to this point.

She tried to push her mind into overdrive. Nothing happened. Instead of coming up with a list of good reasons he should keep her, she was ready to fire herself. If she didn't need this job to pay her bills and put some money aside to go back to school, she probably would, out of fairness to him. To distract herself from such drastic action, she stared at the wood coat-tree in the corner of his office. His coat took one prong of the coatrack. The raffish cap she hated and he loved, probably because it shielded his bald spot, was on the second while the third was empty. For some reason, her mind fixated on what should hang on that hook, instead of how she could continue to hang around the office.

"Sarah?"

She tore herself away from the coatrack. Harlan repeated her name and gestured toward the guest chair near his desk. She sunk into the chair. She had tuned him out. Another moment of being inattentive.

Harlan sat in his high-backed leather desk chair and took a few pieces of paper out of the inner pocket of his blazer. Smoothing them out, he handed them to her.

"What's this?" Sarah scanned the documents. "Bill's will . . . and something about Bill and the animal trust for RahRah. Where did you get these? Did you draft them?"

"No, a Birmingham attorney did. When I was with Peter and Emily at the station last night, Peter gave me these copies to share with you."

"They can't be real!" She dropped them on his desk.

"On their face, they look pretty real to me."

Sarah shook her head, her face screwed in utter disbelief.

"If I read this one right"—Harlan handed her a page with several signatures on it—"it purports to be a codicil executed by Bill giving Jane control of RahRah and the animal trust." He picked up the other papers. "This other document is a will leaving his physical and personal property, wealth, and any unspecified assets to Jane."

She glanced at the paper without reading it. "There must be some mistake. Bill wouldn't leave everything to one of his flings."

"It seems Jane was more than a fling." Harlan gently took the page back from her and dropped it and the other pages on his desk. He put his hands together, prayer-point style. "Jane claims they were planning a wedding and, well, when Bill talked to me about the zoning question, he seemed to indicate he was expecting to make more changes in his life than simply remodeling the big house."

Sarah leaned forward and reached for the pile of papers. She flipped through them again, noting some of the pages Peter had given Harlan were typed, but some were handwritten. "I can't believe this. Surely these are fakes. Besides, you've always said handwritten wills don't fly in Alabama."

Harlan shrugged. "There is one exception and this may meet it."

"But Bill wasn't an exception guy. He wasn't particularly exceptional, either." Noting the look Harlan shot her, Sarah pressed her lips together. She walked to the window and looked out. "As I found out during our divorce, his business dealings might have been just this side of shady, but they were drafted in a foolproof manner. Bill Blair would never have left anything in a state it could be challenged."

Harlan took the papers back from her and dropped them on his desk. "Well"—he tapped the stack of documents with his hand—"from the face of these, I don't think you knew him as well as you thought."

Sarah grasped for another argument. "Surely, knowing RahRah has been with me for three years, a court would decide possession is nine-tenths of the law."

"Nine-tenths is a myth in most areas of law. Definitely so here. Since 2007, Alabama has allowed pet owners to create trusts to benefit their beloved pets. Mrs. Blair created such a trust and named Bill the trustee, giving him control of five hundred thousand dollars and the house she left for RahRah's care after her death. As trustee, Bill had the right to speak on behalf of RahRah and choose who cared for him. If he now believed Jane to be a better caretaker, nothing prohibited him from giving her the care of RahRah until RahRah's death, as well as naming her the beneficiary of any remainder of the trust."

"None of this makes any sense. If that was the case, why give me RahRah?" She bit her lip and shifted her gaze to the floor, holding back the tears that blurred her vision. "Jane was in the picture before we split. I just didn't know it then."

Sarah raised her head and met Harlan's gaze. "Can't you think of something legal to tell Peter so I can keep RahRah? I don't care about getting anything from the trust."

Harlan stared at the pages and shook his head. "Sarah, I'm going to research every angle to argue on your behalf, but if these papers are what they purport to be and the trust holds up in court, you need to consider the worst scenario. In the meantime, Jane demanded you surrender possession of RahRah immediately, but Peter stalled her."

"For how long?"

"Until Sunday."

Chapter Fourteen

Back at her desk, Sarah thought being fired by Harlan might have been less gut-wrenching than being told Peter had only bought her until Sunday to surrender RahRah. She didn't understand it. Until RahRah came into her life, she was a dog person. If asked, she always blamed it on a big cat jumping out of the shadows at her when she was a child, but RahRah had changed her feelings about cats. RahRah wasn't necessarily a warm and fuzzy kitten or cat, but he had a presence that ruled the roost. The roost would be much lonelier without him.

Even though assured she had RahRah until at least Sunday, Sarah was apprehensive every time someone opened the office door. Because so many client appointments were rescheduled when he was at the jail with Sarah and Emily, the door seemed to be in constant use. In fact, the office was so busy neither Harlan nor Sarah stopped for lunch.

Harlan walked the last client of the day to the door. "What are you still doing here?"

"Same as you." Sarah was returning one of Harlan's many paper files into a black metal filing cabinet. "Working."

"Well, get thee from this dungeon."

"Yes, m'lord," Sarah said with a straight face and a mock curtsey. She was relieved things on the surface were lighter between Harlan and her, but it didn't minimize their earlier discussion.

"Are you going over to the Civic Center for dinner?"

"Planning on it. You?" She was relieved when he responded it would be later because he still had things to finish up. Not having to watch for him over her shoulder would make it easier to snoop around the Civic Center. Still, she forced herself to offer, "If you need me to stay . . ."

"Don't even think about it. By now, I'm sure Emily would love seeing your friendly face. Get out of here, but do me a favor, please. Make sure the front door is locked." He walked back into his office.

Sarah didn't have to be told twice. She powered down her computer, cleared and locked her desk, and grabbed her purse.

"See you Monday." She was gone before he could reply.

Chapter Fifteen

Emily had predicted Friday evening would be slow, but the Food Expo was a zoo.

One of three women seated at a long table outside the main exhibition hall collected Sarah's ten dollar entry fee and handed her a plastic bag filled with different-colored poker chips. "Now dear, make sure you hold on to those chips. They're how you pay for everything you want to eat or drink. White chips for wine, blue for coffee, tea, or soda, and yellow to buy food. Lose them and you either go hungry or have to buy more."

Sarah examined the bag. Besides the ones the woman had mentioned, it contained about a dozen red ones. "What are the red chips for?"

"Voting for things you really like. Each exhibitor has a glass fishbowl for folks to leave red chips in. The vendor who gets the most during the weekend will be declared the winner of this year's Food Expo."

The woman beside her leaned over. "Make sure you look around at all the booths before you decide which ones you want to bless with a red chip and don't forget to save one for tomorrow for the best recipe demonstrator."

Assuring her she would choose carefully, Sarah went through the double doors into the exhibition hall. She wasn't sure which way to turn first in the crowded room so she simply walked up and down the aisles between the rows of booths. There didn't appear to be any rhyme or reason to how the product, arts and crafts, food, or drink booths were interspersed. She made note of the fact that from fried green tomatoes to whole fish piled on ice, all different types of food were on display.

Dropping a white chip into an oversize brandy snifter, Sarah accepted a pinot grigio–filled plastic cup from an earnest server who didn't look old enough to drink. She sipped it as she checked out the back room. A curtain partitioned off the work space, exhibitor food table, ovens, and refrigerator area from additional exhibitor booths.

Sarah returned to the main exhibition hall and headed toward the Southwind booth. Today, most of the open space in front of the three-stall booth was filled with patron tables and plastic chairs. Since yesterday, a small raised platform stage had been erected on the far end of the aisle. Southwind was in a perfect position. People watching something on the stage had to pass in front of the booth, as did anyone who sat down to eat or rest.

It certainly appeared that everything in both rooms was going well. Hopefully, Bill's death wasn't from foul play and yesterday's cut cord was an isolated incident.

Her wineglass still half full, Sarah took a seat at a table across from the Southwind booth to watch her sister in action and, perchance, do a little sleuthing.

Emily had a nice crowd in front of her section of

the booth. Mechanically, but with a smile pasted on her face, she alternately popped in or took out casseroles and pies from the microwave and oven. With equally machinelike precision, she cut and placed small servings in the plastic cups that lined her table. From the number of red chips Sarah could see in Emily's bowl, she knew Emily must have used up the serving cups she and Grace set out yesterday.

The other two Southwind stations apparently were getting far less traffic or hadn't been able to convince voters to drop their red chips as successfully as Emily had. Unless she'd emptied it, the bowl in front of Jane's area had half as many chips as Emily's. Sarah smiled at her observation but frowned when her gaze moved to Jane. She quickly shifted her attention back to listening to her sister interact with the crowd rather than risk a confrontation with Jane. Sarah wasn't sure she could control herself if they exchanged words. Hopefully, Harlan would figure out a way to resolve everything so RahRah could stay with her.

Emily's nonstop patter was quite impressive. Without missing a beat while restocking cups, forks, or food, she smiled, maintained eye contact, and engaged the people standing in line in front of her station by flitting from topic to topic.

After listening to Emily for about twenty minutes, Sarah realized she was merely repeating variations of the same remarks over and over. She described the dish she was serving, gave cooking tips, and personalized her remarks to bring the ever-changing crowd in on the joke with her. Once people laughed and ate, they invariably dropped one or all of their precious red chips in her basket.

In the few minutes Sarah watched, Emily managed to charm a group dressed in cowboy gear who roared about how many helpings of rhubarb crisp it would take to fill a portly gentleman's ten-gallon hat and equally big belly, as well as a church book club who hung on to Emily's cooking tips.

The crowd was waiting for Emily to serve them a spinach pie hot out of the oven when people from the back asked folks to move aside, allowing a girl barely as tall as the serving table to reach the front of the line. While Emily and the shifted line of folks watched, the pigtailed girl, clutching her teddy bear, carefully dropped her food chip in the basket and then ran back to her mother with her claimed taste of spinach pie. A moment later, she squeezed through the crowd again and put a red chip in Emily's basket.

Sarah envied Emily. She could never entertain a crowd like Emily was doing. When talents were given out, Sarah hadn't been in line for the gifts of gab and grace that made Emily a perfect cheerleader and now an engaging chef and food entertainer. She grimaced. If Harlan hadn't gotten Emily away from Peter in time to be part of the Expo today, Sarah would probably have had this crowd laughing, too, but it would have been at how inept she was in the kitchen.

"Are you finished?" Sarah looked up at the uniformed waiter who posed the question. He nodded toward her empty wineglass. Rather than answer, she stared at the seemingly familiar tattoos on his fingers and then shifted her gaze back to his face.

"You're Richard, aren't you? We met yesterday."

"Yes, that's right. May I take your glass?"

She handed it to him.

He thanked her and started to walk away when she called him back.

"Yes, ma'am?"

"Sarah, please. Ma'am is my mother."

He laughed. "Mi . . . Sarah, did you want something else? Perhaps one of Jane's flavored expressos or scones?"

"No, but yes, I was wondering why you're clearing instead of cooking?"

A frown crossed his face, but he converted it to a partial smile. "Good question. Chef Marcus rented extra space for Southwind's booth and divided it into three distinct sections. He's letting each of his cooks take turns showcasing throughout the weekend. Jane has the space on the left, Emily and Grace are in the middle, and Jacob and I are sharing the far side. When we're not cooking, we're making sure the exhibitor food and drinks are stocked and these tables are bussed. Grace and I had the opening few hours in the booth and, as you can see, Emily and Jacob are being featured now. We've got it worked out so we each have a few prime hours."

"Isn't Jane sharing?"

Richard grimaced in Jane's direction before rearranging his features into an unreadable mask. "No, Mr. Blair decided she didn't have to share her booth space."

Of course he did. Sarah rolled her eyes. "That's a shame. I'm sure we all would have enjoyed more time to taste your food. Do you have a personal specialty?"

"Comfort food. I don't cook again until late tomorrow, but if you come around then, I promise you some of the best chicken and waffles you've ever eaten."

"I'll make sure to stop by when you're working in the booth." Sarah remembered her promise to Emily and slipped back into her investigative mode. "I gather Jane insisted Chef Marcus honor Mr. Blair's wishes?"

Richard smiled and dipped his head once. "Speak of the devil, I better get back to work." He raised the decibel level of his voice. "If there is anything else I can get you, please let me know."

He briskly walked away. Distracted by Richard's abrupt departure, Sarah jumped out of her skin when she realized Chef Marcus, wearing flat yellow plastic clogs, a white Southwind jacket, and balloon chef pants, loomed above her.

"May I join you?" He pointed at the extra folding chair at her table.

"Of course." She moved her purse from the chair. Even seated, she had to look up at him. "Your Southwind food certainly seems to be a big hit."

"Thanks to your sister. I am very fortunate to have a chef of her talent working for me." He gestured toward Emily. "You should be very proud of her."

"Oh, I am. I've known for a long time what a marvelous chef she is. But, I guess you must think Jane is an even better cook because you aren't having her share her portion of the booth with anyone."

Marcus frowned. "Jane is good, but after Emily wins Sunday's contest, all of Wheaton will know how lucky they are to have her back in town."

"From your mouth to God's ears," Sarah teased. "It sounds to me like there will be many excellent chefs, including Jane, competing."

"None stand a chance against Emily."

Sarah shuddered, chilled by Chef Marcus's words. It was a feeling her grandmother described as "Someone just walked over my grave."

She bent forward, her voice no more than a whisper. "I hope you're not telling me the competition is rigged. That wouldn't be fair to the other competitors or to Emily."

He seemed to try to relax the contracture of his dark brows. They were thick and almost startling against his alabaster features. "Of course not." He threw her words back at her as he scrambled to his feet. "Rigged? To think that is to besmirch both my honor and your sister's talent. I have confidence in her. Obviously, you don't!"

Turning on his heel, he walked straight toward Emily's portion of the Southwind booth. Sarah sat dumbfounded. She wondered if she needed to use her hand to close her mouth while she made a mental note to discuss his short fuse with Emily.

Ignoring Jane, waving from the far side of the table separating her work space from Emily's, he pushed his way to the front of the diners standing in line for Emily's food. Chef Marcus picked up one of the sample cups on her table and held it above his head. Looking back, he stared at Sarah. "Chef Emily's food is marvelous, isn't it?"

A murmur from members of the crowd showed their agreement. "Probably the best food here or anywhere in Wheaton."

Even from where she sat, Sarah saw Emily blush. Chef Marcus ignored both the way Emily stepped back from him and the glaring daggers Sarah thought were jumping from Jane's eyes. There might be trouble in paradise the way it was going because, by now, Chef Marcus had managed to get the attention of many of the nearby exhibitors and Expo visitors. "I want to take this moment to introduce you to Southwind's newest and youngest sous chef, Emily Johnson."

Sous chef? Sarah's lips spread into a grin—thrilled that Emily had just received the promotion she wanted. She heard an intake of breath coupled with an "Oh, no!" The exclamation was so loud it took Sarah a few seconds to realize the same words had been uttered by both Emily and someone else in the booth. Sarah wasn't sure which of Emily's coworkers was so verbally dismayed by this development.

Chef Marcus grabbed Emily's hand and raised it in the air as if she had just won a prizefight. People waiting in line applauded.

Sarah heard a loud "woohoo" she realized came from Jacob. Although still at his station, he had stopped cooking long enough to let out a whistle and a cheer. At the other end of the Southwind booth, Richard stood silently by a sullen Jane. Seeing the diverse reactions of the Southwind cooks, Sarah wondered where Grace was and how she would react to Chef Marcus's surprise announcement. Not knowing the answer, she tucked the question into the recesses of her mind as she rose to join the crowd congratulating Emily.

Chapter Sixteen

When the crowd dissipated, Chef Marcus suggested Emily go home and celebrate or simply relax from her two late nights at the police station, but Emily refused. Basking in Chef Marcus's surprise announcement, she insisted she would remain until the Food Expo closed for the night. Sarah couldn't blame her. Chef Marcus's naming of her as his new sous chef gave Emily a short-lived mystique that Emily already was capitalizing on in terms of collecting red chips.

To Sarah's delight, it appeared that Emily's thoughts of them playing detective at the Expo seemed driven from her mind after being named Southwind's sous chef. Not wanting to remind Emily, Sarah tasted her sister's spinach pie and dutifully dropped all her red chips, but one, into her sister's basket. She offered to get Emily something to eat, but Emily declined, noting if she got hungry, she could nibble on one of her spinach pies or rhubarb casseroles or snack from a plate of brownies Jane had placed in the back of the booth in case any of the staff needed a sugar boost.

"Brownies are one of the few things she makes that are delicious."

Down to one wine chip, Sarah was debating whether to use it or go home to RahRah when Emily, without missing a beat in serving customers, whispered, "Don't worry about hanging around here tonight. Go home and try to piece things together about what really happened to Bill before the newspaper comes out."

"Sure." Sarah understood. Normally, both Emily and she complained that the decision to make their local paper available only three days a week made it a sham of a paper, but this time, having an extra twenty-four hours until the Sunday paper was published could work in their favor. It gave Sarah tonight and tomorrow to get to the bottom of things while Emily worked on making a good impression that hopefully wouldn't be dinged too badly if the Sunday headline read: "Local Sous Chef Allegedly Poisons Former Brother-in-Law."

Moving away from her sister's booth, Sarah used her last wine chip and found another seat. She tried to observe what people were doing while she considered what she knew:

1) Bill Blair was dead—and while it was shocking, a lot of people didn't necessarily believe it was a bad thing.
2) Bill apparently died from an allergic reaction after eating Emily's rhubarb crisp casserole—or something not yet determined.
3) The police believed Emily made the rhubarb crisp that Bill ate. Peter hadn't said it outright yet, but Grace and Emily both brought up the idea it was Emily's rhubarb crisp.

4) Emily and Sarah knew Bill would never eat Emily's rhubarb crisp because he hated rhubarb and, more importantly, he knew she used nuts in her recipe.

5) On Wednesday night, Bill called Emily to come to the Civic Center because there was a major problem that couldn't wait until morning. According to Emily, he didn't say what the problem was.

6) Emily discovered Bill lying in front of Southwind's Food Expo booth. She called 911 and then tried to resuscitate him.

7) The police found Bill dead, clutching a fork that had remnants of rhubarb crisp on it.

8) The police observed rhubarb stains on Bill's and Emily's clothing and hands.

9) The only fingerprints on the fork belonged to Bill and Emily.

10) Jane, Bill's girlfriend (fiancée?), had her job because of her relationships with Bill and Chef Marcus. Since Bill's death, Sarah had seen Jane cozying up to Chef Marcus, indicating the two might be having an affair or there had been a quick change in allegiance.

11) Jane claimed Bill was going to fire Emily because she caught Emily rifling through company business records. Emily still hadn't told Sarah the story behind that accusation.

Sarah stopped making her list. She added a mental note to ask Emily about what might be behind Chef Marcus's short fuse, the other chefs, and why, with Bill dead, Chef Marcus didn't make Jane share her station with anyone else. She also decided her sister needed

to explain why, when Jane was adamant Bill wanted to
can Emily, Emily didn't defend herself. As fiery as
Emily normally was, especially if she felt she was being
wronged, she'd never denied the accusation. Something about Emily's response didn't feel right to Sarah.

She forced herself to shift her focus back to the
facts she knew.

12) Someone sabotaged the refrigerator/freezer
    that held the food for a private dinner party
    Southwind was catering and the partially
    cooked casseroles and pies Emily had pre-
    pared for the Food Expo. Could it have
    been Jane, Grace, Jacob, Richard, or one of
    Richard's friends? Were there any compet-
    ing restaurateurs who might have it in for
    Southwind? Either avenue could be a way to
    develop more suspects for Peter.

13) If Harlan hadn't stuck with Emily and essen-
    tially forced Peter's hand so that she'd left
    the station in the wee hours of the morning,
    Emily wouldn't have been able to remake
    enough food to participate in the Food
    Expo. Whether Emily liked it or not, they
    had to consider who from Southwind would
    have benefited if Emily hadn't been able to
    be in the booth. Richard certainly hadn't
    seemed happy about being restricted in his
    cooking time. Jane seemed threatened by
    Emily's competency. Sarah wasn't sure about
    Grace or Jacob—or even Chef Marcus.

14) Chef Marcus promoted Emily in the public
    forum of the Food Expo after having pre-
    dicted to Sarah that Emily would win Sunday's
    cooking competition.

Thinking chronologically wasn't producing any revelations, so Sarah decided to try something Harlan taught her. He claimed every life decision was tied to a relationship. As he said, love, hate, greed, and jealousy were the things that kept him in business. Reactions to emotional stimuli prompted business decisions, made people create trusts, wills, and prenuptial agreements, and dictated how people behaved during divorces. Time and again, Sarah had seen Harlan calm ruffled feathers or hold the hand of a person going through a difficult time.

She took a deep breath and shifted gears to think logically about Bill's murder and Emily's involvement with him. The obvious connection between them was their former family relationship because of Sarah and Bill's marriage. There was no secret that his treatment of Sarah had resulted in tension and bad words exchanged between Emily and Bill during the divorce proceedings.

It appeared, except for Jane's accusation that Bill was going to fire Emily, they'd found a way to work together professionally. Apparently, Emily put aside any bad feelings to realize her dream of working for Chef Marcus and Southwind—or had she? That, Sarah realized, was probably the million-dollar question that Peter, in his official police role, was investigating.

Using Harlan's method, she brainstormed beyond Emily for suspects. What about Chef Marcus and his economic woes? Bill saved the restaurant by investing in Southwind, but that meant Chef Marcus no longer controlled his own business. Perhaps that riled him, or was Marcus angry because his hands were tied when Bill wanted to promote Jane and he favored Emily? Maybe someone else was upset when it seemed Jane likely would be promoted? Unfortunately, for Peter's purposes, that question pointed the finger back at Emily, but surely some of the other line cooks could have been angry, too.

From watching everyone in action, it seemed Jacob was okay with Chef Marcus's promotional decision, but she couldn't say the same about Jane, Richard, or Grace. Then again, maybe appearances were deceiving. Grace seemed nice, but she also appeared to know a lot about questioning and bookings in criminal matters. Maybe she was the type of person who would kill someone else. Sarah needed to find out more about Grace's past. Richard obviously had issues with Bill's favoritism of Jane. Perhaps he wanted to clear the way for his own promotion. And just because Jacob was clean-cut and oh-so-cute and had yelled "woohoo," she shouldn't jump to let him off the hook.

What bothered her the most, though, was how Jane fit into everything. There was no question she wanted the position and might have been on her way to being more than Southwind's sous chef. Marrying Bill, would that have made her an owner of Southwind and given her a better hold on her position in the kitchen, but didn't she get all that with him dead, too? If the documents were real, once the will Harlan showed her was probated, Jane would inherit everything of Bill's and become the majority owner of Southwind. From what Sarah had seen of Jane, she was surprised Jane wasn't already trying to exert her authority over everything, especially who was promoted to sous chef.

Sarah's head was beginning to spin. She wondered how much of this she could verbalize for Peter or for Harlan and whether they'd take any of these possibilities seriously. And silly as it might seem, did RahRah fit into the murder equation somewhere?

Sarah sipped the last dreg of her wine and pushed her glass away. She had a buzz, lots of questions, no answers, and a cat waiting at home for what might only be an indefinite period of time.

Chapter Seventeen

Sarah was about to swing into her driveway to park near the garage when she saw an open parking spot in front of her house. Because her apartment was converted attic space that could only be reached through the front foyer, she always preferred street parking to having to walk back to the front door from the dark driveway. Feeling lucky, she parked, locked her Honda, and went up the walkway.

The street door was ajar. She would have to talk to her downstairs neighbor about it. Both rarely locked their own doors, but that was because they were careful to keep the outer door locked. She thought about knocking and reminding her neighbor but decided it was too late to bother him tonight. Looking up the stairs from in front of his door, she noticed the bulb by her door was burnt out. As she climbed the steps, she added calling her landlord and her neighbor to tomorrow's to-do list.

As Sarah reached the dark part of the stairwell "When the Saints Come Marching In," her ringtone, resounded through the hallway. She rummaged through her purse, hurrying down the stairs until she reached one illuminated by a working bulb. Yanking her phone from the bottom, she hit the green answer icon. Before she could say "hello," she was pushed hard from behind. The last thing she heard before she hit her head and passed out was her own scream.

"That should do it. Expect to have a pretty good bruise on your face." The paramedic, who had arrived just as she regained consciousness, finished smoothing the Steri-Strip over her left brow. Without thinking, Sarah reached for her forehead, but an out-of-uniform Peter, who sat on the step next to her, intercepted her hand. She didn't hurry to move it.

"You need to leave that alone and keep it dry tonight," the paramedic said. "Because you won't go in with us tonight, give your doctor a call tomorrow or go in and see him on Monday." Taking off his purple gloves, the paramedic pulled a sheet of paper out of the pocket of one of his two bags. "From the looks of it, you're lucky you weren't hurt worse."

"I'm lucky I was answering a call from the chief of police, who responded so quickly."

Ignoring Sarah's gushing and the faintly blushing chief, the paramedic thrust the piece of paper at Sarah. "This is a concussion checklist. I don't think you have one, but I don't know. You were unconscious for a few minutes, so it would be a good idea to have someone keep an eye on you tonight." He snapped his bags shut and stood up. "Call us if you feel ill or need us again."

"Thank you," Sarah said. As the downstairs door slammed behind him, she scanned the checklist. "It probably isn't necessary, but I guess I can set an alarm to wake me up every few hours." She stuck the paper in her pocket as she stood, then stumbled.

Peter caught her and eased her back onto the step. "I don't think you should be alone tonight. My techs are finished with your apartment. Nothing seemed out of order. They got a few prints off the doorknob, so we'll see what that shows, but that's about it."

Sarah nodded.

"Can I take you to your sister's place?"

"She doesn't have a place. She's been staying with Mom. And no, even if my mother wasn't at a spa in Mexico this week, that's the last place I would go tonight. This would frighten her too much." Sarah's free hand again found its way up to the bandage. "Plus, I doubt Emily's even back from the Food Expo yet. Besides, all my things are here and . . ." She jumped to her feet, steadying herself with the rail as she became light-headed.

"What is it?" Peter asked.

"RahRah. The door was open all this time and RahRah hasn't come out." With Peter behind her, she went into her apartment and called for her cat.

There was no response.

"Does anything seem out of place?"

She looked around. Nothing seemed disturbed. The drawers were closed, the closet was cracked exactly as she had left it, her bed was unmade, and a bracelet she had left on top of her dresser still sat there. "The only thing missing seems to be RahRah. Would you please check under the bed for me? He likes to hide there. Maybe the techs scared him so he's hiding."

Peter leaned down and used the flashlight on his phone to make sure there wasn't a curled-up fur ball under the bed. "Nothing here."

He put a hand on Sarah's rumpled double wedding ring quilt for leverage to stand. "I haven't seen one of these in years."

"My grandmother made it. She was afraid she wouldn't be around when Emily and I got married so she made a quilt for each of our hope chests."

"It's beautiful."

"I always thought so, too, but Bill preferred a down comforter. After our divorce, I couldn't see keeping it pristine for the future. I decided the new me would use things I love."

"Makes sense. Quilts like yours are made with love and meant to be used by people who love them." Peter looked around the apartment and pointed to the closet. "Let's check that out."

Sarah walked into the closet ahead of Peter. She settled herself on the floor amidst her shoes and boots. Peter stepped in front of her and stretched his arm up to shine his flashlight across the upper shelves.

From her position on the floor, Sarah looked up, slowly taking Peter in. His leather boots, probably the same ones he wore with his uniform, were almost as tall as her seated eye level. Instead of the usual baggy appearance created by his uniform, his dark jeans, tucked tightly into his boots, emphasized his muscled legs, calves, and lack of a tush. When he turned and raised his arms to scan the nooks and crannies at the top of her closet, she saw his chest muscles ripple under his black cotton T-shirt.

The man obviously worked out. In fact, despite being a few pounds heavier, he was more buff than when they were in high school. If he had looked like this back then, Emily might have stayed home some of the times he came around. Tearing her eyes from his chest, Sarah took in the square jaw jutting out beyond his neck and his shock of thick black hair. She even liked the smell of his cologne. It was muskier than the sweet stuff Harlan used. Maybe it was the bump on the head or her angle from the floor, but she hadn't ever viewed Peter this way before.

Embarrassed, she bent her head so he couldn't see her face as she moved her shoes, tote bags, and other clutter around the closet floor. Regaining control, she started to stand but again became dizzy and grabbed for his arm.

With one hand, Peter scooped her to her feet. He guided her out of the closet and back to her bed. "Are you okay?"

"I am, but I'm afraid RahRah isn't."

"It looks like RahRah may be what whoever broke into your apartment was after. Could the person who pushed you have been holding RahRah?"

She shook her head. "I don't think so. Whoever pushed me used two hands."

Above them they heard a faint sound.

"RahRah? RahRah!" Sarah yelled.

The shuffling sound came again. Peter rapped his knuckles on the ceiling and waited. Nothing.

"RahRah." Peter opened the closet and again shone his light upward. "Look, there's an opening I missed. Above the shelf."

Jumping from the bed, Sarah squeezed into the closet and pressed against Peter so she could see the small space where a ceiling tile had been dislodged.

"Could he fit through there?" Peter asked.

"You'd be amazed the spaces he can get into."

"Do you have a step stool?"

"In the closet, near the sink."

Opening the two-step ladder, Peter set it up next to

Sarah in the closet. He reached up but couldn't move the tile to create a larger opening. Backing out of the closet, he retrieved the stepladder and placed it near where they heard a scratching sound.

Sarah steadied the ladder as he gently pushed up one of the ceiling twelve-by-twelve-inch squares. The tile gave. Carefully, Peter slid it to the side and used his flashlight to illuminate the attic area over the dropped ceiling. He handed her his flashlight and reached his arm into the open space.

"It's going to be all right," he whispered. He moved slowly, speaking softly. Finally, he pulled his large hand through the opening, grasping one subdued-looking cat. Peter extricated the finger he'd tucked under RahRah's collar and handed him to Sarah.

Once in Sarah's arms, RahRah alternately purred and hissed, but he didn't try to escape Sarah's engulfing hug. Cuddling him, she sat at her kitchen table.

"You must be a cat whisperer." She stroked RahRah gently behind his ears while Peter replaced the ceiling tile, climbed down, and put the stepladder away. "RahRah is usually so squirrely. It's amazing he let you bring him out of the attic without a fight."

"I got lucky. Apparently, you have a fraidycat who prefers flight to confrontation. Whoever broke into your apartment must have scared RahRah, so he fled up into the attic through that opening in your closet. I'll block it with some of your purses, but I'd get that closed soon. It looks as if he's used that route before."

"I'll show it to the landlord tomorrow."

Peter rubbed the top of RahRah's head before plopping into the other kitchen chair. RahRah turned toward Peter as if affronted the rubbing had ceased. "RahRah either went farther into the attic than before or was simply so scared he froze. It sure was easier retrieving him frozen than biting and scratching."

"I gather you've done this before."

"Usually from trees, not attics."

Sarah squeezed RahRah closer to her chest. "Maybe being frozen saved him. We couldn't find him nor could the person who broke into my apartment."

"Speaking of that person, did you notice if the person was male or female?"

"I thought it was a man, but I really don't know. The light at the top of the stairs was out so I had gone down a few steps to where it was lit to answer my phone. My back was to the door of my apartment, so I didn't see anyone before I was pushed. I think I blacked out quickly. All I remember is a black image flying past me."

"It's a good thing I heard you scream. If you'd simply not answered, I wouldn't have come."

Sarah lightly touched her head. "As my mother would say, 'your call was meant to be.' But, why did you call me?"

"You were upset when you left my office. I was hoping we could talk."

Peter got up and walked into the hallway.

Suddenly, she saw light outside her door. "It works?"

"Yup. Looks like someone wanted to make sure it was dark if you came home."

"They planned to hurt me?"

"Maybe not hurt you, but at least be able to hear you fumbling at the door. That's the only way in or out, isn't it?"

Sarah nodded. She put her face into RahRah's fur as she screwed her eyes tightly shut, trying to avoid another crying spell. "I wish I could remember more, but I can't."

"Tell you what. Let's make this easy. Don't try so

hard. Simply close your eyes and think about being on the stairs. You told me you heard your phone ring, went down a few stairs, and answered it. What else did you smell or hear?"

She closed her eyes and slowly stroked RahRah's fur, willing herself back in time. "After I felt the two hands on my back, I lost my balance. I fell forward, turning my head to the left. When I did that, I saw a flash of black out of the corner of my eye, probably as the person ran to the downstairs door. At that moment, I felt pain. It must have been when I hit my head."

"Did you see anything else as the person ran by?"

"No and I don't know if the flash of black was me passing out or a person dressed in black." Sarah thought for another moment. "When the person pushed me, there was a sweet smell."

"Perfume? Aftershave?"

"I don't think so. It was something pleasant, but I don't know what." She looked up from RahRah at Peter, a tear escaping from her eye. She brushed it away. "I'm sorry. I really wish I could remember, but my memories are all mishmashed. Nothing seems solid."

"That's okay." Peter's soothing tone calmed Sarah. He cleared his throat. "I think RahRah and you need a good night's rest. Are you sure you don't want me to stay and wake you every few hours?"

"Stay here? Tonight? Thank you, but no. I prefer to not be fussed over." She grinned. "Don't worry. I'll make sure the door is locked."

"But the directions about you sleeping . . ."

"RahRah and I will be okay. I'll set an alarm for every few hours. Besides, I won't be sleeping late. I need to be at the Civic Center to help Emily before the Expo opens tomorrow morning."

"I need to be there early tomorrow, too. There are a few more people I want to talk to about the malicious mischief with the refrigerator. It would make me feel better, though, if you'd let me watch you. I could sit in this chair."

"Thanks, but no," Sarah said. "Besides, I'm sure your family will be looking for you."

"Not tonight."

"Oh, are they on some kind of trip?"

"No. Hi and Peter Jr. are with their mom. It wouldn't be a problem for me to stay."

So, he was divorced or separated. She wondered which one. "That's very kind of you, but I'll be okay tonight." She glanced at RahRah, seemingly asleep in her lap. "Peter, am I going to have to be alone?"

He turned his face away from her. "I'm working on it. I'm not sure yet."

Chapter Eighteen

Too early the next morning, Sarah covered most of the bruises on her face with makeup, but she couldn't hide the area surrounding the Steri-Strip. It was nearly as blue as the shirt she wore with her jeans. Thankfully, she didn't have the horrible headache she'd expected. She wished she could hide until the bruise faded, but she'd promised Emily she'd snoop today. Besides, she needed the money Emily was paying her to work at the Expo.

In the kitchen, Sarah carefully stepped over RahRah. She put fresh food and water in his bowls.

He purred but didn't move from his linoleum square.

"Right back to your special place as if last night didn't faze you for a moment. You're not fretting about anything, are you, RahRah?" Sarah ignored the fact that their conversation was one-sided as she checked his kitty litter. For one more night, it didn't need changing.

She picked up her keys. "RahRah, I'll be home late tonight, but you don't have to worry. I'll make sure the door is locked. Just remember, Peter blocked the closet opening, so if anything scares you, hide under the bed."

On her way to the Civic Center, Sarah wished she felt as secure as RahRah.

"I guess I didn't get the message about today's dress code," Sarah said to Emily, twenty minutes later, after finishing an abbreviated rehash of her fall without mentioning she was pushed.

Emily smiled at the dress code reference. "I forgot to tell you." She gestured at the other chefs working in the Southwind area. Except for Jane, who was wearing black balloon pants with a black Southwind chef's jacket, everyone, including Emily, wore black jeans and a button-up black shirt with the word SOUTHWIND stitched on the top of the pocket.

"And Jane?"

"Being a server isn't in her repertoire."

"Well, outfit or no outfit, it doesn't make a difference to me. You and I know I'm the last one who belongs in a kitchen. That said, what can I do to help today?"

"Not much right now. We'll be setting up for the next hour, getting ready for the Expo doors to open at nine, but Grace and I have my area under control." Their discussion was interrupted by a timer beeping.

Not moving from the front of the booth, Sarah watched Emily slip her hands into two black pocket potholders lying on her back table and carefully grab a hot spinach pie from her oven and put it on the empty top of her microwave to cool.

Coming back to where Sarah stood, Emily stopped to peek over Grace's shoulder to see how she was doing at a makeshift cutting board station they had placed on their area's side table. Emily patted Grace on the shoulder and said something too quiet for Sarah to hear.

Grace looked up and brandished her knife in Sarah's direction by way of greeting before returning her attention and sharp knife to deftly separating the leaves from the rhubarb stalks. As Grace tossed the leaves in the trash and added the stalks to an almost full storage container, Sarah marveled at the swiftness of Grace's strokes without slashing a finger in the process.

"As you can see, we're using every inch of our space. Let's see what we can do with you." Emily looked toward the smaller end of the Southwind exhibition space, where Chef Marcus and Jacob had their heads together. "I don't think those two can squeeze another person or thing into their area."

Sarah followed the line of Emily's vision. Mounds of different vegetables, spices, and salad ingredients were separated into distinct stacks on Jacob and Marcus's table. Sitting in front of the two chefs was the largest bowl Sarah had ever seen. It appeared to her that Jacob, as guided by the older chef, was slowly adding various layers of ingredients and spices to whatever he was mixing in the bowl.

"Those two look like they work well together."

"Definitely. Jacob is a sweetie and very talented. He worked under Chef Marcus in San Francisco. In fact, I got his job when he left to try something on his own. His new venture failed right about the time Chef Marcus opened Southwind, so Marcus gladly made a place on staff for him."

Glancing behind her, Sarah couldn't help but think how much Jacob and Marcus's neatness contrasted with Jane's workstation. In Jane's work space, plastic containers glistening from condensation were interspersed with discarded bowls and utensils. Three grocery bags sat on the floor. Sarah could see the tips of leafy greens protruding from two of the bags. Unlike in Jacob's and Emily's areas, there didn't appear to be a clearly defined prep area in Jane's section of the Southwind booth.

Jane and Richard stood near Jane's front table, which was covered with fresh spices and a small pile of vegetables. They obviously were engaged in a heated exchange. Each held a knife.

Sarah's attempt to ascertain if one might have pushed her the night before by observing them was interrupted by Emily. "Uh-oh. I better break this up before he wastes his knife skills on her."

While Emily squeezed through a small opening between Jane and her display tables, Sarah moved closer to hear the fighting couple.

". . . I'm not an errand boy. I can't help it if things haven't worked out at Southwind the way you planned, but Bill and you promised I'd get my own Expo station."

"Bill . . ." Jane stopped in midsentence when she noticed Emily approaching from behind Richard. She slashed her finger across her throat.

Richard turned his head and looked over his shoulder "The cavalry arrives." He threw the knife in his hand onto the table. It missed, making a clattering sound as it fell to the floor. Grabbing his cinched knife roll, the prized possession of most chefs, from the table, he ignored the fallen knife as he pushed by Emily. "I need a smoke."

Sarah thought Emily would follow Richard. Instead, Emily bent over and retrieved the knife from the floor. Handle first, she handed the knife to Jane, who placed the knife on the table with her other knives and thrust her flushed face toward Emily's.

"This is the last straw. He's got to go. I can't work with Mr. Drama anymore. All he's done since he got here is gripe. You've got to fire him."

Emily crossed her arms over her chest but didn't try to stop Jane's tirade.

"It's not fair. If it wasn't for you, I wouldn't be behind." Jane moved closer to Emily. "I shouldn't have to pay the price because you can't manage employees."

"Your lack of organization is my problem?"

"Yes! I'd be prepped if Richard hadn't been so busy complaining. He's talked more than he's worked." Jane twisted her mouth into a pout.

"Somehow, I doubt that." Emily turned her back on Jane. She rolled her eyes at Sarah, who bit her lip to stifle a laugh.

"Emily," Jane said in a suddenly sweeter tone, "you look like you've got your station going smoothly. Why don't you let Grace help me catch up before the Expo opens?"

When her sister turned around again to face Jane but hesitated to respond, Sarah peeked over at Grace. She could swear she saw Grace shake her head "no."

"Under the circumstances, I'm sure Marcus wouldn't mind you letting Grace work for me."

"I'm tied up right now," Grace said. "I need to cover this stuff and take it out to the back refrigerator. Chef Marcus also asked me to make sure we have enough ice and drinks at the employee table." She swept the last leaves from her cutting board into the garbage, threw the remainder of the usable rhubarb into the storage container, and fled the booth.

"Grace is busy right now, but Sarah can help you."

Too late, Sarah tried to keep her face from registering surprise. Had Emily lost her mind? Help Jane? She was about to remind her sister about her ongoing dispute with Jane over RahRah and Jane's accusations she'd stolen Mother Blair's bracelet, but because of Emily's now-widened stance and relaxed shoulders, she waited. Sarah wondered what her sister's crazy thought process was.

Emily certainly couldn't be envisioning Sarah's prowess in the kitchen would help Jane or make Jane and Sarah bosom buddies. Maybe Emily thought Sarah could learn something useful from Jane? Perhaps Emily hoped Sarah would screw something up for Jane? Or, it could be both.

"Sarah? Not on your life." Jane closed her hand around one of the knives. She took a step forward. "You're just trying to ruin my presentation this afternoon. You're not going to get away with it."

Sarah held her breath. She feared this might be a rerun of the other night, but without police officers to hold Jane back. She scanned the room for one of the Civic Center security guards or, if she was lucky, Peter, but didn't see either. As Jane stepped toward Emily, Jane knocked over one of her grocery bags. Its contents spilled under Emily's table.

Sidestepping the spillage, Emily placed her hand near the knives on the table.

"That's enough!" Chef Marcus yelled.

Sarah didn't know where he had come from, but she was relieved. His bulk filled the space between Jane and Emily.

He stared at Jane. "This isn't the way chefs behave in my kitchen. Go wash your face and cool off."

Jane started to protest but apparently had a change of heart. She left without another word.

After Jane was gone, Chef Marcus turned to Emily,

who was smiling at him. "And you, I expected better from you. You need to learn how to manage your staff."

Amazed, Sarah watched Emily stiffen as she clearly struggled to keep her temper in check and not respond.

"Get back to your station," Chef Marcus directed. "I'll work with Jane."

Emily stood frozen.

"Go."

Emily went, but not to the part of the station where Sarah stood. Rather, she headed toward the back room.

In all the years of their sisterhood, Sarah didn't think she had ever seen Emily so forcibly restrain herself from speaking her mind. It didn't suit her.

Chapter Nineteen

"What are you waiting for?" When Chef Marcus didn't get an answer, he snapped his fingers in Sarah's direction.

She jumped.

"Emily told me she asked you to help us out today. If you're here to work, get to it. Pick up Jane's things from under the table and help your sister with whatever she needs while I see to Jane."

"Yes, sir." Not waiting for further directions, Sarah crawled under the front table of her sister's section of the booth. On her hands and knees, Sarah stuffed Jane's vegetables back into Jane's partially torn bag. Chef Marcus's intervention on Jane's behalf surprised her. Had Marcus or Jane—or both—killed Bill to get him out of the way so they could be together while keeping Jane as Bill's heir? If Jane inherited Bill's estate and Marcus then married her, he again would have full control of his restaurant. Maybe he promoted Emily to cover up his relationship with Jane to prevent the police from suspecting them of conspiring to kill Bill?

Squeezing the last tomato into the bag, Sarah

wondered how long she could safely hide under the table before Chef Marcus noticed. She prayed Emily or Grace would return soon. She had no idea what needed to be done. The idea of explaining to Chef Marcus why she wasn't being productive wasn't something she relished.

"Are you planning to stay under there all day?"

Sarah peeked under the edge of the tablecloth. The disembodied voice belonged to a pair of Docksiders almost covered by khakis standing in front of the booth. She rose, carefully balancing the restuffed grocery bag.

"Hi, Harlan. What are you doing here so early?" She slid the bag carefully onto the table in Jane's station.

"I'm on the Food Expo steering committee, so I'm obligated to make an appearance."

"But the Expo isn't open yet."

"The better to make sure all the exhibitors note I was here. Being on the committee let me come in early. I can say hello to everyone and be out jogging by the time the Expo officially opens. What are you doing under this table? But first, what in blazes happened to your face?"

Sarah gave him the abbreviated version of her adventure from the night before and then added a quick summary of what had just happened between Emily, Jane, and the vegetables. He listened without interrupting. His gaze never left her face.

She'd always thought it cliché when authors wrote someone's eyes were the same shade of blue as their shirt or that a character's eyes twinkled, but anyone seeing Harlan's blue eyes today would have to agree they met the stereotypical descriptions.

"Isn't my office enough for you? Or are you here snooping, despite what I said about playing detective?"

"Now, Harlan, would I do that? How could I ever think of leaving the wonderful boss I have?"

He laughed. "That's flattering, but I'm serious. Look what happened to you last night. Maybe Emily or your sleuthing is why you were attacked? You need to go home and leave the investigating to the professionals. Neither Peter nor I want anything to happen to you and we can't always be around when you play detective."

Sarah's eyes narrowed. She'd been so focused on RahRah that she hadn't considered the attack might have been personal. "Honest, I'm not here playing detective. I didn't have to work or be at the animal shelter today and the Southwind staff is so short-handed, Emily thought some extra hands onboard would help." She held hers up. "Have hands, will work. I bet she could use you, too, if you'd like. You should know, though, she barely pays minimum wage."

He waved his right hand in protest. "When it comes to cooking, I plead the Fifth. I'm simply here to be seen, nibble a bit, and be gone before it gets too chaotic."

Sarah caught sight of Chef Marcus staring at them as he peeled the skin off plump eggplants with quick knife strokes. He looked away as Jane sidled back into the booth. "Uh-oh. I better get to work before I get more than the evil eye."

Harlan glanced in the direction Sarah was staring. "Okay, but don't get too comfortable in this environment. I expect to see you in the office Monday morning."

She gave him a mock salute.

Grinning, Harlan walked over to speak with Jane and Chef Marcus.

Sarah wished Emily or Grace would come back

and tell her what needed to be done next. Turning her back to Jane's section of the booth, she slipped her phone out of her pocket and texted Emily. No response. She peeked back at Jane, Chef Marcus, and Harlan. Judging by how physically close the three stood, Sarah concluded Harlan had engaged them in a serious discussion.

To stall, but still appear busy, Sarah decided to fall back on her childhood kitchen habits. She grabbed Emily's overflowing trash bag from the can and cinched it closed. "Any garbage you'd like me to take out for you?" she called to Jacob.

Jacob looked up from carefully transferring bunches of carrots from a big box into his mini-refrigerator. While she'd hidden under the table, he'd apparently gone and changed into a nicer chef's jacket. "That would be great. I've got plenty."

She left Emily's near the back of the booth and went to get his. Seeing his neatly stacked carrots and how clean his work area was, she marveled at how much he'd gotten done while managing to stay out of the fray with Jane. His giant bowl, filled to the brim, was centered on his front table surrounded by tasting cups and forks. Once he removed the Saran Wrap covering the bowl, he'd be ready to serve.

With a dramatic flourish Sarah was sure was for her benefit, he pulled his garbage bag from the can, tied its flaps into a knot, and handed it and the now-empty box from the carrots to her with a slight bow. "Thank you."

"You're welcome." She dropped the bulky bag into the box and carried both back to where she'd left Emily's garbage. Rather than immediately heading to the Dumpster, she tried another justification for staying in the booth until Emily or Grace returned. The idea of leaving Emily's area unguarded didn't sit well with her.

Her gaze lit on the nearby plate of Jane's brownies. Only a few remained—and they were calling to her. Sarah weighed her options: take out the trash or succumb to temptation. No matter how delicious the brownies were, and they certainly looked good, she wanted nothing to change her tainted opinion of Jane. She decided the more noble choice, and the one with fewer calories, was the garbage.

Still hoping Emily or Grace would come back so someone would be in Emily's part of the booth, she left the two filled bags and the box where she had dropped them and leaned across the side table Emily shared with Jacob. "Jacob, do you know where the clean garbage bags are?"

Instead of answering her, he reached under one of his tables and dragged out a large roll of oversize trash bags. He peeled two off and handed one to her.

Sarah was tucking the edges of the bag around the sides of Emily's can in slow motion when Grace returned. She, too, was wearing one of the nicer Southwind chef jackets.

"Boy, am I glad to see you!"

Grace smiled. "Aw, I guess absence really does make the heart grow fonder." She started to pick up the garbage, but Sarah stopped her.

"I'll take it, if you don't mind. It would be better if you stayed here and finished setting up the booth. I don't know what to do next but this way everything will be ready when Emily gets back."

"No problem." Grace glanced at the clock on the wall. "Do you know where she is? We've only got about fifteen minutes until the doors open."

Sarah shrugged and pulled her phone from her

pocket. No new texts or missed calls. "I'm sure she'll be back soon."

She bent to double-check the bags were cinched.

"Our food is ready, but there still are some little tasks to be done before service begins." Grace peered around the room. "It's not like Emily to leave things to the last minute."

"No, it isn't," Sarah agreed.

Grace dragged the box marked TABLECLOTHS from under the table. Opening it, she rummaged through the box until she found one the right size to cover her prep station area. With a quick flick of her wrist, Grace flipped the clean tablecloth onto the table. As she smoothed it into place, Sarah marveled at how easy the younger woman made everything look.

"I can't tell you how glad I am you know what to do. You seem like an old pro. How long have you been doing restaurant work?"

"Ever since I can remember. My mother was a waitress in a restaurant that couldn't hold a candle to Southwind. She worked a split shift."

"A split shift?"

"Yeah. She came in around eleven for the lunch shift. When the crowd thinned, she hung around to do food prep and set up the salad bar. I came to the restaurant when school was out. Once everything was set up, we went home until she went back for dinner service. She stayed until closing."

"Those must have been long evenings for you or did you stay home with your father?"

"That's a laugh. I never knew my dad."

"Oh, I'm sorry."

"Don't be. Because Mom's boss didn't want kids around during the evenings, I stayed at the apartment.

Homework, a bite to eat, TV, and bed. Mom's hours weren't great, but the tips were good."

"But surely you didn't learn everything I've seen you do in the kitchen from being at your mom's restaurant a few hours a day?"

"Hardly. I'm a student in the junior college's culinary program, thanks to Harlan."

"How's that?"

"I was at a party during high school that Chief Mueller busted. He took everyone in, whether we were doing something or not. I was just there, but it was my word against some of the other kids."

Now Sarah understood why Grace adored Harlan. "And Harlan was your attorney?"

"Right. Mom and I couldn't afford an attorney, but I got lucky when the court appointed him to represent me. He dug holes in the other kids' stories and got me off. Then Harlan convinced Chief Mueller and Mr. Blair to help me go to culinary school as a work-study student. I promised I wouldn't let him down." She wiped her cheek and turned her head away from Sarah. "I don't know where I'd be without him."

Grace cleared her throat and pointed at the garbage. "Enough. We have work to do. Better go take care of that trash."

Sarah picked up the two garbage bags and Jacob's box. "I'll throw these out and be right back to give you a hand."

"Okay." Grace covered the now-cleaned prep area with more cups. "The closest Dumpster is the temporary one on the loading dock. Go through the back door." She pointed to the room where Sarah and she had worked yesterday. "On your way back, grab a couple of Emily's spinach pies from the fridge we threw the stuff away from."

Sarah froze. "Excuse me?"

"Don't worry. They replaced the cord last night and cooled it down so we could use it today. Emily has the top shelf and the two on the bottom. They're marked."

Sarah let out the breath she hadn't realized she'd been holding.

"While you're gone, I'll cut these pies up for the first onslaught of visitors. We'll warm the pies you fetch in the oven. That way, Emily will have a steady flow once the Expo opens."

Sarah nodded in agreement. That would be Emily's plan, too, if she was here. Where was she? All Sarah could think was whatever Emily was doing, it had to be important to keep her away from her booth this close to the beginning of the Food Expo. Even though she'd already been named sous chef, Emily had to know that as fast as he gave her the job, Chef Marcus could take it away. Chef Marcus didn't seem like a person who played around in the kitchen.

Emily wasn't stupid. So where was she?

Chapter Twenty

Sarah carried the trash into the back room. Out of sight, she checked her phone again. Where was Emily? For a moment, Sarah listened to the purr of the repaired refrigerator. Its hushed whisper comforted her because it made her think of RahRah when he was in one of his deep sleep cycles. She couldn't believe how attached she had become to that cat or how upset she was at the possibility of RahRah living with Jane. Jane might not harm or starve RahRah, but she didn't impress Sarah as someone who could share love with a human, let alone an animal.

It made her wonder what kind of relationship Bill and Jane had really had. She wasn't being catty, Sarah convinced herself, as she dropped the box with the bag of garbage and unlatched the Civic Center's rear door. Unless Bill's tastes had changed greatly after their divorce, Jane was the antithesis of the willowy long-haired brunettes Bill typically fell for.

Sarah stepped onto the loading dock. She twisted backward to drag Jacob's box and the bags over the threshold. It wasn't only that Jane was different from

Bill's normal type, Sarah thought as she inched backward. Jane was such a mean, manipulative, and unpleasant person, Sarah couldn't imagine what Bill saw in her.

"Aah!" Sarah screamed as she tripped. Arms flailing, she slammed onto the ground, right on top of one of the garbage bags, which split, its contents spewing. Looking up, she realized the culprit behind her fall was her own sister's leg.

"Emily?"

Emily sat spread-eagle on the ground, shaking. Tomato sauce and other trash mixed with tears on Emily's face.

"What are you doing, Emily? I could have broken my neck!"

Her twin didn't move.

"Em?" Sarah put her hands down for balance as she inched toward Emily. Her hand touched something damp underneath her. Instinctively, she wiped it on her jeans and reached out toward her sister.

"Stay away from me!" Emily backed farther away from Sarah, alternating a high-pitched mixture of sobs and the word "No!"

"What is it? What's wrong?" Sarah craned her neck from her shrieking sister to look over her shoulder. Eyes bulging, she twisted around and rose on her knees, trying to comprehend what she saw. Not three feet away, Richard lay on his side. A pool of blood surrounded him, a knife protruded from his back.

For a moment, Sarah's brain detached itself from its present reality as she wondered if the tip of the knife might have simply pierced one of his many tattoos, resulting in red ink running to the ground. But that wasn't the case. This was far worse.

Sarah raised her hand to her forehead and gagged. The sticky wetness she'd wiped on her jeans hadn't come out of the broken trash bag. She'd put her hand into the puddle of Richard's blood. It took everything she had to not be sick. Swallowing hard, she forced herself to turn away from Richard and focus on Emily. Her twin, now silent, sat hugging her knees to her body.

Between the light casting shadows on the loading dock and how tightly Emily had her knees drawn to her chest, Sarah couldn't discern if there was blood on Emily's black clothing, but she saw stains she was certain weren't rhubarb on Emily's exposed hands. "Emily, what happened?"

Emily shook her head.

Trying to penetrate her sister's silence was useless. Frustrated and frightened, Sarah turned back to help Richard. His mottled pallor and the amount of blood on the ground told her it was too late. She forced herself not to touch him, knowing it would only annoy the police if she disturbed anything else. As it was, she doubted Peter would be too pleased with her garbage shower over his crime scene.

Avoiding Richard, she crawled to Emily and embraced her. With a sob, Emily collapsed against Sarah.

Sarah forced herself to ask, "Did you?"

"No." Emily held on tightly to her twin.

"Did you touch the knife?"

Emily nodded. "He wasn't moving. I tried to help him."

"Hush." Keeping one arm around Emily, she reached into her pocket and pulled out her phone. She punched the icon for recent calls and hit the number she hadn't recognized the other day.

When Peter answered, she didn't identify herself. In a monotone, she said, "There's been a murder on the loading dock of the Civic Center. I think you'd better come over here." She hung up and speed-dialed Harlan. He probably wouldn't be very happy to hear Emily had been a Good Samaritan again.

Chapter Twenty-One

The Civic Center's security chief arrived first, followed by Peter. The damp collar of Peter's shirt and the slick hair protruding from his cap made Sarah think he had probably just jumped out of a shower and into his uniform. It wasn't a bad look for him. She pushed that thought from her mind.

Ignoring Sarah and Emily huddled together in the corner of the loading dock, Peter pulled on a pair of rubber gloves and joined the Civic Center security chief closer to where Richard lay. Since the security chief's arrival, he'd stood a few feet from Sarah and Emily, keeping an eye on them, as if worried they might make a break for it. Watching Peter now, Sarah sat silently while holding her still-shaking sister.

"Chief Mueller, I came out here as soon as you called." The security chief pointed to the twins. "Other than telling those two to sit over there until you got here, I've limited access to the loading dock and preserved the scene beyond what they already disturbed. I thought about locking down the Expo, but it didn't seem necessary. Besides, I was afraid of what kind of crowd problem we might have."

Peter frowned. He squatted near Richard. "Is this the way you found the body?"

The security chief didn't even turn to look at the unnatural way Richard lay, his legs and head twisted as if he had been running in the hope of jumping into the Dumpster. "Yes. Everything's just as I found it. I figured you'd want your techs and the coroner to see him exactly as I found him. Only problem is, it looks to me as if those two touched everything and moved him around a bit."

"What else can you tell me?" Peter stood and brushed his pants off.

The security chief pulled a notebook from his pocket but didn't open it. "His name was Richard Brown."

Peter shot a look at the security chief, who fumbled with his notebook.

"Richard was in high school at the same time as my boy. That makes him about twenty-five or so. He ran track with my kid until about midway through his junior year, when he quit the team after failing a drug test. I know he's in the junior college's culinary program and did odd jobs for Mr. Blair. He must have been a decent cook or I doubt Chef Marcus would have hired him."

"Thanks." Peter motioned for his techs to begin photographing the scene. "You'd better get back into the exhibition hall."

The security chief nodded and shoved his notebook back into his pocket while Peter again knelt by the body, careful to avoid the pooled blood. He didn't say anything as he gazed at the torso.

Sarah bent forward, trying to ascertain if Peter was seeing more than what was apparent to her. Other than the knife sticking out of Richard's back and a partially smoked cigarette dropped next to him, she hadn't observed anything that seemed out of place. There were no apparent pulled-off buttons or tears other than the one made by the knife.

Peter stood and headed in the direction of the Dumpster. He peered at the ground as he walked slowly backward from the body. Sarah, with Emily's head still pressed into her chest, watched him.

A few feet from the doorway, almost at the point where Sarah landed after her fall, he bent and stared at the ground.

"Did you find something?" Sarah called out to him.

He ignored her but waved a tech over to join him. Sarah could see him point at something the tech took a few pictures of before Peter carefully picked up and bagged whatever it was Sarah couldn't make out.

Leaving the bag with the tech, Peter walked over to the twins. Sarah met his gaze, but Emily kept her head tucked against her sister.

"Did you find something, Peter?"

"Another cigarette butt. Probably not important." He didn't try to sit or kneel near them. "Tell me, what were the two of you doing out here?"

"I was doing a garbage run."

Emily didn't answer. Sarah prodded her with her hand.

"My job," Emily finally said. "Richard said he was going out for a smoke. It was getting close to the Expo's starting time and he wasn't back, so I came out here. . . ."

A commotion at the loading dock distracted her from continuing. It was Harlan and one of the police technicians.

"You can't come in here."

"Those are my clients." Harlan tried to push his way past the taller man.

The tech easily held the smaller man at bay.

"Don't say another word!" Harlan squirmed against the man's grasp of his sweat suit.

Sarah noted the damp marks his wet hair made where his head hit the tech's shirt.

"Peter! You know better than this."

Peter signaled with his hand for Harlan's release. The tech let him go so quickly Harlan stumbled, almost falling. The tech caught and steadied him before releasing his grip.

Harlan glared at the tech but transferred his attention to Peter and his clients as he stormed over to them. "Anything my clients might have said can't be used against them." He stuck his balding head upward, almost butting Peter's chin. "I don't know what they've said, but I bet you didn't read them their rights."

"Harlan, relax. There hasn't been a need for Miranda rights. I haven't focused on anyone as a suspect." Peter took off his cap and wiped beads of sweat from his forehead with the back of his hand.

Sarah made a choking sound, suppressing a giggle. Harlan and Peter both looked at her. She didn't know why but, under the circumstances, Harlan's sports casual and Peter's uniform and hat hair struck her as out of sync.

Although she didn't say anything, Peter's gaze lingered on her for a few extra seconds. "Harlan, my guys will finish up here. I think the four of us should continue this discussion at the station house."

Chapter Twenty-Two

The interrogation room looked the same as it had earlier in the week, except extra chairs had been pulled into it. Peter stood behind a chair placed directly across from the twins and Harlan, who had angled his chair on the corner next to Emily. Peter held a thick manila folder. Sarah wondered if it was the same one from the other night being recycled for effect.

"Coffee anyone?"

Harlan shook his head. "This isn't a social visit."

Peter slammed the folder over a dent in the table. "For Pete's sake, Harlan, I'm only asking if anyone would like a cup of coffee."

While the two men stared at each other, Sarah leaned forward. Watching them having their ministandoff, she honed in on Peter's offer of coffee. "I'd love a cup."

She peeked over at Emily, who was shaking her head. Cold as Sarah was from having been on the loading dock, she was surprised Emily, who had been on the dock far longer, was turning down a hot drink.

Sarah's mind raced, trying to sort out the deeper meanings of everything going on in the interrogation room. Maybe Emily's refusal was tied to the fear that, like in a bad TV show, Peter's kind offer was a ruse to get her fingerprints from the cup. Maybe . . . it didn't matter. Sarah was too cold and upset about Richard to care. A cup of coffee wouldn't take away the image of Richard's body, but it might physically warm her.

When it was placed in front of her, the coffee smelled divine. She immediately wrapped her hands around the hot cup, absorbing its warmth.

Peter took a long sip from his mug. "Look, I'm simply trying to figure out what happened and how, once again, the two of you seem to be in the middle of finding another body."

He ran his hand through his hair, causing it to stand up in a few odd places. "Believe me, I'd much rather be tasting food at the Expo."

"Me too, and we should all be able to do that soon because, Peter, there isn't much to tell."

Harlan cleared this throat.

"I was taking the garbage out to the Dumpster when I tripped and fell."

"Over me," Emily said.

Sarah nodded.

"I couldn't help him," Emily's voice quavered. "I tried."

Harlan put his hand over Emily's. She looked at it and stopped talking.

"Was he moving or talking when you tried to help him?" Peter asked.

"No. He was just lying there. I tried to help him, but there was the knife and so much blood." She covered her face with her hands.

Sarah immediately put her arm around Emily, almost knocking her coffee over in the process. "Peter, that's enough. Emily has had it. She told you she went outside looking for a coworker, who was supposed to be taking a smoke break and found him smoked. Instead of interrogating us, you need to figure out who beat Emily to Richard."

"Sarah—"

Sarah ignored Peter. "I think it's safe to say neither Emily nor I stuck that knife into him anymore than Emily force-fed Bill something he would never willingly eat. It's time you leave us alone and look for the real killer or killers."

Harlan stood. "It doesn't seem like we're getting anywhere here. I think that, unless you want to charge my clients, it's time for them to leave."

Peter licked his lips and pressed them together. He shook his head affirmatively. "We'd like to keep their clothing for processing. You know I can have them wait around while I get a warrant."

Harlan glanced at Emily and Sarah and then back at Peter. "That won't be necessary. I doubt there's anyone we can find to bring them a change of clothing, so why don't you give them something to change into so we can get out of here."

Sarah knew Richard's blood was on their clothing, but she didn't relish the idea of going home in a prison jumpsuit. She couldn't see how agreeing to have their clothes examined was going to do anything but put them in a worse position than they already were in.

Harlan leaned toward Sarah. "We know both of your outfits are stained with Richard's blood. I also know no matter how much I rant and rave, any judge they approach will grant them a warrant. Better to be cooperative now than appear obstructive."

Sarah nodded but her stomach twisted. She was glad they'd be getting out of here quickly, but she still felt Harlan should do more to protect Emily than pat her hand.

Chapter Twenty-Three

Emily stepped over the orange jumpsuit on Sarah's floor. Standing outside Sarah's walk-in closet with a towel wrapped tightly around her, she shivered. "Aren't you freezing? I thought you were going to put the heat up while I was in the shower."

"I did. It's not that cold in here." Still wearing her orange jumpsuit, Sarah sat on the floor with RahRah in her lap.

With her free hand, Emily opened the underwear drawer in Sarah's dresser. She made a face as she rummaged around and pulled out a pink thong. "Saving this for anyone special?"

"I only wish. But that's not important now. Considering everything that has happened this morning with poor Richard, the Civic Center is the last place I want to be." Sarah shook her head. "I can't believe you. You don't make sense to me. Even though Harlan told us to stay put, you're insisting on being back there before one."

Emily threw the thong back into the drawer and grabbed a pair of beige underpants, with the tag still on it. "We can't figure out why Richard was killed staying here."

"That's not our job. It's Peter's."

"Look, Sarah, I don't know if Richard's murder has a connection to Bill's death or to the sabotage of Southwind's refrigerator, but how hard do you think Peter will look for another suspect when he has me as the only person at the scene with both dead bodies?"

"You're selling him short. Maybe you were too upset to hear Peter and the chief of security talking. Grace told me the same thing. Richard hung around with a bad crowd and still has some of those guys as his friends. Surely Peter will investigate whether he had any enemies or shady connections that might be involved in what's been happening." *Including attacking me last night,* Sarah silently thought as RahRah fled her grasp and jumped onto her bed.

No longer balancing RahRah, she rose and walked into her closet. She quickly came back out clutching a black blouse and pair of black jeans. She handed them to Emily. "Try these. You'll have to roll the jeans up, but they're the shortest pair I own."

"Thanks." Emily pulled the shirt over her head. "You know, it really is cold in here."

Sarah went to the thermostat and adjusted it. "It's on seventy-two, but I turned the heat up to seventy-four. Em, I think your body is reacting to the shock it had. Maybe we should stay here and talk instead of running back to the Civic Center."

Emily slipped her feet into a pair of Sarah's black rubber-soled loafers and held one foot up. "As always, a perfect fit."

No surprise. Although opposites in terms of height, coloring, personality, and talents, when it came to shoes, both had inherited their mother's size six triple A foot.

"You don't need to come with me." Emily looked at her watch. "But, if you are, please hurry and take your shower. I really have to be back by one."

"Why one? I'm coming with you but, for Pete's sake, remember this is a cooking competition at a mini–food expo in Wheaton, Alabama. You're acting like it's life or death."

"For me, it might be. It's Marcus's rule that the only way any of us can cook in tomorrow's competition is to make a recipe presentation onstage today at two. I still have some things to prep."

"That's stupid. Surely, under the circumstances, Marcus can change or break his rule."

Sarah grabbed a towel and headed for the shower but paused near the sink when Emily followed her into the bathroom.

"I don't want him to. I need to win this cook-off by the book so no one can question the results."

Emily's somber tone scared Sarah. "Does this have anything to do with the monkey business with South-wind Jane accused you of?"

Emily put the toilet seat cover down and sat on it. She played with the toilet paper. "Marcus is an excellent chef, but he isn't a great businessman."

Sarah hung her towel and clean clothing on the shower rack and proceeded to take her shower. She waited for Emily to fill the silence. When she didn't, Sarah shouted over the running water, "So, how do you play into this?" Not hearing anything, Sarah repeated her question louder.

This time, Emily called back an answer. "When Southwind became available, Chef Marcus took it over on a shoestring. We never thought it would be so hard to get folks to drive here from Birmingham proper. Marcus was barely holding it together, despite working around the clock, when I accepted his job offer."

Sarah turned the water off and reached for her towel. Dried, Sarah threw the towel onto the floor and put a foot on it. She dressed while Emily, still seated on the toilet, leaned her arm against the porcelain sink. "Well?"

Emily cocked her head toward Sarah. "Marcus and I have known each other since he was an adjunct teacher at CIA. He already was working under some of the finest chefs in the country and teaching on the side. Starting a restaurant costs money. Money Marcus had yet to save. That's why, when some investors approached him with the opportunity to be a part of Southwind, using his cooking and everyday management skills in exchange for his interest, he asked my opinion because he knew I was familiar with Wheaton. With all the foodies in Birmingham, I thought it would be a no-brainer to open another excellent restaurant for the same clientele. Driving fifteen minutes from the City Center to a fine dining restaurant is no big deal in San Francisco, but that didn't turn out to be the case in Birmingham." Emily twisted her mouth into a smile. "Marcus relied on my opinion. That's why I feel guilty he's had such a hard time with Southwind."

Sarah ignored the guilt, opting to go right for the jugular. "So you've been in on Southwind since the beginning?"

"Not exactly. Back then, all I did was assure Marcus Wheaton was a nice town. It wasn't until I came home for the Fourth of July last year and mentioned things in San Francisco were souring that Marcus suggested I work for him at Southwind. He said he was juggling everything and felt like he was being pulled in too many directions so this could be a win-win situation for both of us: I could come home to get my head together and ease his responsibilities, while adding a respectable credential to my résumé."

"This is the first time you've said there was trouble in San Francisco. I thought you simply wanted to work for Chef Marcus."

"It wasn't a big enough deal to mention to you. Personalities. Like I've told you before, it was the opportunity to train under Chef Marcus that attracted me home."

Because of Emily's closed body posture, Sarah was certain there was more to Emily's return home, but she didn't interrupt when Emily resumed talking.

"Everything was great until I found out about Bill's involvement."

"And when was that?"

Emily ignored the question. "Before I managed to move to town, someone brought Bill to Southwind. He must have recognized how much talent Marcus has because he started coming into the restaurant three to four nights a week for dinner, staying until closing and chatting up Marcus. Their conversations about Marcus's dream to move the restaurant into one of the old houses on Main Street somehow evolved into Bill giving Marcus financial advice. Eventually, Bill made Marcus an offer that seemed like the answer to his prayers."

"That sounds like Bill. He could take the shirt off your back and make you believe you'd given it to him. What was Bill's good-hearted offer?"

"Bill would buy out the partners and assume all of Marcus's debts. He'd also provide him with a six-month infusion in exchange for being a silent fifty-one percent partner. Marcus would have total control of the day-to-day operations, plus the opportunity to buy back the controlling percentage if the restaurant was a success."

"Those aren't great terms."

"They got worse after Marcus signed the legal paperwork. Bill insisted on expanding Southwind's outside business by taking on the Civic Center contract and increasing their catering. He also stuck his nose into adding staff until, after a few hires like Jane, Marcus put his foot down. Bill agreed choosing cooks had to be Marcus's domain, but—"

"He tied Marcus's hands on everything else because the legal contract gave Bill fifty-one percent ownership," Sarah finished for her.

Emily nodded in agreement.

"Not surprising." Sarah walked into the kitchen area and picked up RahRah's water bowl.

Emily followed.

"If I've learned anything working for Harlan, it's that you'd be amazed at the predicaments people get into by simply trusting other people to live by the Golden Rule." Sarah put fresh water into RahRah's bowl and returned it to the floor. She wiped her wet fingers on her pants and positioned herself so she could see Emily's face. "Come clean. What predicament did you get yourself into with Bill?"

Emily looked away, but Sarah kept her eyes focused on Emily's face. "What was Jane talking about the other night?"

"Nothing."

"Don't lie to me." Sarah crossed her arms over her chest. "You froze at the police station when Jane mentioned whatever it is and you're avoiding making eye contact with me now. I may not have gone to CIA or any other college and my life got a little messy with Bill, but I know when someone isn't shooting straight, especially you."

"It wasn't a big deal. I told you part of my job was the business side of things." Emily fixated on a spot on the floor. "Once I started working with Marcus, I knew exactly what our food and labor costs were. I took over scheduling everyone and handling the purchasing and distribution of all inventory used in the restaurant, Civic Center, and catering jobs. After a few weeks, I realized the profit and loss numbers were off. Either supplies were going out the back door or someone was playing with the books."

"Marcus?"

"Definitely not."

Sarah noticed how fast Emily came to Chef Marcus's defense. "Maybe you missed something. After all, you've said Marcus was under a lot of stress this past year."

Emily shook her head. "The only people having access to the supply areas where inventory was off were Marcus and me, who I knew weren't involved, and Bill and Jane. Despite Bill's history, he was handling the final accounting. I didn't want to accuse him outright. Consequently, I bluffed. I told Bill my first thought was Jane and maybe one of the cooks were playing with the supplies and numbers."

"What did he say?"

"Instead of saying he'd look into it, he got mad and accused me of being a troublemaker. He told me if I wanted to keep my job, I should mind my own business and leave the finances to him and the cooking to Marcus."

"What a bastard to threaten you like that. That had

to be like throwing down a gauntlet in front of you. I
bet you saw red."

"I did. I took my suspicions to Marcus. When he
wouldn't hear of Bill cheating him, I decided I needed
concrete proof to show Marcus. That's what I was looking for the night Jane caught me."

"What were they doing there?"

"That's the same thing I asked Jane and Richard.
Jane gladly told me they were meeting Marcus and Bill
to discuss a new contract Southwind was signing. She
gloated she and Richard were in charge of the new
deal."

"I can picture her now."

"Magnify whatever you're picturing. The minute
Marcus and Bill got there, she took great joy in tattling
on me. Bill blew up, but I defended myself by explaining I was going through the books for the good of the
business. I explained I was trying to figure out why
the numbers weren't adding up, but Bill wanted to fire
me on the spot."

"Why didn't he?"

"Because Marcus latched onto the fact I was only
trying to protect him and Southwind. He argued, even
if I had gone about it in the wrong way, I really hadn't
done anything wrong. After all, my job allowed me
access to the inventory numbers. Besides, Marcus
noted, between the Expo, restaurant, and catering
jobs, Southwind needed all hands on deck during the
next week."

"Bill gave in? That doesn't sound like the old Bill
I knew."

Emily snorted. "Bill relented, but the first time he
got me alone, he suggested I start looking for another

position because he couldn't guarantee how much longer they could afford to keep me around."

"And now?"

"Now?" Emily's gaze wandered from the spot on the floor to a plant sitting on the window ledge above the sink.

"With Bill dead?"

"Except for Jane's involvement, the world is right again. Marcus is in charge of Southwind and his debts are paid off."

"Isn't that convenient?" Sarah opened a can of tuna cat food and put it in RahRah's bowl. The cat crawled out from under the bed and nosed around his food. Sarah rubbed his back but he shook her away in favor of his bowl. "I would think that would mean you could stay home and forget today's cooking demonstration and tomorrow's competition."

"No. The Expo has attracted chef entries from Birmingham and other nearby cities so there are going to be plenty of Birmingham foodies in attendance."

Sarah threw Emily a quizzical look.

"This is a chance for Southwind to have a new start. Once the foodies taste our food, we hope they're going to realize it's no big deal to drive an extra fifteen minutes for a great meal."

Sarah put her hand on her chin and wrinkled her brow. "We? Our? I thought this is Marcus's restaurant."

"It is, but I still feel obligated to help him make a success of it."

Sarah held her tongue. As Emily hastened to defend her position, Sarah tried to hold her face in a neutral position. From experience, Sarah knew Emily could usually tell from a glance at Sarah's face what she was thinking.

"The Expo gives us a chance for more people to sample our food."

"Too bad Jane's involved." Sarah had previously tasted Jane's food at Southwind. Even to her simple palate, it lacked the complexity and layers of Emily's dishes.

"No kidding. Chef Marcus got around that problem. He's letting Jane offer her samples from one end of the Southwind booth, but she's entered in tomorrow's competition under her own name. I'm the Southwind entry. That's one of the reasons Bill and Jane were gunning for me. Jane wanted to be the Southwind entry."

"And to be named sous chef?"

"Yes. But without Bill, Marcus is back in control. He can do what's right for Southwind."

"Like promoting you?"

Chapter Twenty-Four

"You're back?" Jane stared at Emily but didn't acknowledge Sarah's presence. "I didn't expect you to be here this afternoon."

"When you're innocent, the police make it a practice not to detain you."

Jacob, who had started in their direction from his end of the booth, stopped. Jane cleared her throat but refocused her attention on the food she was preparing. Emily snatched a napkin from Jane's table and dabbed her face as she slipped into her own part of the booth.

Emily threw the napkin into the nearby trash can and removed her jacket. She stowed it under her table. "I wonder where Grace is."

Sarah glanced up and down the Southwind booth. Although Jane and Jacob had samples ready for the next wave of tasters, there were only a few cold samples remaining at Emily's station. "Grace was here earlier. She had both of your tables covered with tasting cups. From the looks of what's left, your food was a big hit during the lunch hour. Maybe she's in the back room checking the employee's table."

"I don't know." Emily threw out the remaining samples. She wiped the plastic tablecloths and put out small plates with new tastes from a quiche Grace had left warming in the oven. As she moved her well-filled bowl of red chips to a more prominent position, she checked her watch and frowned. "We'll wait a little while to heat anything else up. I'm sure Grace will be back for the next rush, but, in case she's not, let me show you what to do if you have to handle things while I'm doing the demonstration."

"Sure." Sarah stared at her sister. "Em, are you certain you're okay? You look flushed and you're sweating."

"I just told you, it's warm in here."

"Not that warm. And you were freezing at my apartment." Sarah touched her sister's forehead, but Emily squirmed away. She sat on a folding chair in front of Sarah.

Jane leaned over from her side of the booth and said loudly, "Emily, are you sure you're not sick? You know you shouldn't handle food if you're ill. Grace went to the nurse's station a little while ago because she was feeling sick to her stomach. She started by sweating, too. You were working together. Maybe you've both got a bug."

"I'm fine, but thanks for your concern."

Sarah watched a person who held one of the plates from Emily's station eye it and put it back down. The person continued to where Jacob was handing out tastes of his Super Duper Seven Layer Salad. After a swallow, she left a red chip in the basket in front of Jacob.

Once the taster moved away, Sarah motioned to Jacob. He put down his serving ladle and came over to where she was sitting. "Did Grace really go to the nurse's station?"

"Yes. She thought she ate something bad because suddenly she started having stomach cramps."

"Maybe Jane's right about Grace having a bug."

Jacob flicked a crumb off the table separating his station from Emily's. "I don't think so. Grace is the type who scares germs away."

They both laughed.

"By the way, Sarah, Grace wanted me to tell you she ran over to the store and picked up the items you might need. She also whipped up a few samples, just in case. Everything is in the refrigerator near the stage."

Emily, still seated, but listening, interrupted. "I don't understand."

Sarah raised her shoulders and put her hands somewhere between an "I give up" and "Just stay put" position as she watched her sister grimace and wipe her forehead with the back of her arm. "You remember me checking with you the other night about what things you needed for today's demonstration?"

Emily nodded and tilted her head in Sarah's direction as if that would make it easier to catch the rush of words Sarah mumbled. "Well, Grace and I weren't sure if you'd make it back or be stuck at the police station. To be safe, Grace offered to pick up the few things in case I had to do a funny food demonstration. Apparently, she also whipped up a few samples of my recipe."

"Grace or I could have done a real demonstration if you hadn't gotten back." Jacob flicked his finger at another crumb. He put his head back down, but not before Sarah glimpsed his features were settled into a pout. He grabbed a sponge and vigorously rubbed the tablecloth.

"Of course you could have done it perfectly." Emily's stomach rumbled. She pressed her hand against it. "I was only kidding when I told Sarah she'd have to do a funny presentation, Jacob. I wouldn't have had her take my place."

Jacob looked up again, his boyish good looks restored. "Well, none of us thought you were kidding, did we, Sarah?"

Sarah shook her head.

Jacob leaned forward. "Before Grace went to the nurse's station," he whispered, "she told me she didn't have time for lunch so she ate a few of Jane's brownies. When her stomach started hurting, she wondered if they were Ex-Lax brownies."

"That would be a mean trick to play," Emily said, "but we all ate the brownies and nobody else is sick."

Sarah stared at Emily. "Are you sure of that? I was too nervous to eat a brownie when I first got here. When I finally considered having one, I decided to save my calories and take out the garbage instead."

"I didn't eat one, either. I had so many ingredients to taste in my dish that I wasn't hungry." Jacob started to add something but noted two people approaching his serving station. "Need to get back to work." He flashed a showman's smile at Sarah.

Emily stood, her hand resting on her stomach. "I'm going to check on Grace."

"And maybe," Sarah suggested, "have the nurse examine you, too?"

Chapter Twenty-Five

Forty-five minutes before the food demonstration, Jane left the booth. Emily had yet to return. A sensation of déjà vu ran through Sarah. She couldn't help but remember the last time Emily hadn't been back well in advance of a scheduled activity, Sarah found her sitting with a dead body. She certainly hoped that wasn't the case again.

Even though Sarah and Grace had prepared for the possibility of Emily not being able to handle the demonstration, neither of them thought it would really be the case. Now Sarah prayed she wouldn't be pressed into service today. She wasn't sure she could do it. The idea made her feel sick to her stomach, even though she hadn't eaten a brownie.

She pulled out her cell phone and dialed her sister. Emily's ringtone sounded from somewhere to her right. Looking down, her eyes rested on the edge of Emily's purse and jacket, where she'd tucked them under the table. Sarah hit the end button on her phone and glanced at the time. She decided she better find Emily.

Because Emily had said she was going to the nurse's station, Sarah headed in that direction. As she turned into the hallway near the medical area, she heard people arguing. She slowed to avoid popping into the middle of their fight. Sarah was about to make noise so they would hear her coming when she realized it was Marcus and Jane. She inched forward, hoping to hear more clearly.

"You're not going to say anything." Jane's disembodied voice was controlled, but harsh. "Not if you want your restaurant to succeed."

Sarah couldn't hear Marcus's reply, but from the sound of Jane's voice, she was moving in her direction. Sarah looked for somewhere in the hall to hide, but there wasn't an opening to slip into. Instead, she decided the best defense would be to go on the offense.

She stepped into the hallway. Marcus was entering the nurse's station. He had his back to Jane, who still was talking. "Do you understand me?"

Sarah didn't wait to be noticed. "Hi, Jane. Have you seen Emily?"

"She's in there." Jane nodded toward the nurse's station and squeezed her way past Sarah, barely missing making bodily contact.

"Thanks," Sarah called to Jane's moving back. She peeked through the glass panes in the door of the small room being used as a nurse's station. Neither Grace nor the nurse was in sight, but her sister was sitting on a gurney, crying. Marcus now stood over her, waving his hands wildly.

Sarah pushed the door open.

Emily turned her head toward the door, but Marcus, intent on his rant, apparently didn't hear Sarah. "I can't let you."

"You don't have a say in this. You're not in charge of me!" Emily stood but swayed. Sarah moved to catch her, but Marcus was faster. He grabbed Emily and held her tightly, his legs pressed against the gurney.

"You mustn't." He ran his hand across her hair and down to her chin. Gently, he tilted her face toward his. "You've done so much for me. It's enough already. I'm going out there and call this charade off. I'm to blame and it's time I admitted it to everyone."

Emily held his arm, but he shook her off. As he turned toward Sarah and the door, Emily shouted, "Marcus, stop! You can't. That will be the end of you and Southwind."

Sarah tightened her leg muscles and put her hands forward, anticipating the bulldozing effect of Marcus's weight because he'd started into motion before realizing she was there. The impact never came. Instead, he crumpled onto a wheeled stool next to the gurney and stared at the floor. Deciding he wasn't having a heart attack or other medical emergency, Sarah stepped around him to reach her sister.

"Em, what's going on? Did he hurt you?"

Emily shook her head and wiped her eyes with her hands. Keeping Marcus in view, Sarah pulled a tissue from a box on the counter and handed it to Emily.

"I'm fine or will be in a few hours. I just hope Grace will be, too."

"Grace? Where is she?"

Marcus lifted his head, his face contorted. "Poor Grace." From the way he blinked, Sarah wondered if he was about to cry, too, until he said, "I swear I'm going to kill Jane."

"Marcus!" Emily said sharply. "Don't make threats

like that! With everything that's happened, someone could take them the wrong way."

The intensity of her sister's reaction shocked Sarah. As she weighed Emily's retort, it dawned on her what Marcus's anger, the absence of the nurse, and her sister's pallor and tears could mean. For a moment, she couldn't get the words out. "Oh, my God! Is Grace dead, too?"

"No. Or at least we hope not."

Marcus stood, his fists clenched. "I will personally wring Jane's neck like a chicken if Grace dies."

Emily leaned around Sarah and put her hand on Marcus's hand.

At her touch, he eased his fist open.

"Don't even think like that. The doctors at the hospital won't let Grace die."

"Hospital? Could one of you please tell me what's going on? What happened to Grace?"

Emily started to answer but bent and grabbed her stomach again. Both Sarah and Marcus moved to help her, but she waved them away. She took a deep breath and sat up straight again. "I'm okay. It's just a cramp." She focused her gaze on Sarah. "Ex-Lax brownies."

"Jane's?"

"She won't admit it, but we think so."

"We know so. Grace wouldn't have poisoned herself or you."

Emily nodded. She banged her hand on the gurney. "Although Jane claims she ate a few of them, it appears Grace and I were the only ones who actually snacked on them. I nibbled two I took to the station with me this morning, but Grace lunched on them. We began having similar symptoms at almost the same time, except Grace's are much worse."

"It could be a virus."

Emily shook her head. "If that was the case, I doubt we would have started being sick at almost the same time. I can't prove it, but I'm convinced Jane poisoned us to knock us out of the Expo. Not that that matters now. Other than a twinge or two, I'm okay. It's Grace we're worried about. She's diabetic and this knocked her for a loop." Emily winced again but then relaxed.

"But you said they took her to the hospital?"

"The paramedics did. Normally, Grace is well controlled, but she really messed up having the brownies instead of a decent lunch," Marcus said. "The nurse here thought her sugar level was way off, probably because when the Ex-Lax kicked in, she dehydrated."

"Grace objected, but the nurse called the paramedics. They'd started an IV and were taking her to the hospital when I got here."

If there had been another chair, Sarah would have sat. Instead, she backed up and held on to the counter the tissue box sat on. "Oh, no. I feel horrible. She skipped lunch to get everything ready in case I got stuck having to cover for you. If I hadn't asked her to help me out, she would have had time to have eaten something other than the brownies."

"It's not your fault. We all gave her things to do."

"The only person at fault is Jane," Marcus declared.

"But we can't prove that," Emily sighed.

"Maybe we can test one of the brownies?"

Emily shook her head. "I don't remember the brownie plate still being in our booth. The main thing we can do is pray Grace will recover quickly. With just the little bit of fluid from the IV, she already claimed to be feeling better. In fact, she wanted to stay and help, but I convinced her we'd be okay and her health was more important than this expo."

"That sounds a bit like the pot calling the kettle black."

Marcus bent his massive body, putting his face close to Emily's. "Sarah's right. You need to take your own advice. You don't need to make a presentation today."

"But I do. For Southwind." She squeezed his now-relaxed hand, keeping hers resting on his for a moment. "I'm fine, honest."

Sarah doubted that, but at least her sister didn't look like she was in major danger. The same couldn't be said about Grace. "What about the cost of going to the hospital? Does Grace have insurance?" Having had six months without insurance after her divorce, she was sensitive to the potentially devastating economics of being uninsured.

"Grace has student insurance."

Sarah cocked her head at Emily, totally confused. "Student insurance? I thought she's a line cook doing an internship."

"She's good enough to be a professional, but she's still a culinary student at Carleton Junior College. She works at Southwind under a work-study system. The restaurant pays her a set student stipend, Marcus grades her work, and she receives college credit. Luckily, any term a student is enrolled, the college requires them to carry a college health policy."

"Thank goodness."

"Even so, Jane needs to take responsibility and pay for what she's done." Marcus slammed the fist Emily wasn't holding against the gurney.

Releasing his hand, Emily pointed to the clock. "Come on. We need to get over to the stage. Let's get even with Jane the best way—beating her at her own game."

Marcus and Sarah jointly blocked her path to the door.

"Em, I agree with Marcus. Shouldn't you go to the hospital like Grace?"

Marcus, talking over Sarah, was more definitive in his assessment of the situation. "Your health is worth more than this expo. Don't be a martyr."

Emily waved them both off. "Other than a few cramps now, I'm fine." She laughed. "Honest, a smelly fart isn't going to endanger anyone's health, so I'm good to go. Guys, we can't roll over and play dead for Jane." She again rested her hand on Marcus's pulpy fist. "Look, I may not win, but after everything, we can't give her the satisfaction of doing whatever she wants to Southwind and all of us. If I can help it, she's not going to automatically end up with everyone's red chips in her basket."

Chapter Twenty-Six

The crowd for the recipe presentation was much larger than Sarah anticipated. She didn't know where all the people had come from for the Saturday afternoon session. If this was a final cook-off, she might understand it, but merely to learn a few new recipes? She hadn't realized Wheaton and, of course, Birmingham, had so many foodies. Under normal circumstances, this wasn't where she would be spending her Saturday afternoon.

She couldn't say the same thing about Emily. At least, Emily wouldn't be onstage constantly. When Marcus had been unable to dissuade her from participating, he had decided, as emcee of the recipe demonstration, that the chefs should alternate their performances like today's reality television singing competitions. This way, Emily would have a break from being in the public eye between her two presentations.

So far, Emily had shown the audience her version of making a rhubarb crisp and then escaped off the stage while Jane and the other presenters took their turns. Other than a couple of times when Emily smiled tightly and gripped the table or hid her face by bending into the refrigerator, both, Sarah guessed, to hide a wave of pain, Emily's rhubarb crisp demonstration had gone well. Watching Emily leave the stage after it, Sarah was very proud of her two-minutes-younger sister.

After Emily's presentation, while the sisters stood in front of the stage as Jane presented the art of making corn pudding, Harlan joined them. He was back in his lawyer attire of bow tie, well-creased slacks, and a blazer.

"I thought you preferred to avoid crowds." Sarah waved her hand at the folks packed in around them.

"Normally, I do."

"Well, at least you found time to squeeze your exercise in today," Emily said.

Harlan raised an eyebrow in her direction. "Till it was cut short."

Sarah laughed but abruptly stopped when she caught sight of Peter coming in their direction. Harlan shifted his stance and muttered something under his breath. Sarah didn't catch his comment because, once again, she was reflecting on the fact that while most men looked sharper in uniforms, Peter's didn't flatter him anymore than the frown on his face.

"What did you say?" she asked Harlan.

When he failed to reply, she glanced at him. His jaw was tight and the little vein on his forehead had popped out.

Ignoring her question, he stepped between the twins and Peter. "Peter, what are you doing here? I thought we agreed you would wait until after this was over."

Peter glanced beyond Harlan to where Emily stood. "That was before I knew there'd been another murder attempt."

Sarah stared from Peter to Harlan and back again.

Onstage, Marcus thanked this round's competitors and reminded folks that, even though there were more presentations to come, samples were available at each of the exhibitor's booths. "Don't forget, at the end of today's demonstration, you'll be able to add to your favorite chef's vote count by dropping a red token in the bowl on the edge of this stage marked with that person's name."

Peter ignored the action on the stage. "Emily Johnson, you need to come with me."

"Peter. What's going on?" Sarah asked.

He didn't respond to Sarah. Instead, he kept his focus on Emily, whose motionless arm he was now holding.

"Emily, I'd rather walk you out of here without handcuffs, but it's your choice. You're under arrest for the murders of William Taft Blair and Richard Brown. You have the right to remain silent. Anything you say can and will be used against you in a court of . . ."

Emily simply stared at him as he recited her Miranda rights, but Sarah tugged at Peter's shirtsleeve. When he shook her off, she jerked around to Harlan.

"Harlan! Do something!"

"I'm sorry," Harlan said as he took Emily's other arm.

She didn't pull away. Instead, Emily stood frozen, with her eyes wide open.

Sarah stuck her face in front of Harlan's. "You knew about this, didn't you?"

He hung his head. "Yes, but Peter and I agreed he would wait until after the food demonstration and give me an opportunity to talk to both of you so Emily could turn herself in. Something must have changed."

Peter began to push the crowd aside.

Forced to move, Sarah grabbed the back of Peter's shirt. "Peter, no."

He shook free and kept moving, using one large arm to support an almost limp Emily.

"Harlan, do something!"

Wordlessly, Harlan and Peter began escorting Emily away from where Sarah stood.

"I'll come with you, Emily," she yelled.

"Is something wrong?" one of the men standing closest to them asked.

"No." Emily dug her feet into the floor and pulled away from Peter, swiveling back to face Sarah. "Stay here and try to find out what's really going on. Finish for me."

"I can't. I can't go up there."

"Yes, you can. I've done my main recipe. All you have to do when Marcus calls for me is go onstage and pretend you're doing a comedy routine with that recipe you found. Do this for me. Please."

"Em . . ."

Emily smiled at her frowning twin. "Okay, boys." She linked her arms through Harlan's and Peter's, making it appear they were three jovial friends exiting the Food Expo in style.

Chapter Twenty-Seven

Sarah watched the three of them work their way through the crowd. Sarah wanted to follow them. Her sister was more important than some stupid food demonstration or some idiot's restaurant. Speaking of the idiot, she strained to hear what Marcus was saying from the stage.

His intermittent hold over her sister bothered her. Sarah couldn't understand what kind of relationship they had. Unlike Sarah, who from the time she met Bill fit her actions to being part of a couple, Emily never had kowtowed to any man.

It had disgusted Emily whenever Sarah made excuses for Bill's behavior. When Sarah finally woke up to the reality of her relationship, Emily became Sarah's nonstop cheerleader. Emily was the one who encouraged her to stand up for herself against Bill's mental abuse. When Bill walked out, it was Emily who repeatedly assured Sarah she had self-worth and deserved to do things that made her happy.

Marcus's voice announcing the next demonstration would be by Emily Johnson interrupted her thoughts. When Emily didn't bounce onto the stage, Sarah observed the anxious way Marcus scanned the crowd for her. For a moment, his darting eyes made her think of her own petrified reaction when Bill almost died on their honeymoon after eating something with nuts. But it was absurd to compare Marcus and Emily's yin and yang business relationship to that of newlyweds.

"Emily Johnson," he called again.

Against her better judgment, Sarah let her feet carry her up the stairs to the stage. Marcus stopped in midsentence. She gave him a half smile. Taking the microphone from his hand, she turned to the crowd. She opened her mouth, but nothing came out.

To steady herself, she thought back to the two tricks her high school speech teacher had taught the class to calm nerves. She could never sustain an image of one hundred people being naked. Instead, she looked around for a friendly face to pretend to be having a conversation with. Her eyes landed on Jacob. He smiled at her and she took that as a sign of encouragement.

She started again. "Um, hi, everyone."

"We can't hear you!"

"Hold the microphone closer to your mouth," someone else yelled from the audience.

She glanced to Marcus, who pantomimed holding a mic directly in front of her mouth. "Sorry." She moved the microphone. "Is that better?"

Even before voices from the audience responded, she could hear the difference in her sound level. She tried to see who had shouted at her but couldn't tell. She swallowed and started again. Her voice was louder, but quivery, in her ears.

"My name is Sarah Blair." She hung her head in shame. "I am a cook of convenience."

She raised her head, appreciating the few people who laughed. The laughter made her remember the other rule of public speaking: smile as if you're having fun. She plastered a smile onto her face. "Emily Johnson is my twin sister. Unlike Emily, who is CIA-trained and a master chef, the kitchen, to me, is like a foreign country. I cook purely out of necessity."

Someone clapped. Sarah moved across the stage and pointed in the direction of the person who'd clapped. "My type of person." Sarah warmed up to her topic. "You know what I'm talking about, don't you? We're the ones who time our cooking minutes to the length of songs and only make recipes with pictures. That way, we can take the picture to the store to make sure we buy the right ingredients." There were a few more chuckles from the audience.

"I know my sister, Emily, and most of those who've been on this stage, believe in gourmet cooking, but I bet a lot of you are more like me. Our cars instinctively know the way through drive-in windows. At the grocery, we buy prepared chickens and we personally keep our local pizzerias in business. That's right, we only turn on our stoves when we need to warm something up. During this segment, I'm going to demonstrate a true recipe of convenience. If you like it, please feel free to drop a red chip in my sister's bowl."

"This isn't fair!" Jane ran up the steps to the stage. Ignoring Sarah and the audience, she went straight to Marcus. "She shouldn't be up here, let alone sharing Emily's basket. In fact, Emily should be disqualified for not presenting two recipes."

Marcus tried to guide her off the stage by her elbow. "Jane, this isn't the competition. I don't see a problem with Sarah demonstrating a recipe. After all, Emily already has presented one. Would you like a substitute for your second recipe? I'm sure Jacob could handle it."

"Definitely not."

She started to protest again but stopped when someone booed from the audience.

"Get off the stage and let her make her presentation."

When others picked up the refrain, Marcus took advantage of the commotion to usher Jane from the stage.

Sarah couldn't hear what Marcus said to Jane as he eased her down the steps and she didn't try. She turned away and fixed her gaze on Jacob. She could have sworn it was his voice that had started the distraction, but why?

As she looked at Jacob, knowing he probably would have preferred to make this presentation himself, he pointed to his watch. She didn't understand what he was trying to tell her. It made no more sense the second or third time he held his watch up and tapped it. Perplexed, she worked her way closer to where he stood. She pointed at him. "I'd like to introduce you to Jacob Hightower, one of the Southwind's fine cooks. He's trying to tell me something, but I can't understand him. Jacob, why don't you wave to everyone and share whatever it is with my other friends here."

Jacob waved as instructed. "Get to your ingredients before you run out of time!"

"Good point." Sarah walked over to the refrigerator/freezer and searched for where Grace had placed her ingredients on a shelf labeled with Emily's name.

Sarah held up a large metal can of Dole pineapple rings and a package of gelatin. "My recipe is Jell-O-in-a-Can."

Several members of the audience laughed until she hushed them with a hand. "It really is a 1955 recipe created by Dole Pineapple and Jell-O. All you need to make it is a can of pineapple rings, a package of gelatin, and some water." She placed the ingredients on her workstation. "Believe me, if I can make this, y'all can, too."

She opened the can of pineapple and drained the liquid. "Center the remaining pineapple rings in the can." She shook the can. "What you poured out of the can was about three-quarters cup of juice. Boil that much water and add gelatin to it. FYI, that's about half of what you normally would use with gelatin. Pour the mixture back into the can so that it goes between and around the pineapple."

Sarah put the can with the mixture she had just prepared in the refrigerator and took out the one Grace made earlier in the day. She turned back to the audience. "As you can see, I've put our can into the refrigerator. Normally I'd keep it there for a minimum of four hours, removing it before it settled." She held the cold can high enough for the crowd to see it. "Voila! With a little magical help from another South-wind chef, the hours have passed."

She wrapped a towel around the can. "We need to gently warm the sides by either putting warm water on them directly or using a towel, like I'm doing. Then we'll open the bottom of the can and use the bottom lid to push the mold out from the top of the can."

With exaggerated fanfare that generated some pockets of laughter from the audience, she mouthed a semi-silent prayer before she tapped the can and eased the contents out of it. "Whew! Luck was with me today."

She picked up a long, sharp knife. "Now all I have to do is slice between the pineapple slices and . . ." She angled the plate toward the audience. "That's all there is to making a perfect Jell-O-in-a-Can Jell-O mold."

Sarah put the plate on the table, took a small bow, and handed the microphone to Marcus. Waving to the applauding audience, she walked off the stage and out of the Civic Center. She had more important things to do than stay around until the end of the afternoon session.

Chapter Twenty-Eight

Sarah clicked the lock button on the key fob of her Honda. She pushed the fob and her hands into her pockets while she walked to the front of the building that co-housed the fire and police stations and the jail. Expansive glass doors and windows framed the main lobby, but upstairs, the windows narrowed to slits too narrow for a prisoner to slip through and below the main level was a small parking area with reserved spots and private office entrances for the fire and police chiefs.

Before she reached the end of the parking lot, Harlan came through the double glass doors. He stood outside them, his head down and shoulders rounded, warding off a nonexistent blast of wind. Emily wasn't with him. Sarah hoped Emily was already gone.

She picked up her pace. Harlan spotted her when she was about a car length from him. He waited for her to reach him.

"Where's Emily?"

Instead of answering, he took her hand and led her back into the building.

"Harlan?"

He put his finger to his lips and guided her to a cushioned bench on the side of the lobby.

"You're scaring me, Harlan. Did you bail her out?"

"She's upstairs." He pressed forward, his words running together. "I'm working on it, but unless something works out, there won't be a bail hearing until next week."

"You can't leave her in a cell over the weekend. She didn't do anything. Surely you can explain that to one of the judges and get some type of bail set today."

He shook his head. "Peter agreed to keep her in a cell by herself tonight, but not indefinitely. I'm doing the best I can to expedite things. Sarah, you have to understand, the forensic evidence is stacked up against her."

"I don't believe it. Harlan, someone is framing her with this so-called evidence."

"If they are, she isn't helping me prove it. She won't talk to me."

"I'll speak to Emily. I don't know what's going on in her head."

Harlan rubbed his hand against the back of his neck and shirt collar. "They won't let you in to see her right now. Best thing you can do is go home and try to get some toiletries or other things she might need."

"Harlan, how can you say that? You're her lawyer. Surely you can get me in to see her."

A pained expression crossed Harlan's face, but he didn't cut her tirade off.

"You don't seem to be doing much to help her!"

He reached for her hands, but she pulled away from him. "Sarah, please, I know it may look like I'm not doing much, but believe me, I'm trying to find her a way out of this mess. The problem is that the accusations keep mounting." He shrugged halfheartedly. "A lawyer isn't a mind reader. Without her cooperation, I'm pulling at straws."

Tears slipped from Sarah's eyes. "But you got her out last time."

"That was easier. She wasn't under arrest then. Plus, there were a lot of things available for me to use to poke holes in the theory of their case." He raised a finger to underscore each argument: "One, Bill avoided recipes with nuts and he knew Emily's recipe had nuts. Two, there was a believable explanation for how her fingerprints were on the knife, and three, Bill hated rhubarb."

Harlan took Sarah's hand. This time, she didn't take it away. "A jury can be convinced to give a person one bite of an apple, but it's beginning to look like Emily has had one taste too many. Reasonable doubt doesn't seem so reasonable. Peter's simply got too much evidence and there are too many coincidences."

"I don't understand."

With his free thumb, Harlan wiped away the tears staining her cheeks. Sarah flinched as he rested his finger a moment more than he needed. "Think back to the minutes before the Expo opened. When I got to the Southwind booth, you were under the table, but I could see it was crazy in the booth with all of you trying to get things set up."

Sarah nodded in agreement.

"That close to the Expo starting, considering what she was responsible for, Emily should have been there."

"She'd . . ." Sarah stopped, remembering how Marcus commanded Emily to "go back to her own station," but Emily left the booth.

"Sarah, imagine how it will play to a jury. Most people will say she should have fired Richard on the spot for insubordination. From what I've heard, it wasn't the first time he'd acted out, and he was the one who stomped out of the booth. They'll also say, considering her management responsibilities, rather than look for him, she should have manned up and helped Jane. Instead, Peter has witnesses, including you, who will testify she got into it with Jane and Marcus ordered her out of Jane's part of the booth."

"It was all Jane's fault. Besides, Marcus sent Jane to wash her face. He stepped in to help her be ready in time."

"That's the point. He stepped in. People will wonder why Emily didn't assist Jane, for the good of Southwind, plus, it really was her job."

"You know all the things Jane has done to Emily and me."

He rolled his eyes toward the ceiling. "A jury doesn't and probably won't. More importantly, Jane came back to the booth. The next time anyone saw Emily, she was alone with Richard, her hands and clothing covered in his blood."

"I got his blood on me, too."

"True, but your fingerprints aren't on the knife that killed him."

"Emily touched the knife when she tried to help Richard. You can explain that!"

"Not if Emily doesn't testify. Right now, she isn't talking to me, let alone indicating she'd testify on the stand. Fingerprints on two different murder weapons won't sit any better with a jury than being found allegedly giving CPR to both men killed by those weapons." He put both hands on her shoulders and stared Sarah straight in the face. "Even for a good lawyer, like me, it's hard to shift attention away from the coincidences and the fingerprints—especially if Emily won't help me understand them."

"I'll make her talk to us."

Harlan stood and looked at Sarah. "I hope you can shake some sense into your sister when Peter lets you see her, but, in the meantime, I'm going back to the office while they're booking her. I have a client coming in at four and I need to be back here at four thirty."

"On a Saturday?"

"It's a special matter. Before then, though, I need to look up a few things I might be able to use on Emily's behalf."

"Let me come with you. Maybe I can think of something you're missing."

"Tell you what, go get your sister a few toiletries or other things she might need. Bring them to me at the office. Hopefully, we can think of something. If not, you can always catch up on your filing."

Chapter Twenty-Nine

With a farewell tip of his briefcase, Harlan left Sarah sitting in the lobby. She shut her eyes and tried to focus on what he'd told her, rather than the sinking feeling in her stomach. None of this made sense. Emily was the good twin who won all the Girl Scout merit badges and shared everything with their mom—or at least she always had.

She took a deep breath and tried to think how Perry Mason might analyze what was happening. There was no question he'd have Paul Drake check the facts and then he'd pull back, think, and tie everything together. Maybe she could do the same thing.

When had things changed? Were there changes in Emily's behavior that Sarah had ignored? Sarah opened her eyes. San Francisco. Since Emily came back from San Francisco, things had been different. Unlike during the period of Sarah's divorce, she and Emily no longer finished each other's sentences or, for that matter, knew instinctively what the other was thinking.

Even Emily's eating habits had changed. In the past, the twins always narrowed restaurant menu choices to two they shared. Since San Francisco, Emily ordered her own dish, except for the few times Marcus was with them. Then, he and Emily shared. Sarah had thought Emily was playing up to her boss, but now she wondered if there was more to it than that. The problem with her hypothesis was his obvious chumminess and involvement with Jane. Was it real or not? If she couldn't get Emily to talk to her, Sarah decided she would confront Marcus. Maybe he could shed some light on what had really happened in San Francisco.

In the meantime, Sarah was determined she wouldn't leave the building without trying to see Emily. Every moment they delayed talking was a moment lost in finding the true murderer. It was unthinkable that the real killer was at large and no one cared. She shuddered at the thought of Emily being fingerprinted, photographed for a mug shot, and locked away in a cell.

Remembering how Harlan bluffed them into the interrogation room earlier in the week, Sarah decided old-fashioned bluster might be the answer again. The only thing was whether to start with the desk sergeant or go straight to Peter. She ran through different possible scenarios in her mind. Unfortunately, they all ended with the same conclusion Harlan had voiced: "Not now."

The elevator across from where she sat chirped as its doors opened. Sarah didn't pay attention to whether anyone she knew got on or off until she heard her name repeatedly called. It was Peter.

"Kismet. I was just thinking about you."

"Oh?"

"I need to talk to Emily."

He tilted his head away from her and ran his hand through his thick black hair. She waited. This was the body language she was beginning to associate with him just before he delivered bad news. Sarah wondered if he was conscious of it. She was certain of one thing, she had no plans to clue him in about his giveaway behavior.

"She doesn't want to see you."

"That's ridiculous. I'm her sister."

He fingered the stitching over his holstered gun. "Sarah, I know this is difficult for you, but Emily couldn't have been any clearer."

"Emily?" She craned her neck toward him and frowned. Harlan had told her it was Peter and the process preventing her from seeing Emily. "That doesn't make any sense."

He eased himself into the space on the bench vacated by Harlan. "I know how it must feel to you, but sometimes people who've done something bad can't face their loved ones."

Sarah slid a few inches away from him. She tried to focus on what he was saying, but none of it sounded logical. "Peter, I don't care what Emily said. We're sisters and I want to see her."

"I'm sorry. She was emphatic that she doesn't want to see or talk to you. Like I said, sometimes people feel guiltier for not living up to expectations than for the crime they've committed."

Sarah rose. She faced him stiffly. "Peter, my sister isn't guilty. I don't know if she's in shock or thinking she's protecting me, but Emily didn't kill anyone any more than I stole Mother Blair's bracelet."

Peter didn't flinch from her gaze.

"You seem to take every accusation Jane makes as being truth. Maybe you should examine her veracity. What if, instead of being loyal to Bill, Jane moved on to Marcus? Perhaps they wanted Bill out of the way to have the restaurant and trust for themselves? Or, maybe Jane, for some unfathomable reason, is simply jealous of Emily and me?"

"That's not what the evidence says."

"Then it's time you look for more evidence." Sarah stalked out of the building.

He called after her, but she ignored him, hoping he hadn't seen the tears obstructing her vision. She absolutely refused to give Peter the satisfaction of seeing her cry.

Sarah held herself erect until she reached the safety of her Honda's front seat. As the windows fogged up, she rested her head on the steering wheel and let the tears flow until there were no more to cry. She pulled a tissue from a pack she kept in the console and wiped her eyes and nose. Although she turned on the ignition, she didn't pull away.

Being shut out by Emily made no sense. True, lately they hadn't been as close as in the past, but just as she knew Emily would always have her back, she firmly believed Emily instinctively shared the same knowledge. Emily's excessive deference to Marcus and her failure to mention Bill's involvement in the restaurant were totally out of character, but not so far as to make her a murderer. It reminded Sarah of when Emily tap-danced around the truth to keep their parents from finding out Sarah had done something bad. Perhaps that was the answer. For some misguided reason, maybe Emily thought she was protecting her.

But there was nothing Emily could be protecting her from this time. Her relationship or lack thereof with Bill since their divorce was out in the open. No, it couldn't be her.

She ran through the cast of other characters. Obviously, it wasn't Jane, but who could it be? Grace, Jacob, and Richard competed against Emily for the sous chef position but only Richard seemed angry when Emily was promoted. The other two hadn't displayed any negative reaction to the announcement. In fact, both Grace and Jacob helped Emily with everything that came up after she was named sous chef and the two came to Sarah's aid after Emily's arrest. Could they be hiding so much anger and disappointment at Emily's selection to have sabotaged her?

And what of Marcus? In the last few days, he'd run the gamut of emotions. Completely in despair, far more than a seasoned chef should have been, when the refrigerator cord was cut and the prepared food ruined and then ferocious when he thought Grace and Emily were poisoned.

Was Emily risking her own future to protect someone who not only had sabotaged Southwind but might be a murderer?

Maybe, once she got back to his office, Harlan and she could brainstorm something from all of this. She pulled out of the parking lot. Emily's stuff was at their mother's house, but that was the last place she was going to go. She didn't have time. Sarah turned toward her own apartment. She had enough extra toiletries at home to easily make a care package for Emily. Besides, she could take a few minutes to check on RahRah before heading to Harlan's office.

Unlocking her door, Sarah smiled. RahRah lay stretched out in his sunny patch on the linoleum near the kitchen sink. He made a noise when she walked in but didn't move.

"Hey, RahRah. Are you having a good day?" She laughed at the series of sounds her cat made. No matter how bad a day she was having, RahRah could always make her smile. She plopped down on the small rug next to him and petted his head. "Talking to me, huh? Was it too quiet for you while I was gone?"

Her finger caught in his red collar. She hadn't noticed it had a small split in the leather. "You must have caught this on something the other night during your attic escapade." She thought about changing it but decided playing with him was more fun than standing up and getting one of the many decorative collars Mother Blair had bought him.

Sarah grabbed a pink rubber mouse lying nearby. She squeezed it until it emitted a squeak. Once she caught RahRah's attention with the toy, she held it up so he could swat at it. Moving it around, she laughed at the intensity of his play. "That's better, isn't it?"

After a few minutes of good playtime, she sighed and let him have the toy while she picked up his empty food bowl. She opened the cabinet she used as a pantry. To save time, she reached for the dry food container while keeping up a running conversation with the chattering cat. RahRah jumped up and stomped around the kitchen. "Don't want this, huh? Rather have your other kind of food?"

She put the dry food back in its place in the cupboard and showed him a can of his wet food. Sarah guessed he preferred it because she could swear RahRah's purr sounded content as he curled himself into a ball and sat on her feet. He didn't budge as she reached for the manual can opener lying on the counter.

The can opener had belonged to her mother. It hadn't worked well when she and Emily were kids and it was even less effective now, but she couldn't bring herself to buy a replacement. With effort, she manipulated the opener until its lip caught the can's edge and circled the top. She put the wet food in his dish.

Extricating herself from RahRah, who was now interested in his meal, she searched her bathroom drawers for sample-size soap, deodorant, and toothpaste and a toothbrush to take to Emily. Or, she thought, at least for Harlan to deliver to Emily.

The bag for the jail zipped, she checked if RahRah was finished. His food was barely touched. He looked at her and meowed. "I'm sorry, guy. I'd like to stay and play, but duty calls. Even if she won't help us, Harlan and I need to find a way to get Emily out of this fine mess she's gotten herself into."

Chapter Thirty

"First you let Peter arrest my sister and now you want to talk about Jane taking RahRah." She banged the drawer of the filing cabinet in the reception area shut. "I thought you are supposed to be representing Emily and me."

Sarah crossed the room with three quick strides and followed Harlan into his office. Keeping the manila file folder he held clutched to his chest, Harlan retreated to the far side of his desk.

"What are you doing?" She pressed her palms into the desk and leaned forward on them. "Do you really think you can shield yourself from me with that flimsy folder?"

"Of course not." He laid the folder on his desk. "I'm simply giving you a moment to calm down and listen to reason."

"The only thing I want to hear from you is 'how.' How you're going to get my sister out of jail and how you're going to keep Jane's hands off RahRah."

"Sarah, you're not being fair. I've been working on Emily's case, but like I already told you, she refuses to help me." He pointed to a stack of law books piled on his desk. "I've looked for a precedent or something to use as a defense, but nothing seems to fit. Your sister may be obstinate, ornery, and unhelpful, but no one would believe she is crazy, temporarily insane, or acting in self-defense."

"But—"

"The evidence Peter has looks bad. Maybe it won't justify a finding of premeditated murder in Richard's case, but between the fingerprints on the weapons and the blood and rhubarb all over your sister and her clothing, and Richard and Bill apparently having enough dirt on Emily to get her kicked out of South-wind and maybe even the cooking field, Peter had good reason to arrest Emily."

Sarah jerked away from Harlan's desk. "What about the tox reports? If they're not back, how can he be sure Bill was murdered?"

"They're not back. Hopefully, the reports will exon-erate Emily, but we can't count on it. That's why we should view this case from all angles. If I can't find grounds for reasonable doubt, we also should consider what kind of a deal we might be able to strike."

"Are you talking about a plea bargain?" Sarah backed into Harlan's guest chair, as if he had pushed her into it. "Harlan Endicott, you're supposed to be on her side."

"I am. I really am." He rubbed the back of his neck as a pained expression flitted across his face. "If there was something I could use to raise reasonable doubt . . ."

"You're missing something. I'm sure of it."

"Believe me, I've racked my brain over this." He again pointed to the books on his desk.

"Maybe the answer isn't in those books." She took

a deep breath and swallowed before letting the words rush out. "I know you said we shouldn't do any sleuthing, but Emily and I felt we had to. In fact, that's why I was working in the Southwind booth."

"You don't say." He peered over his glasses. "It didn't take a detective to figure that one out. Did you think I really believed Emily put you on the payroll for your culinary skills? So, what did you two super sleuths discover?"

"Well, we realized Marcus and Jane are involved in something together." She filled him in on the conversation she overheard outside the nurse's station. "Control of Southwind could have been a motive for Marcus. By the same token, claiming the carriage house, RahRah's trust, and a piece of Southwind might have made Bill's death attractive to Jane. Emily and I haven't even scratched the surface on Jacob and Grace yet, but we know Grace has had some dealings with the criminal justice system. We didn't get time to compare notes before Peter arrested Emily. We've got to go back to the jail and talk to her."

"I'll try but . . ." He lowered his voice and kept his eyes glued on his desk. "Emily doesn't want to see you."

"I've heard." She sunk back in her chair. "It doesn't make sense to me. Until she came back from San Francisco, we've always shared everything."

"People change."

"Not as much as you're saying. We're missing something."

"Perhaps." Harlan came around his desk. He parked himself on its edge, in front of Sarah. "Help me here. Your sister isn't. You keep telling me you know something is different, but what is it?"

He leaned into Sarah's personal space. "I can't sell

a judge on your intuition. I need something concrete. What have you noticed? What is it that feels good or bad to you?" He bent so close to her that when Sarah raised her head, she could smell the sweetness of his aftershave. "Well?"

Sarah ran the events of the past few months through her head. Nothing specific came to mind. In every instance she could think of, things had started as they always did and then Emily had drifted away. Work excuses were her main reason—hours on duty or a minor crisis. Come to think of it, Emily's issue of the day always distracted her from whatever she planned to do with Sarah but wasn't so major Emily, who normally never shut her mouth, felt the need to use Sarah as a sounding board. Until this moment, Sarah hadn't understood how far outside Emily's inner world she now was. "Secretive and silent—she's the exact opposite of the Emily I've known since the day she started talking."

Harlan crunched his eyebrows, narrowing his eyes. "That certainly doesn't help. Think of how the prosecutor will play that to a jury." He stood and puffed his chest as he walked around the room and then assumed almost the same posture Emily struck when she'd been role-playing earlier in his office. "Ladies and gentlemen of the jury. The defendant and her sister were always close. They shared everything. That is, until lately, when she began holding her feelings and thoughts close to her heart."

Sarah jumped up and gave him a hug. "Harlan, you're a genius!"

"I think I'm missing something here. I've gone from slacking devil to genius?" He looked at his watch. "In the space of two minutes?"

"Not even." She laughed at his solemn frown and crossed arms. "Relax, you're giving away your feelings in your body language. That's exactly what Emily's been doing. We simply didn't see it."

"Sarah, go back a step. I don't know what you're talking about."

"It's simple. You're one hundred percent right about her holding things close to her heart." She waited for Harlan to catch up with her but then pressed forward. "Think about it. Emily has always been out there—hiding nothing. If Mom asked, 'How was school?' I'd say 'fine,' but Emily would lay out her day hour by hour. Why suddenly no run-on descriptions or random thoughts?"

Harlan stared at Sarah, eyes wide.

"Don't you see? Emily hasn't changed. She's just sharing her feelings and everything important in her life with someone other than Mom or me. Someone close to her heart who she's protecting."

"Someone close to her heart?"

Sarah nodded. "Emily couldn't wait to get out of Wheaton, but she came back willingly. Chef Marcus is up-and-coming, but she's worked for bigger names. I don't know exactly what happened in San Francisco, but figure it out. They're both here now."

"And Emily is—"

"Sharing food with him instead of me. We need to talk to Chef Marcus."

Chapter Thirty-One

"Whoa! Sarah, where do you think you're going?"

"To talk to Chef Marcus," Sarah called over her shoulder, already in the reception area where her coat and purse were. "I just need to grab my jacket."

"Sarah, come back in here." Harlan went behind his desk and sat down.

Sarah returned to his doorway.

"Chef Marcus? I thought you said Jane and Marcus were involved with each other? And now you're pairing him off with Emily?"

"I hadn't thought about that. But logically, he's got to be the one she's protecting."

"While you think about it, please sit down again. We need to talk." Harlan focused his attention on the file on his desk that he'd shielded himself with. Opening it, he shuffled the papers. He held a piece of paper up so she could see it from where she still stood in the doorway. "This is what we need to address, now."

RahRah's name was at the top of the sheet. She couldn't believe it. With everything else going on, how could Harlan and Peter still expect her to give up RahRah tomorrow? For a fleeting moment, she wondered what would happen if she simply refused. Would they arrest her, too? At least that might give her access to Emily.

The front door chimed. Sarah shoved her thoughts about RahRah away while she walked back to her desk and checked the monitor. She buzzed in George Rogers, the nosy across-the-street neighbor from when she lived in the Main Street house with Bill. Not wanting to have him pry about Emily or Jane, she greeted him and returned to Harlan's doorway, leaving Mr. Rogers cleaning his feet and the tip of his cane on the little carpet by the door.

Harlan got up and poked his head around Sarah. "I'll be with you in a few minutes, George. There should be a new *Sports Illustrated* on that table by the lamp."

Sarah barely moved out of the way quickly enough to keep Harlan from clipping her heels as he closed the door between his office and the waiting area. "Harlan?"

He reached across his desk and picked up the sheet he had dropped. "Sarah, I run a business. For the past few days, it's been the last thing getting my attention." He looked at his watch. "I've got to discuss a few things with George and still be over at the courthouse in forty minutes."

"Court today?"

"Judge Larsen is going on vacation next week and asked me to run by his chambers this afternoon."

Sarah nodded. She didn't know what it was about, but she knew that if the only active judge in town asked you to stop by his chambers, even on a Saturday, you went.

"I know you don't work on Saturdays, but would you do me a favor and please stay here and man the phone until I get back? I've been expecting a really important call this afternoon and it still hasn't come in."

"But if I can catch Marcus, he might be able to help us find out who is framing Emily."

"Believe me, that's not the issue for Emily this afternoon. Don't worry," Harlan hastened to add, "I promise I'll help track down Chef Marcus later today. For now, we've got to take a minute to talk about RahRah."

He again held the document out to Sarah, who put her hands over her ears and squeezed her eyes shut, hoping no tears escaped them. She heard him drop the sheet on the stack in his folder and felt him place his hands on hers. Gently, he guided her hands away from her head and put a finger over her mouth.

Eyes tearless and opened wide, she jerked her mouth away from his finger. "What do you think you're doing?"

"Nothing. Nothing, that is, except stopping you from wasting the little bit of time we have. You need to understand that Jane's testamentary documents appear to be valid. Accordingly, she has the right, under state law, to take RahRah from your possession to live in the carriage house." He paused as Sarah stumbled crossing the room to his guest chair. "Are you all right?"

She brushed loose strands of hair back behind her ear. "I don't care what Alabama code says. Bill gave RahRah to me. Jane can't just waltz into my house and take him away. Can she?"

"I'm afraid she can. Alabama has a statute for creating an animal trust. Under it, Bill's mother could legally set up a trust, which she did, leaving money and even a home for RahRah. She named Bill as the trustee. Under the old trust law, if she didn't establish a successor trustee, the court would have to name a successor, and we could have argued in court you should be the new trustee. The modified statute is more lenient. Bill was within his rights to make provisions if RahRah survived him. Whether we like it or not, it appears he appointed Jane RahRah's trustee upon his death. Peter held Jane off to give you time to surrender RahRah voluntarily, especially with everything going on, but Jane is adamant about picking RahRah up tomorrow morning."

"Can't we fight this? Maybe you can file some kind of legal challenge? After all, I've been taking care of RahRah with Bill's blessing all this time."

"I can go to court on your behalf and at least make the argument that you've cared for RahRah for years and you have a mutual loving relationship, but we still have to be realistic about what state law dictates. If we make the argument, it won't help us if it can be demonstrated you defied the law by refusing to give RahRah up. This is a two-edged sword: your loving relationship against the documents. I can argue how fit you are to be a trustee, but the other side may question your abilities by saying you were so naïve Bill scammed you into caring for RahRah while he rode RahRah's legacy to the bank. The court may pity you or acknowledge your love and care of RahRah, but the judge will be compelled to rule against you in the face of these documents." He closed the folder and dropped it on a stack on his desk. "I'm sorry, Sarah. Everything seems properly executed and they name Jane, not you."

"But surely we can show Jane can't take care of RahRah like I do."

He nodded affirmatively. "Unless we can demonstrate that Jane is unfit to take care of RahRah, and we don't have any evidence to that effect, the court must go by the letter of the law. Fighting this might be good emotionally, but it isn't worth your time or money." He closed a black-covered book that lay open on his desk.

Sarah struggled against breaking down. It shouldn't matter if Jane was fit or not. What should matter was what RahRah wanted, what was best for RahRah. In her home, RahRah was comfortable and loved. Surely love needed to play into the equation. Harlan often talked of the letter and the spirit of the law. If she lost RahRah, she wasn't sure if she wanted to continue working in the legal profession.

Awash with her thoughts and struggling to keep her cool, Sarah simply shrugged at Harlan, at a loss for words she could say to change things.

Taking advantage of her silence, Harlan grabbed a worn book and the briefcase she carried for him at the police station and headed for the door. "Sarah, I've got to go, but you need to turn RahRah over to Jane when she comes to pick him up tomorrow morning."

She stared at him, an emotionally void calm replacing her prior trembling sensation. Her mouth set in a straight line, she followed Harlan's steps into the waiting room. She stopped short when Harlan paused without warning.

"George, walk with me. I'm running late, but we can talk on the way to the courthouse." He turned his head back toward Sarah. "Please don't leave until I get back. I won't be gone long. I promise that the minute I get back, we'll find out if there is anything to your hunch about Emily and Marcus."

She nodded, but Harlan didn't see it. He and George were already gone.

Sarah squared her shoulders, deciding to focus on practicality. She might not be able to help RahRah, but she could still be there for Emily. Her choices were simple. Wait for Harlan and keep her job, considering how little work she'd done of late, or leave the office, find Marcus, and lose her job. Confronted with this choice, the answer seemed like a no-brainer. She knew what she wanted to do emotionally, but she needed her paycheck.

Being rational, which she didn't want to be right now, she couldn't argue with why Harlan asked her to stay. As much as she hated waiting to find Marcus, Sarah's pragmatic side dictated she do some work while she was here.

She doubted Emily, if faced with the same dilemma, would make the same choice. Her reaction probably would be a combination of "Damn the torpedoes" and "Let the chips fly." The big difference between the two of them was Emily would leave the office unattended, save the day by coaxing the truth from Marcus, and then convince Harlan to reemploy her with a raise. Sarah would simply muddy things up and end up canned.

A sudden blaring of the University of Alabama's fight song startled her. It took her a moment to realize it was the ringtone of Harlan's phone coming from his office. She followed the sound and saw his cell phone sitting on his desk. Apparently, in his rush to leave for the courthouse, he'd left it behind.

Concerned it might be the important call coming in on his private cell instead of the office number, she picked up the phone but before she could punch the answer button, the ringing abruptly ended. Worried, she hit recent calls. Like her cell phone, Harlan's recent call listing showed the name of the caller if the person was listed in his contact list. She heard her own slight intake of breath because the bold letters spelled out the caller as JANE CLARK.

Why was Jane phoning Harlan? Sarah wanted to hit the call back button but instead stared at the name. If this call was to arrange when and how RahRah would be turned over to her, Sarah wanted no part of it. Perhaps she could stall RahRah's departure if she hid the phone. She looked around the office for a hiding spot. Rationally, she knew it wouldn't change things to hide the phone, but the temptation was so great she held it in her hand for a moment as her eyes scoured the room.

Her eyes were drawn to the built-in bookcase behind Harlan's desk. Two shelves were devoted to black cloth–covered books like the one he took to the courthouse. She moved closer to examine them. The Code of Alabama.

Most of the books were in pristine shape, but a few were obviously well handled. That made sense. From her work as Harlan's receptionist, she knew that although he pretty much took any case that came in the door, most of his work was confined to wills, divorces, property transactions, and DUIs. Leaving the phone on Harlan's desk, she traced her finger across the spines of his books, more closely examining the ones he used the most.

As she touched the books, she noticed from their dates they weren't current. She remembered Harlan telling her he'd inherited the books, but she hadn't realized how out-of-date his version of the Code of Alabama was. Now she understood why Harlan received tear sheets in the mail every month from a subscription service—small booklets that covered current changes in state law.

The monthly updates arrived wrapped in plastic shrink-wrap already three-hole punched. When she first started working for him and they came in the mail, she asked him what binder or notebook he wanted her to put them in, but he responded he preferred reviewing them before they were filed away. From that point forward, when the updates arrived, she put them neatly in his "in" basket. She hadn't realized, until now, he stacked the still-wrapped packets on the bottom shelf of his bookcase.

Considering his obvious backlog of reading material, she wondered, because she didn't remember ever typing paperwork for an animal trust, how current he was on that kind of law. Maybe there was a loophole she could use? She didn't know the code section to check, but she was sure if she keyworded different search engines on her computer with "animal trust" and "Alabama," something would come up.

She smiled as she woke her computer from sleep mode. Harlan had asked her not to leave the office, but he hadn't forbidden her to use his office equipment for personal research.

Chapter Thirty-Two

Nothing. Sarah tried all the tag words she could think of: "animal trust," "cat trust," "wills and animals," and "animal trustees," but every article or statutory reference she found didn't vary from what Harlan told her. Maybe the paper updates were stacked in his office, but whether by computer or some seminar, he was, it seemed, sadly current on animal trust rules in Alabama.

With a sinking feeling in the pit of her stomach, Sarah thought about what else she could do until Harlan got back from court. Filing? Typing? Harlan might want—make that need—both things done, but neither was good for her to do now. Between her worries about Emily and RahRah, she was sure she'd screw up anything she touched. At least, without Harlan being there to overhear her avoiding work, she could call and check on Grace.

As she punched in the hospital's phone number, she realized she didn't have to look it up. She still had it memorized from dialing it daily when Mother Blair was hospitalized for her final stay. How such a warm and good woman had raised a jerk like Bill was hard to fathom. It was also puzzling that she'd named Bill as RahRah's trustee. She knew how allergic he was to cats. Given how close Mother Blair and she were and Mother Blair knew how much Sarah cared for RahRah, Sarah was surprised she hadn't named her as RahRah's caretaker.

"Wheaton General Hospital. May I direct your call?"

"Patient information, please."

"One moment." There was a *click* and a few bars of generic music before a voice came on behind a second *click*. "Patient information. May I help you?"

"Would you please connect me with Grace . . ." She paused, uncertain of Grace's last name. She remembered Grace telling it to her. "It's on the tip of my tongue," she said to the voice asking if she had a last name. She mentally ran through her previous meetings with Grace.

"I'm sorry, I need a name please."

"It's . . . um . . ." The image of their introduction came back to her. "It's Winston."

"I'm sorry. We don't have a patient admitted by that name."

"She came in through emergency earlier today."

Again, there was a pause on the other end of the line. "No, we don't have anyone admitted or in emergency at present by that name."

"Does that mean she checked out?"

"I'm sorry, but I'm not allowed to give out that information. May I help you with anything else?"

"No, thank you." Sarah hung up. Apparently, Grace was okay or she would have been admitted. Sarah felt relieved. Now she could concentrate on worrying about her sister and finding something to do during the rest of the time she waited for Harlan.

Looking around, she decided the mail seemed like a good thing to tackle. It would take a lot to mess that up. Chanting "Mail is Mindless" to herself, she turned her attention to the unopened mail from the past two days. At least getting rid of the overflowing mail bin on the floor next to her desk would make Harlan think she'd worked during his absence.

As she emptied each envelope, she put its contents in one of three places. The advertisements and junk mail she dropped directly into the circular file. Any correspondence Harlan needed to read went into a second pile of letters she would put in his "in" basket. Sarah stuffed anything that needed filing, like copies of court orders and pleadings, into a folder she kept hidden in her desk drawer to be worked on at a future time.

Once she'd distributed the mail, except two checks, she went back into Harlan's office and pulled the firm's ledger from a wood-grained filing cabinet. She took the ledger back to her desk and on separate lines entered the numbers of the respective checks, their amounts, what case they referenced, and who had made the payment. After updating the ledger, she filled out a bank slip to deposit the two checks.

She knew the firm's balance was in the black, but she couldn't help but notice that these two checks, the only two received this week for work completed, weren't enough to cover her weekly salary. Seeing such a low cash flow, she could understand why, with all the pro bono time Harlan had put in helping Emily and Sarah this week, he was concerned about having some billable hours, too.

Sarah checked her watch. Four thirty. If this was a normal day, she would only be scheduled to work another half hour. If the call Harlan was waiting for was a business call, it should come by five, too. Hopefully, Harlan would get back soon. If he didn't, she was torn between leaving on time to search for Marcus or going straight home because RahRah was alone and it might be their last evening together. Then again, Harlan had specifically asked her to wait for him. She opted to give Harlan an extra thirty minutes beyond her normal quitting time before she powered down her computer.

The reception desk computer screen had just gone black when she heard Harlan's private entrance being unlocked. She rose to check if it was Harlan.

"I'm glad you're still here," he called from his office. She heard him drop his coat and briefcase on his desk. "I was afraid I'd missed you."

"What?" she began, but words deserted her when Emily walked out of Harlan's office.

Without waiting, Sarah ran to hug her. Emily hugged back, holding on tightly.

"Are you okay?" Sarah held her twin at arm's length. Emily looked tired, but there was something else, too. For a moment, Sarah couldn't pinpoint the difference. Then she realized the furrows in Emily's brow were relaxed. Emily was smiling—something Sarah had rarely seen her do since coming back from San Francisco.

"More than okay. Harlan got Judge Larsen to hold a special hearing and let me out."

"Temporarily, on bail," Harlan hastened to add as he watched their reunion from the safety of his doorway.

"A bail hearing on a Saturday? Who put up the collateral for Emily?"

Harlan blushed. "It wasn't a big deal. I ran into Judge Larsen when I went for coffee this morning. Because he's going out of town next week and our other judicial post is vacant, Judge Larsen agreed it wasn't fair to make Emily sit and wait for a bail hearing until he got back. Neither Peter nor the city prosecutor raised any objections with what Judge Larsen wanted to do, but the case hasn't gone away. Emily still isn't a free woman."

"We'll simply have to work harder to find the real killer." Sarah gave her sister's shoulders another squeeze.

"Or at least some grounds for me to use to create reasonable doubt." Harlan motioned them into his office. He sat down in his leather wingchair and indicated they should take seats on the matching brown couch.

As Emily settled herself onto the couch, Harlan made a show of leaning back and resting his booted feet on the coffee table. Sarah was so busy trying to decide whether his feet would touch the floor if he sat all the way back, she almost missed his drawling cowboy imitation. "Time to 'fess up, Emily."

Emily and Sarah looked at each other.

"Sarah, I'm sorry. I know I should have told you earlier about Marcus and Bill and what's been happening at Southwind, but I didn't want to complicate things any more than they were."

"I'm confused. How can things be more complicated than they now are?"

Harlan snorted but Sarah ignored him. She kept her eyes glued on her sister's face.

Emily returned her gaze. Emily held her head high, with her chin jutting out. "I came back from

San Francisco because Marcus and I were seeing each other exclusively."

"What is this, high school? You couldn't tell me you're going steady?" Sarah stood.

"We didn't want to hide it, but it was a business decision."

"I don't understand." Sarah walked to the front window and stared outside.

Emily came up behind her. She placed her hand on Sarah's shoulder, but Sarah shook free.

Now she fully understood why Emily had stopped sharing food and thoughts with her. "You didn't trust me enough to tell me you were dating?"

"It wasn't like that. It wasn't a matter of trust. It was business."

"Business? Do you think I'm an idiot?"

"No. I was the fool. Because of Southwind's precarious financial situation, I was afraid for us to admit we were a couple."

"I don't understand." At the sound of Harlan clearing his throat, Sarah jumped on him. "Harlan, did you know? Is that why you didn't want me to talk to Marcus this afternoon?"

Harlan held up both hands in mock defense of himself. "I didn't know before this afternoon. In fact, with Emily refusing to help me with her case, I probably never would have considered the possibility of them having a relationship but for your hunch she was shielding someone. Because of another matter, Judge Larsen delayed Emily's hearing by thirty minutes and I ran with what you suggested to bang some sense into her head. I called her out on keeping secrets and making matters worse by trying to shield everyone and ending up protecting no one."

Emily again reached for Sarah.

This time, Sarah didn't resist.

"Honest, Sarah, I was only doing what I thought was best. In San Francisco, our boss had an unwritten rule against staff members dating." She made quotation marks with her fingers. "He believed 'Kitchen romances create undue tension and feelings of jealousy.' Once I got back here and found out Bill was involved in keeping Southwind afloat, I was scared. Knowing Bill, if he was mad at anything I said during your divorce, he wouldn't care how much money he lost or who he hurt to get even with me or as a way of still getting to you."

Sarah nodded in agreement.

Emily picked up the thread of her story. "Marcus and I were trying to get Southwind turned around enough that Marcus would be able to buy back his restaurant when Bill decided that in addition to our limited catering business, we needed to handle food services for Civic Center events."

"And you didn't say no?"

"They couldn't," Harlan said. "Think about it. Bill controlled them."

Emily clenched her fists in the same way Sarah remembered seeing Marcus do at the nurse's station. "If Marcus didn't go along with Bill's business plan, Bill threatened to pull his financing and shut Southwind down. He'd bought out the other investors, so there was no one else Marcus could enlist to his side."

"In true Bill fashion, he had you over a barrel."

"Yes. We didn't have a choice but to take on the Civic Center gig after Bill signed the contracts over Marcus's objections. By that time, Bill had made him add Jane and Richard as line cooks . . ."

"Jane, I understand, but Richard?"

Emily nodded. "When Richard was getting his act together, he did odd jobs for Bill around his office and the Civic Center. After he started the culinary program at the community college, he asked Bill for an internship. The school is picky. It doesn't want to place students at restaurants staffed only with students. Because Grace was already scheduled by the junior college to do a work-study program, Richard was going to have to wait until next term. Bill wasn't happy with that. Instead, he insisted Marcus put him on the payroll."

"Got it."

"Even if I wasn't afraid of what Bill might do, keeping our relationship a secret made sense. There wasn't extra money to pay another supervisor, and Marcus didn't trust Jane or any of the others to take charge. Instead, he was doing everything."

"And probably nothing well," Harlan observed.

"Right. So, we decided he'd handle cooking for the restaurant and all of the catering while I managed the daily restaurant operations and Civic Center activities."

"I understand that arrangement," Sarah said. "But I still don't understand why you kept your relationship a secret."

"If anyone knew we were dating, they might have thought I hadn't earned my position because of my cooking and kitchen management skills. We didn't need any extra tension in the kitchen while Marcus resolved the control issue with Bill."

"But even with Bill dead, you've never gone public as a couple."

"Because there's no longer anything to go public with."

"Huh?"

"We're just good friends. Between the hours we've

been working and my commuting to live with Mom and that lack of privacy, plus the financial stresses of Southwind and all the garbage with Jane, I realized being business partners fit us better than a romantic relationship."

"Did Marcus agree?"

"He protested, but then things got crazy with Bill and Jane."

"Wait a minute," Sarah interrupted. "What exactly has been going on between Marcus and Jane? They've seemed awfully cozy since Bill died."

"It's purely business."

"Monkey business?"

"No. When Bill was dating Jane, he apparently promised her she'd be top dog. Consequently, she tolerated and played up to Marcus because of Bill and his business arrangement, but she resented taking orders from me. With Bill gone, she's gunning for my job again."

"Or," Harlan said, "for the entire business. By Bill's will, it looks like she is Marcus's partner, even if she isn't acting like it. Considering everything, I might be able to suggest to Peter Jane had a financial reason to kill Bill, but it doesn't solve the problem of your prints on the fork and knife."

Sarah tried to digest everything while watching Emily shrug and stay silent. It still didn't make sense. "Emily, Jane said Bill was going to fire you. What was that all about?"

"I told you. Jane and Richard were the ones who caught me searching the office for an extra set of books or something that truly affected the financials."

A movement from Harlan caught Sarah's eye. She glanced over and saw he was again raising his pencil.

"You're not the bookkeeper. What made you suddenly look at the books?"

"It was a gut feeling."

Harlan and Sarah exchanged glances.

Cowboy Harlan put his boots back on the floor and resumed the role of Harlan the lawyer. "There is one thing I still don't understand. Emily, why refuse to see Sarah or help me with your case?"

Emily didn't answer.

"You were afraid Marcus killed Bill to protect you," Sarah said.

Emily nodded affirmatively and stared at the floor. "That's why I needed you to stay at the Civic Center. I was hoping you'd find something to force Peter to consider someone other than Marcus or I could be the murderer."

Chapter Thirty-Three

Emily and Sarah walked down the cement sidewalk from Harlan's office. His admonishment to "please keep a low profile through the rest of the Food Expo weekend" still rang in their ears. Sarah headed toward her apartment, but Emily veered in the opposite direction.

"Em, where do you think you're going?"

"Drat, there goes Mom's back." She pointed to a crack in the sidewalk and then toward the Southwind signage posted at the edge of the shopping center down the street. "I'm going back to work. It's Saturday night and dinner service is just starting."

Sarah closed the gap between them and planted herself in front of her sister. She crossed her arms tightly across her chest. "I don't get it. Didn't you hear anything Harlan told us?"

Emily held her ground. Hands on hips, she matched her sister's stance. "Of course. He told us to keep a low profile at the Food Expo, but Harlan didn't tell me I couldn't work at the restaurant. We're booked solid tonight."

"It's Chef Marcus's and maybe Jane's problem. Not yours." She pressed on in a low but determined voice. "Emily, I don't know what's going on in your head anymore, but you don't have a financial stake in Southwind and, from what you've said, Marcus and you don't have a current connection either."

Emily yanked a black scrunchie from her pocket and cinched her hair into a ponytail. "You don't have to be an owner to be responsible. I still have a job to do."

"For a possible murderer?"

"That's a low blow. We don't know who's responsible, but I do know the restaurant is short-staffed and needs me tonight." Emily pushed past Sarah toward Southwind.

"Nobody, not even you, is indispensable." Sarah grabbed at Emily's fast-retreating back. She caught the edge of her jacket. "Think of yourself for a change."

Emily tried to twist free. "Let go. You're not my mother . . ."

Sarah held on, her foot turning as it slid into the edged space between the sidewalk and the grass. Her balance off, she fell, pulling Emily down with her. They landed on the grass with a thud.

As they extricated their overlapping arms and legs, Sarah and Emily began to laugh uncontrollably. Emily's "If Mom could see us now!" comment produced a second wave of giggles.

Finally catching their breaths, Emily jumped up and offered her hand to Sarah. Instead of taking it, Sarah leaned back, pulled her knees closer to her body, and wrapped her arms around them.

She looked up at her sister, whose hand remained outstretched. "Em, we've got to figure this out."

Emily sat back down on the edge of the street curb,

her back angled to where Sarah sat on the lawn. "I know, but other than trying to find suspects, too much of it has been too terrible and unreal to think about."

"Ignoring everything hasn't made it go away. Things seem worse than the other night."

"I know. I'd hoped that if I kept my head down and stayed in the kitchen, someone else would figure things out for me."

"Well, that hasn't happened." Sarah scooted beside Emily and the two sisters leaned on each other. "Peter is too convinced you're the guilty party to look clearly for any evidence that doesn't fit his conclusion and Harlan, bless his heart, can't seem to figure out a creative way to get around the letter of the law. Unless we do something, you're going to go to jail for two murders you didn't commit, and I'll probably be joining you because of a missing piece of jewelry I haven't seen in years."

"Huh?"

"It's another Jane story. Not something we need to get into now."

"So, what do our next steps need to be?"

"I'm not sure," Sarah said. "Is there anything else at the Civic Center tonight?"

"Not that the Southwind crew is involved in. With all the confusion, Marcus is closing our booth at seven tonight so everyone is going to work Southwind's dinner service. We'll all be at the Civic Center when the cook-off kicks off tomorrow afternoon."

Sarah gave her sister a nudge. "I guess you'd better get going. Promise me, though, instead of focusing on cooking and being a restaurateur, you'll keep your eyes on everyone. Treat it like one of those reality shows. You tend to be task-oriented, but tonight, put on your private detective cap and figure out who the alliances are and what everyone really wants."

"What about you? Don't you want to come and get something to eat or drink?"

Sarah checked her watch. "Not tonight. I'll do some more thinking, but I have a cat that needs me tonight."

Chapter Thirty-Four

"Believe me, RahRah, if I thought Peter wouldn't remember to look for you there tomorrow, I'd hide you back in the rafters and tell everyone you ran away." She made a face at RahRah, who lay in his spot on the kitchen floor, batting at his rubber mouse toy with one paw. He had no interest in her.

Sarah stepped over him and turned on the mini-television on the counter above where he lay. She flipped the stations until she found the one showing local news. The broadcast had just started so she watched it for a moment before she resumed packing RahRah's food, vitamins, and collection of collars and toys into an old cardboard box she'd set on the kitchen table. Picking up RahRah's scratching post, she examined it carefully. "You've certainly used this well."

Instead of putting it with RahRah's other things, she laid it on the table. "I can't do it, RahRah. I want you to be happy, but not as happy with her as you are with me. Maybe if you drive her a little crazy with your obstinate rotten ways, she'll opt to give you back to me. Want to try?"

RahRah turned his head in her direction but continued swatting his toy.

"Harlan and Peter only told me I have to give you to Jane. Not that I have to make this any easier for her than it is for me." She took the scratching post and an unopened bag of food and hid them in the cupboard under her kitchen sink. Dropping to the floor next to RahRah, she rubbed the short fur behind his ears. "Don't worry. I've given Jane enough for your first few meals, but she's going to have to do grocery and toy runs fairly quickly to keep you happy."

RahRah let his toy go and stretched his body as he purred in a rhythm that almost sounded like a one-sided dialogue. Sarah smiled as the intensity of his conversation ebbed and flowed with the speed with which she petted him.

"Are you going to remember to show Jane what happens when you're not happy? Remember, no honeymoon period. Let Jane see the real you when you're not happy." Sarah could have sworn RahRah bobbed his head "yes."

They both stirred at the sound of a siren rushing up their street. Subsequent earsplitting sounds came from different response vehicles following the path of the first. She grabbed RahRah and went to the window. Although she could see the rear of a fire truck in the distance, nothing on her block seemed out of place.

She put RahRah back on the floor. With his tail partially upraised, he sashayed back to his spot. She followed him into the kitchen. A picture of a burning building on the TV caught her attention. White letters flashed across the bottom of the screen—"Shopping Center Fire—More at Ten."

Sarah stood transfixed by the television picture, hoping the newscaster would say something about the fire. She was afraid to say aloud what she was thinking. In the distance, she heard more sirens, but rather than going back to the window, she grabbed her cell phone and punched in her sister's number. She held the phone to her ear, mumbling, "Emily, answer. Answer me, Emily." The call went to voice mail. Sarah again looked at the television screen. When a stock picture of the shopping center where Southwind was located showed on the screen, she strained to hear the voice-over. She didn't catch all the words, but she caught enough to pick up her jacket and keys and run from the apartment.

Sarah thought about taking her car but made the snap judgment she could get closer to the shopping center on foot. She ran the two blocks. Even from her street, she could see smoke billowing into the air in churning gray-black puffs obscuring the white clouds dotting the sky.

She went faster. When the full center came into view, Sarah scanned the people milling around the parking lot. No Emily. The stores near Sarah appeared intact, but the billowing smoke had to be coming from somewhere. She prayed as she dashed toward Southwind at the opposite end of the strip center.

Oh, no! Firemen stood in front of the building, their hoses trained on the restaurant's façade.

"Emily," she screamed. She sprinted toward Southwind, but sawhorse barricades stopped her. "Emily," she cried again, as she looked for a way around them and the people held back from the fire zone.

No one acknowledged her or moved aside to let her through.

"My sister," she shouted, as she elbowed through the crowd.

Wildly looking in all directions, she saw flames shooting up through the restaurant's roof. Several people, a few in Southwind attire, were being ushered beyond the parking area. Sarah craned her neck but couldn't tell if Emily was with them. Hoping, Sarah pushed her way through the crowd and around the various parked emergency vehicles and fire trucks. "Emily," she called out again and again, a cold sweat wetting her back when she didn't see her sister in the crowd.

Sarah spotted the fat officer from the station house shoving and guiding people away from the building onto the grassy area. She grabbed at his arm. "My sister?"

He stared at her for a moment until recognition softened his features. "Haven't seen her, but most everyone is already out of the restaurant." He motioned to where another crowd of people were gathered across the parking lot.

Most everyone? Most wasn't good enough. If Emily made it out, where was she?

Sarah squeezed past him and started toward Southwind.

The officer grabbed her shoulder and dragged her back as low pops erupted from the building. "You can't go any closer. There are hotspots in there."

Sarah squirmed but froze at the sound of a sharp crack and sizzle. Southwind's front façade began to crumble. The white plastered wall twisted as it slowly danced downward. Glass windowpanes shattered.

"Emily!" She jerked from the officer's grasp.

Staying out of his view, Sarah inched her way closer toward the end of the building but stopped cold when a trembling hand reached up and yanked the sleeve of her jacket. "What?" Recognition dawned on her as she looked down.

"Jacob!" She bent to where he sat on the ground, pressing a once-white monogrammed handkerchief to an oozing slash on his forehead. The handkerchief slipped as he shivered uncontrollably. She helped him reposition it. Observing his chattering teeth, she slipped off her jacket and draped as much of it as she could around him. "Help! We need help over here." She waved frantically, hoping to catch the eye of a nearby EMT.

"In a minute," an EMT yelled at her.

Relieved to have caught his attention, she focused on Jacob. "What happened?"

"I don't know. I was in the front of the house serving tonight." A coughing spell interrupted him. He began again, his voice low and scratchy. "I heard a whooshing noise and when I looked toward the kitchen, I saw flames coming from there."

"Emily?"

He shrugged. "She and Chef Marcus were in the kitchen. Grace and I were in the main dining room. When we saw the flames, we tried to get everyone out immediately."

Sarah looked around, praying she would see Emily. "Grace was working?"

Jacob coughed again. "Of course." He pointed across the lawn. She noticed Harlan on the sidewalk ringing the grass. In the center of the grass, Grace sat holding a child.

"I guess Grace must be better."

He dabbed his forehead with the blood-soaked

handkerchief. The bleeding had slowed, but not stopped. "She's tough. They wanted to keep her for observation, but once she was hydrated, she insisted on being released."

"I'd have thought she'd go home, not to Southwind."

He stared at her. "She knew how shorthanded we were. She came to help. Chef Marcus tried to send her home, but she insisted on staying."

"He let her?"

"Yeah. We really needed her. Jane decided to take tonight off and well, we didn't think Emily would be working."

Sarah nodded. She knew where they all thought Emily was going to be. But where was she now?

"Chef said . . ." Jacob struggled to catch his breath as he coughed. "Chef said Grace could sit behind the bar and run the cash register. He told her if he saw her do anything else, he was sending her home."

An EMT hurried over. Sarah stood and backed away, relinquishing her charge into his care. As he eased the handkerchief from Jacob's head, Sarah hoped the wound wasn't deep enough to mar Jacob's soot-covered but good-looking face. She didn't have time to wait around to find out. She had to find Emily.

Still not seeing her, Sarah moved closer to the blocked-off area. Emily had to be okay. Her sister was too strong and too bullheaded to be anything but fine.

Firemen hosing down the front of the building prevented her from getting closer. Pieces of the building seemed to float away like chalk dust in the air. A loud crunch refocused everyone's attention to the side of the building.

A firefighter burst out of the building through a break in the wall carrying a soot-covered body. Sarah felt like her heart was in her throat as other firefighters drenched him and the limp person he carried. Behind him, a black mountain lumbered out, dwarfing the fireman.

It slowly registered with her that the mountain with the tattered pants was Marcus. Sarah screeched. She ran toward the fireman. There was no question in her mind that the diminutive figure he carefully laid on a gurney was Emily.

She was within ten feet of the gurney when two other firefighters blocked her, saying even if it was her sister, she needed to stay out of the way. Praying, she kept her eyes focused on the unmoving person and listened as commands were shouted. When she saw the person on the gurney swat an arm at the EMT starting an IV, her legs wobbled with relief. She realized her unspoken words had been answered.

She was alive. Emily was alive and okay.

Sarah let her watering eyes wander to where other EMTs were trying to work on Marcus. He appeared to be refusing their help, his attention on Emily. Only after she was being loaded into an ambulance did he let himself slip into a seated position on the ground so the EMTs could tend to him.

"Where did they take her?"

"Wheaton General," the EMT working on Marcus replied.

"Thanks." She was relieved the ambulance wasn't rushing her to the University of Alabama Hospital in Birmingham. If she'd been badly burnt or hurt, she'd have been taken there. Her only thought now was hurrying to Emily.

"Sarah." The gravelly voice belonged to Marcus.

She tried to get through the group of people working on him but couldn't.

"Please, I need to speak to her. Please."

Someone shifted her position to let Sarah near him.

Marcus looked at Sarah with glazed-over eyes. "Tell Emily, I'm sorry. I'm so sorry."

Sarah knelt beside him. "Why, Marcus? What happened?"

"I don't know. I opened the back door of the kitchen and there was a loud whoosh. Flames jumped into the kitchen. The fire moved so fast near where we were working. Cabinet doors and things on shelves started falling. I tried to shield her, but . . ."

Rough hands pushed Sarah away. Others helped him into an ambulance. Sarah took one more look around before she ran to get her car. Her sister needed her.

Chapter Thirty-Five

Sarah tried to get her bearings in the emergency room. It was a zoo. Clumps of people, who obviously had come from the shopping center fire, were interspersed with run-of-the-mill emergency room patients. She didn't see her sister anywhere, so she pushed her way to the front desk and asked for Emily. The triage nurse, who Sarah faintly recognized as someone she'd gone to high school with, sent her back to room three.

The first thing Sarah saw in room three was Peter's back. He obscured Sarah's view of Emily. "What are you doing here? Haven't you already browbeat Emily enough?"

"Hi, Sarah." He stepped aside so she could reach Emily's side.

Sarah gazed at her sister. Soot stained her face. The few exposed parts of skin on her face were redder than usual, but Sarah didn't see any major burns or wounds.

"Are you okay?"

Peter answered for her. "She was one lucky girl. They've already checked her out thoroughly and, while they think she inhaled some smoke, not enough to do any major damage. The doctor is writing a prescription for an inhaler and some salves. You'll be able to take her home in a little while."

Ignoring him, Sarah addressed her sister. "Does anything hurt?"

Emily pointed to her throat.

"Other than a raw throat and some redness to her face that's no worse than a sunburn, the doctors say she's fine." Peter smiled.

"Marcus saved me. He pushed me away from the flames and covered me with his body, but I guess I fainted. Is he . . . ?"

"He's okay, too. I talked to him in the parking lot. You both were lucky."

"Is he here?"

"I don't know. He was being put in an ambulance when I left. Now that I know you're safe, I'll try to get you an update on his condition. Do you want to come with me, Peter?"

"Sure. I'm finished here."

Sarah was surprised at how quickly Peter acquiesced to her invitation.

He took a step toward the door but turned back and faced Emily. He fumbled with his cap. "Emily, I'm really glad you're okay."

"Thank you." Emily lay back on the pillow.

Sarah shot a look at her docile sister. "I'll be right there, Peter."

"Um, I'll be outside the door."

After he left, the twins looked at each other and tried not to giggle. "He hasn't changed since he used to come over to the house. I do believe he still has a sweet spot for you, Emily."

"I think you're wrong on that. Besides, he's married and has a family."

"They're separated or divorced. But that's not what's important right now. What did he want?"

"He was only doing his job. Peter wanted to know my version of what happened, even though he probably thinks Marcus or I burned down Southwind for the insurance money."

"Did you?"

Emily sat up on the gurney, her blues eyes glaring against her reddened skin. "How can you ask that? Marcus saved my life. Do you think he's the type of person who would chance hurting other people? The restaurant was full of customers and staff."

Sarah glanced at the door. Three bets Peter was trying to listen to their conversation. She leaned in to Emily.

"You're the one who suggested it and who's been afraid he might have killed Bill." She pointed at the door.

Emily nodded. "I was just rambling about Marcus considering that because Bill was ruining the restaurant," she whispered back, apparently understanding Sarah's concern about Peter. "Marcus would never risk the lives of innocent people. Besides, with Bill dead, Southwind is in the best financial shape ever. He might not be able to move into one of the old houses immediately like Bill and he planned, but the last thing Marcus would do is burn down the restaurant now."

She lay down again. "I think Peter is as perplexed as I am about what happened." Emily turned her face to the wall. "I'm tired. Would you please go find out about Marcus?"

True to his word, Peter was in the hallway, just outside the door. Sarah couldn't decide if he was being genuine or playing good cop to take advantage of an old friendship. She started toward the nurse's station, but he stopped her.

"I've already checked on Marcus. He's here and he'll be fine, but they are going to hold him tonight for observation."

"Why?"

"Smoke inhalation and a hairline shoulder fracture where he deflected some falling debris from Emily."

"Will they need to operate?"

"No, but he's looking at about six weeks in a sling and some PT." Peter bent his foot back against the wall. "At least it's his nondominant arm."

"Thanks. I'll go tell Emily." The two of them stared at each other without speaking until Sarah added, "Unless you want to."

"No, I . . ." He again played with his hat. "I'm not the bad guy you've been making me out to be."

"I never said you were."

He didn't answer. Instead, he glanced in both directions down the hallway. Sarah did the same, hoping someone was coming. His behavior was getting her nervous.

"Look, I know you think I've been unreasonable about Emily, but I've had to follow the evidence."

"Don't tell me you think she torched Southwind."

Peter shook his head. "No. I don't think so, but I still can't rule her out completely. My gut says today gives credibility to what she's been saying all along. The problem is someone deliberately set the fire and, once again, Emily was there at the critical time."

"What?"

"You can't tell anyone else, but there's evidence someone started a fire behind the kitchen by putting smoldering coals in the Dumpster area."

"But the fire was in the kitchen?"

"A gas can either in or next to the Dumpster exploded and caught the kitchen on fire. The fire marshal is investigating. He thinks someone deliberately placed coals on the Dumpster, perhaps as a prank to get the fire department called and the restaurant emptied out."

"But you mentioned a gas can explosion."

"Right. We don't know if the gas can was the ignition source or just happened to be in the Dumpster. Either way, the fire ran up the can and it exploded. If the can was happenstance, they still have to rule out whether Marcus opened the door to the kitchen at just the right moment or it simply was a bad prank outcome."

"I don't understand."

"When Marcus opened the door, the air draft may have pulled the fire in that direction. If the coals on the Dumpster were merely a distraction, then, when they finish sorting through things in the kitchen, they may find some other ignition source in the kitchen itself. Either way, once the flames hit the kitchen, there were more than enough fuel sources to destroy the kitchen quickly."

"Could it have been both?"

"Possibly. Right now, everything is speculation."

"I need to tell Emily."

He moved from the wall and cut her off. "No, you can't. Until we know more, you can't share this with anyone." He peered down the hall again. He hushed her from interrupting him. "I'm telling you because I'm scared for Emily. I've known Emily too long to believe she could possibly kill either Bill or Richard, let alone both, and yet, all the evidence has pointed that way. Try as I might, until tonight, I haven't been able to prove anything to the contrary."

"So, what's different tonight?"

"Everything is too simple for me to find it credible."

Sarah waited for him to explain further.

"Emily has a solid alibi for most of today and this evening. Whether she was in custody, with Harlan or you, or working in front of the staff and customers at Southwind, most of her time is accounted for." He ran his hand through his hat-head hair. "What's also evident to me is that if she'd been killed, everything would have been tied up with too pretty a knot."

"So, someone's trying to frame her."

Peter nodded. "If Emily died, my department could close the two cases against her based upon the evidence in our possession without the truth ever being known. That doesn't sit right with me."

"Or me." A thought crossed Sarah's mind, exciting her. "Peter, have you checked on Jane's whereabouts? She wasn't working tonight."

"Sarah, please, leave the investigative work to me. I have someone checking that out. Take Emily home with you and don't let her out of your sight. You need to be each other's keepers until I can figure out what's going on."

Now it was Sarah's turn to brace herself against the wall. "Each other's keepers?"

"I know it sounds dramatic," he said, as a nurse carrying papers headed in their direction. "But if I assume, as you have all along, that Emily is innocent, I don't know who you two should trust, except me."

"No offense, Peter, from what you've said and I've seen, I'm not sure our trust circle is big enough to include you."

Chapter Thirty-Six

Kitchen clatter woke Sarah. She opened and closed her eyes, knowing her few hours of sleep were ended, but she didn't move for fear of disturbing the warm mound pressed against her thigh. There was no knowing how long RahRah would stay still, but Sarah wanted to relish their last minutes before Jane came for him. "RahRah, if this was a movie, the governor would be coming through with a reprieve for you any minute."

"Unfortunately, it isn't."

Sarah reluctantly opened her eyes.

Emily, her face glistening from the aloe vera salve the doctor had given her, stood across the room setting two places at the table. "Get your sorry selves out of bed. It's a beautiful day. Besides, breakfast is almost ready."

Emily turned back to the stove on which Sarah could see an iron skillet sitting. "I've made us a frittata using what we picked up last night."

"A frittata?

"Think of it as a special omelet or a crustless quiche with meat or vegetables. Ours has shrimp and vegetables. Hurry up, it's almost ready."

Sarah jumped up and headed toward the bathroom. "Give me a moment to get washed."

The doorbell rang while she brushed her teeth. She groaned, spit, and grabbed a towel to wipe a blob of toothpaste from her mouth. With one last look at herself, Sarah walked out of the bathroom. Red-faced from climbing the steps, Jane stood in the center of the room next to one of the largest animal carriers Sarah had ever seen.

"I didn't expect you until later today. If you'd let me know you were coming this early, I would have met you so you didn't have to carry that monstrosity all the way up my stairs."

Jane rested her hand on the plastic top of the carrier. "The early bird catches the worm or, in this case, rescues her cat. Where is my little love?" Both Jane and Sarah peered around the room, but RahRah wasn't lying anywhere in the open preening himself.

"He dashed under the bed when you came in, Jane," Emily said. "Have you had breakfast yet? I just made a frittata and there's plenty for all three of us."

She carried the skillet by Jane, who eyed its contents, as Emily put it on the table.

"No, thanks. You do know that using a dairy product would have given you a more airy and creamy texture, darling." Jane drew the last word out as though it had more than two syllables.

"It looks good to me." Sarah sat at the table.

Emily joined her.

Jane cleared her throat. "My cat."

"Oh, how silly of me." Sarah stayed at the table. "I thought you might want to coax RahRah out from under the bed and play with him for a while. After all, you've never been around each other so I don't think throwing him right into that cage would be the best idea. My bad for assuming. You know what they say about the word 'assume.'"

"I do, but I don't really care. Will you please get my cat?"

"Certainly." Sarah rose but made no effort to go near the bed. If Jane wanted RahRah more quickly, let her get him herself. She wasn't going to do anything to make this easier for Jane.

Instead of retrieving RahRah, she went to the corner where she'd left the box of miscellaneous cat things she'd put together for Jane. She brought the box back, set it on the carrier, and reached into it. "I thought you might need a few things to get started taking care of RahRah, especially with being busy with today's Food Expo competition."

Jane's lips were as tight as her back as she watched Sarah take food and toys from the box.

"Oh, and I almost forgot, cats like to scratch and RahRah is no different." She opened the cupboard under the sink and pulled out the scratching post and the bag of food she'd originally decided not to give Jane. She couldn't begrudge RahRah any of his comforts.

"I don't need those used things."

Used, Sarah thought. The things RahRah knew and loved were used things?

"I bought RahRah new food, toys, and this travel carrier at the Pet Place last night. Now, my cat, please."

"I forgot you missed the excitement at Southwind last night."

Jane frowned. She tapped her fingers on the carrier. "I don't know what you're talking about. I was out shopping last night so I'd have everything I need to bring RahRah home."

"We had a fire at the restaurant last night," Emily said.

"Well, there couldn't have been much damage if you're here." Jane turned away from Emily and called out RahRah's name a few times. No cat magically appeared. "Sarah, enough of this game. I don't know where you're hiding RahRah, but I want him now!"

"The restaurant was pretty badly damaged. Marcus is in the hospital."

"I hadn't heard. I better get RahRah and find out what's been going on."

Sarah slowly glanced around the apartment surprised RahRah wasn't standing in the middle of the room with them. This was the moment of truth. Sarah couldn't give him away just yet, so she continued to stall. "Are you sure about the scratching post? Don't you think you should take something he loves so the scent is comforting to him in his new home?"

She picked up the toy mouse and held it out to Jane. "This is his favorite."

When Jane made no effort to reach for the mouse, Sarah let the toy drop to the floor and moved closer to where Emily sat at the table.

Jane scowled at Sarah and bent down on one knee and peeked under the bed. "There you are. Come here, RahRah." She reached for him. "I can't reach him. You try."

"Well, I don't know if my arms are any longer than yours."

Sarah and Jane stood beside the bed in a standoff.

Shaking her head, Emily gave in first. "I don't believe you two." She reached under the bed and coaxed RahRah out. She held him close, rubbing his head. His ears perked up. Slowly, Emily handed RahRah to Sarah, who bent her head into his fur.

"Hey, little guy, I'm going to miss you. You're going back to the house you lived in with Mother Blair. You'll have a lot more room to run and play than you've had here, but don't forget what we talked about."

"Get a life, Sarah. Come on, I've got to get going. Put him in the carrier, please."

Sarah held RahRah out to Jane. "I can't put him in that hard plastic cage. You'll have to do that yourself. He's not one for confinement or change, so maybe you should take a few minutes and make nice to him. Let him become accustomed to you."

Jane made no move to take RahRah from her. Sarah put him on the bed, keeping a hand on him, preventing him dive-bombing underneath it again. She couldn't believe Jane wouldn't even pet him. Maybe they could use Jane's unwillingness to show him love against her in court but, for RahRah's sake, she hoped Jane would warm up to him. "Why don't you sit on my bed for a moment and let him get to know you?"

Jane grimaced but sat. When she finally hooked her finger under the edge of his little red leather collar, Sarah backed off.

"I didn't realize cats wear collars. I thought you only put them on dogs."

"No. People use them for cats, too. I've heard of people who actually connect a leash and walk their cats, but most hang identification tags from the collars or use them to dress their cats up." Sarah rummaged through the cardboard box until she pulled out a plastic bag filled with collars. She grabbed a few from the bag and held them up for Jane to see.

"I remember this red, white, and blue one. Mother Blair always had RahRah wear it for the Fourth of July. She loved changing his collar to match her outfits or for holidays. RahRah has quite a collection."

Sarah leaned over and started to remove the torn red collar.

"What are you doing?" Jane asked as Sarah finished unhooking the collar.

Sarah held the bag out to Jane. "This one is ripped. I thought I'd change his collar. If you have a preference, I'll put that one on him."

Jane randomly grabbed one from the bag. "It really isn't necessary. I'll be buying him a new one." She addressed her next words directly to RahRah. "Time to go, cat. Mama's got to get ready for this afternoon's contest."

Jane started to stand, but a look from Sarah kept her anchored to the bed. She put her face down toward RahRah like Sarah and Emily had done and rubbed his head. "Nice cat. We're going to be great friends."

RahRah angled on his side.

"Nice cat." Jane reached to pat his stomach.

"Don't!" Emily and Sarah yelled in unison, but it was too late. RahRah sprang onto his four paws hissing. Jane recoiled as RahRah swung his front paws wildly and barely missed scratching her. Sarah grabbed him as he went to jump from the bed. How stupid could Jane be? Whispering, she sweet-talked RahRah until he relaxed and snuggled to her.

She exploded at Jane. "Cats aren't dogs. You can't pat their stomachs and expect them to roll over and swoon for you. A belly is the most sensitive spot on a cat so if you go near it, the cat will instinctively protect itself."

"I'll not make that mistake again." Jane opened the wire door of the carrier. "Put him in, please."

Unable to think of a way to stall anymore, Sarah kissed RahRah and placed him in the carrier. "I'm so sorry. I'm going to try to get you back."

Jane snapped the wire door of the carrier shut.

"There's no way that's going to happen." Purse and carrier swinging, she strode out the door.

Sarah stared at the apartment door as it slammed. She had the sensation a bad smell had left the room, but for some reason, a chill as cold as her forgotten frittata still lingered.

Chapter Thirty-Seven

This time it was Emily's turn to comfort her sister. She guided Sarah away from where she stood fixated on the door. Neither of them spoke. Emily began returning RahRah's abandoned toys to the cardboard box.

"It isn't fair!" Sarah said.

Emily looked up and nodded. She added the unopened bag of food to the top of the box.

Sarah watched her sister but didn't offer to help. "That witch doesn't want RahRah because she loves him. She only wants him for his money."

"His money?" Emily stood and wiped her hands on her jeans. "Did I misunderstand you?"

Sarah grabbed a tissue from the box on the windowsill and blew her nose.

"Our furry friend has money?"

"According to Harlan, RahRah is loaded. In her will, Bill's mother left RahRah the carriage house and established an animal trust that provides for him to be pampered and cared for the remainder of his life."

"So what was he doing living with you? Was this his slumming period? I wouldn't consider this living with royalty." Taking the bag of collars from the box, she crowned herself with one of RahRah's jeweled collars. Scooping the dropped toy mouse from the floor, she held it as a scepter.

Sarah was amused at how the makeshift tiara sat firmly askew on her sister's head. It caught the light as Emily pranced around the room, but Sarah's smiling mouth quickly tightened into a flat line as she thought about RahRah.

Emily stopped dancing. She dropped her crown and scepter back into the box. "I'm missing something. Didn't RahRah live here until five minutes ago?"

"Yes."

"Well, this doesn't look like the carriage house and it would seem that your check must have been lost by the post office."

"It was delivered into Bill's bank account. Mother Blair's provision for RahRah's care was simply another thing Bill neglected to mention." She dabbed her eyes with the used tissue. "You know, I should be mad about everything Bill cheated me out of, but I really don't care. One part of me is in shock and can't believe Bill's gone. At other times, I feel like good riddance, he got his comeuppance. I only wish the same fate for Jane, but I don't want RahRah to suffer because of her."

Emily scrunched her eyes at her sister's harsh words. The worry lines in her forehead became more prominent. "I wouldn't say that too loudly. You never know when making a threat might come back to bite you."

"Now you're the one being dramatic. Em, for someone who can be so take charge, you definitely have a histrionic flair."

"And you have a way with words. Histrionic?"

"It's simply a synonym for dramatic."

Emily arched her eyebrows. "Really?"

"Okay, sometimes I spice up what I'm saying, like some of the things I said about Bill during my divorce, but be honest, you do that with the names of your recipes."

"You've got me there."

"Look at it this way. I enjoy playing with words like some people enjoy playing with jewelry."

"That's because you don't have any."

"Tell that to Peter and Jane. According to them, I'm supposed to have hidden a diamond bracelet somewhere."

"Wait a minute," Emily said. "Maybe the bracelet has been in plain sight."

"Are you accusing me of taking it, too?"

"No." Emily pulled the bag of collars out of the box. She poured the bag out on the floor and searched through them until she found the one she'd used as a tiara.

"What are you doing?"

Emily waved the collar at Sarah. "Maybe the bracelet's been here all along?" She handed the collar to Sarah, who stared at it and frowned before throwing it back into the box.

"Good thinking, but the diamonds in Mother Blair's bracelet are far bigger. That's probably why Jane wants it so badly." Sarah picked up another collar. "Maybe Mother Blair separated the stones into different collars to hide them for some reason."

The two flipped through the rest of the collars, but nothing else caught their eye. Frustrated, they put them back into the box.

"Look at the time."

Sarah glanced at the wall clock. "It's only eight twenty."

"I know. I've got to get a move on and get to the Expo.

"Considering the fire, are you going to even bother with the booth?"

"Yes. I called Marcus while you were sleeping."

"How is he?"

"Grumpy and ready to be discharged. He wanted to go to the restaurant before going to the Expo to see what he can salvage, but the fire marshal hasn't declared the area stable enough for anyone to go anywhere near it until tomorrow. I told him to sit tight. Jacob can always handle the emcee duties."

"And you?"

"There are only five hours until the contest. Not only do I have prep work, but there is a ton of stuff to do to make sure the Southwind booth is ready when the Expo opens at eleven. Want to come along?"

Sarah laughed. "Are you asking for my help?"

"No, not this time. We're the only ones allowed to touch our contest dishes from prep to finish. I thought you might want to nose around a bit. Check out the other cooks and our neighboring booths again."

"Thanks, but I'll keep my nose to myself until contest time. I think any sleuthing we do at the Civic Center should be done together."

"I'm going to be too busy to play detective."

Sarah realized that was true. With Chef Marcus in the hospital, Emily, rather than Jane, was taking responsibility for the efficient operation of everything and everyone in the Southwind booth, plus her contest entry. Sarah felt torn. She had promised Peter to stick to Emily's side, but she couldn't see how Emily would ever be alone at the Civic Center. And while others watched her, it would be such a great time to run by

Harlan's office and do a few things. After all, Harlan didn't usually work on Sundays.

Sarah tried to think how she could warn her sister without violating Peter's confidence. "If you don't really need me, it would be a great time to justify my paycheck by typing a response brief I know Harlan needs filed by four on Monday. Considering the confusion of this week, he'll be thrilled if we don't go to the wire with it."

"Fine. You go to the office."

"I will if you promise me one thing."

"What?"

"Until your presentation, you won't go anywhere in the building without staying in at least one person's sight, if not two."

Emily laughed. "I thought Mom was on vacation. Don't worry about me. I'll be too busy to wander anywhere. When are you leaving?"

"Right behind you." Sarah flipped the light switch off as she followed Emily out the door. "I don't have any reason to hang around my apartment today."

Chapter Thirty-Eight

Once outside, Sarah realized Emily's earlier observation that it was a beautiful day was an understatement. Most days she drove to work so she could sleep to the last possible moment, but today she veered in the opposite direction from her parked car. Considering how the morning had gone, taking advantage of the perfect weather seemed in order. Walking would be a stress reliever.

The most direct route to Harlan's office was the one she'd run to Southwind yesterday, but today she opted to meander along the scenic tree-lined section of Main Street she'd once lived on. It had been a long time since she'd studied its big houses, set-back garages, and carriage houses. There were a lot of little changes in the neighborhood.

Because of the zoning law modifications that permitted the strip center to be built, she knew many of the homes near the mall now housed office space, like Harlan's, businesses, or apartments. Most of the buildings on Main Street were still private dwellings, except for one that had been razed.

To Sarah, many of the houses looked tired. There

was one with a FOR SALE sign that appeared to have a fresh coat of white paint on its wooden exterior and some newly planted knockout roses for color. Sarah thought several of the other buildings could use similar tender loving care. She wondered what was planned for the empty lot. Hopefully, whatever it was would bring some vitality back to the street. Personally, she wasn't against the planned entertainment district as long as it was done rationally.

Distracted from her thoughts by a bird sipping from a freestanding bird feeder across the street from the house she knew had been her destination all along, she paused. Staying on the sidewalk in front of Bill's, or should she say Mother Blair's house, she craned her neck to see if, by chance, she could catch a glimpse of RahRah.

The drapes were closed and both houses seemed dark and deserted. She wondered if Jane had given RahRah the run of the carriage house or confined him to that awful carrier. One part of Sarah wanted to knock on the door and find out, but she couldn't do that. Instead, she stood across the street staring at the house.

"Thinking about breaking in?"

Startled, Sarah swung around. "Mr. Rogers."

The wizened neighbor who owned the home across from Bill's stood near her.

"I didn't hear you come up behind me."

The old man laughed again. "No wonder. You were too lost in your own thoughts. Missing the homestead?"

Sarah sidestepped his question by responding with one of her own. "I'm sorry we didn't get an opportunity to visit yesterday in Harlan's office. How have you been?"

"Never better." He tapped his cane on the sidewalk

and then used it to point to Bill's house. "A lot of things going on there."

"You mean construction?" She waited for him to answer in his own good time. Despite his rheumy eyes and failing hearing, there were a few things Sarah knew could be counted on from George Rogers. One was that he was always clad in a three-piece brown suit with a pocket watch he claimed dated back to his grandfather. The second was that, while his late wife and he were always kind to her, they'd hated Bill because of some long ago incident. Not only had they unsuccessfully tried to keep Bill from buying the property, but once he started his post-divorce remodeling project, they repeatedly called the city inspectors to say something in the remodeling wasn't being done right.

"No, the construction has been on hold for a while now. Talking about comings and goings. I wouldn't be surprised if the house isn't put up for sale soon."

Although she couldn't be certain what would happen with the big house, Sarah knew from the documents Harlan had shown her that there was no question about the fate of RahRah, his animal trust, and the carriage house. "I'm sure that won't be the case for quite some time. You know how these legal things are when someone dies."

"Don't kid yourself. Folks find ways to get around the law all the time," Mr. Rogers chuckled. "Mark my words, this will be on the market before you know it."

Sarah shuddered. She didn't much care what happened to Jane or the big house, but even if he couldn't live with her, she wouldn't let anyone monkey with Mother Blair's legacy for RahRah.

Chapter Thirty-Nine

Sarah was surprised to see lights on in Harlan's office. Normally, he avoided work like the plague on Sundays, but maybe, like his Saturday appointment with Mr. Rogers, he was also making up for getting behind this past week.

As she reached the top of the stairwell, the screen door opened, almost knocking her down. Jacob, still talking to someone in the office, stood in the doorway with one hand on the inner doorknob and the other on the storm door's handle. Other than a small white bandage near his hairline, Sarah couldn't help but note that his appearance was back to near perfection.

"Hey," she said.

"Um, hey, yourself. What are you doing here?" Jacob closed the door behind him. He stood blocking the door as they talked.

"This is where my real day job is. And you?"

He pointed over his shoulder. "With me working every day, Harlan was nice enough to come in today to give me some advice."

"Oh, is everything all right? How is your head?"

"I'm fine and yeah, it was just a matter of something

I've been thinking of doing. Harlan's got a good grasp of investment possibilities and their legal ramifications." He jumped down the stairs two at a time. "I better get back to the Civic Center. There's a lot to do before the contest."

"Are you competing, too?"

"No, but I need to be around in case Jane or Emily need help prepping. Plus, I promised Chef Marcus I'd make sure the exhibitors' refreshment tables stay stocked." He gave her a quick salute with two fingers to his bandaged forehead and then took off whistling.

Sarah watched him go. For a second, an unformed thought floated through her mind, but it was gone before she caught it.

She opened the screen door. The wooden door was locked. She unlocked it and pushed it open. "Harlan." She stepped over the threshold.

No answer.

"Harlan?" The hair on the back of her neck stood up. She slipped her hand into her purse and felt for her cell phone. After the past few days, one part of her brain commanded her to "leave and call Peter," but then she thought about the possibility of Harlan lying in his office injured, or worse. She tiptoed to the doorway of his office. From there, she could see pads and files on his desk, but his chair was empty. She inched forward to check the floor behind his desk. "Harlan?"

"Yes?"

Sarah jumped a mile as his voice came from behind her. She turned to see him drying his hands with a paper towel. "I'm sorry. I didn't mean to frighten you."

She dropped her purse onto Harlan's couch and followed it with her body. "I called your name a few times and when you didn't answer, I was afraid something had happened to you."

"I took something to my car and went to wash my hands. I must not have heard you over the water running. What are you doing here today? I thought you'd be helping your sister at the Civic Center."

"The contestants aren't allowed to have anyone help them. I thought I'd surprise you by typing the response brief before tomorrow. I know you hate things to be last minute. What are you doing here?"

"Same thing. There were so many interruptions this week, I came in this morning to take care of a few things."

"I ran into Jacob on my way in."

"Oh, yes. He stopped by for a few minutes."

She waited, hoping Harlan would volunteer the reason for Jacob's Sunday visit. There were lots of possible investments in Wheaton and Birmingham. She was curious what he was considering and if it had anything to do with Southwind.

"I was just getting ready to leave." Harlan walked around his desk, threw the paper towel into his trash can, and picked up his aviator sunglasses from where they lay on the edge of the desk. "Now that I scared you, are you staying or going?"

"Staying."

His sunglasses perched on the top of his head, Harlan swept a few papers into his briefcase and clipped it shut. "I'll take care of the back door. Make sure you lock the front."

"I will." One time. One time she'd forgotten to make sure the door was locked and Harlan never let her forget it. She scooped up the contents of his "out" basket and took them back to her to-be-filed pile and the folder hidden in her desk.

The minute she heard Harlan walk out the back door, Sarah hurried to lock the front door. Once she felt secure in the quiet office, she quickly typed the brief and distractedly began her filing. Other than glancing at the headings on each of the memos and files in her stack to make sure she associated things correctly, her task was mindless. Sarah was surprised at how fast her to-be-filed stash began to diminish.

Seeing how much neater her desk could look without the paper clutter, she wondered why she always put off filing. She promised herself she would try to keep things current in the future, even if it meant coming in here and there for an hour on the weekend when there were no interruptions.

She still couldn't believe Harlan had given up part of his weekend for Jacob. As good-natured as Harlan was, in all the months she'd worked for him, he'd never met anyone on a Sunday unless there was a significant fee involved. Jacob might have a case with a contingency fee, but he couldn't have much disposable income. He was only a line cook so he had to make less than Emily and Emily didn't make much.

Sarah chided herself for accusing Harlan of measuring things in terms of money. After all, he certainly hadn't made a penny for the work he'd done for the twins during the past few days. Moreover, he'd taken a hit in his pocket when he created a job for her when no one else was willing to hire her. Harlan might be small of stature, but he was a big man.

The more she thought about it, the more convinced she was Harlan probably met with Jacob during Jacob's few off hours because he was doing a good deed. Considering all the terrible things that had happened to the Southwind gang since Bill's murder, it was time something nice happened to a member of the staff.

Remembering how Jacob had been her biggest

booster during the exhibition, even though Grace or he could have handled the presentation, it dawned on Sarah exactly what Jacob had said that was bothering her. He'd told her he needed to get back "in case Jane or Emily want some help prepping." Surely, if Emily knew the rules prohibited a contestant from having any help at any stage of today's competition, Jacob was familiar with them, too. Was he covering up something from his visit or did he plan to help someone so that it ultimately resulted in that person's disqualification?

Could that be what he wanted? He'd seemed okay with Emily being named Southwind's sous chef and had been Sarah's rock during her demonstration. It was obvious Chef Marcus depended upon him. No, Jacob had a bright future if Southwind survived. What more could he gain by having Jane or Emily knocked out of the competition?

Maybe he wanted to mess with Jane. Sarah could certainly understand that inclination, considering how mean and selfish she was. Or was he after a non-Southwind competitor? Maybe the fried green tomato maker? Wait a minute. Jacob said he talked to Harlan about investment advice. What money could Jacob possibly have to invest? That had to have been a lie. But why?

Sarah toyed with the different possibilities as she randomly filed the notes Harlan had made in various cases, but nothing came to mind. She squinted at the sheet in her hand, trying to read Harlan's miniature handwriting to determine which case the memo went with. He might not have the best handwriting, she decided, but no one would ever be able to accuse him of not keeping meticulous notes.

That was how she could find out why Jacob had been here. Look at Harlan's notes. She dropped the

sheet of paper back on her to-be-filed stack. There was
no way Harlan wouldn't have made a detailed note of
his conversation with Jacob. Where was it?

Everything from his "out" basket had been on the
top of her pile and she'd already handled and filed
those sheets. If the notes were in his "out" basket, she
should have seen them. The thought that curiosity
killed the cat went through her mind, but she ban-
ished it quickly as her eyes rested on the closed door
to his office. It was a no-brainer that unless Harlan
took his notes about Jacob home with him, they were
still some place in his office.

Chapter Forty

Normally, Sarah respected Harlan's privacy, especially when his office door was closed. Not today. With Bill and Richard dead, the refrigerator sabotaged, someone tampering with the brownies that Grace and Emily ate, and the fire damaging Southwind, she felt Harlan's out-of-character appointment with Jacob made him fair game. Sarah made a beeline for Harlan's office. The door was locked.

She hesitated, surprised and confused Harlan felt the need to do more than close his office door. Was he deliberately keeping her out or had he locked it out of the same skittishness that made her hurry to lock the front door? No matter, she was on a mission now.

Returning to her desk, she found the small jewelry box she kept in the back of her center drawer. She removed the extra passkey to Harlan's office he'd given her on her first day of work. "Sarah," he'd said, "you'll need this only if I want to avoid someone and escape out the back door or if I hit the lock button by accident."

Up to now she'd never needed to use it, but then

again, Harlan had never locked her out before. Sarah slipped the key into the lock. It turned easily.

Inside his office, she closed the door, flipped the overhead light on, and looked around to see where the file or memo might be. She checked his "out" basket first, but it was empty. A quick glance revealed the coffee table and the small, round, marble inlaid conference table in the corner of his office had nothing on them. If he hadn't taken it home, that left Harlan's desk as the logical place for the memo.

Rather than trying to read the few things lying on his desk upside down, she walked around the well-polished mahogany piece. She moved his leather chair back a few inches to allow her to slip her legs under the lip of the drawer. She'd never realized how high Harlan's chair was set.

There were no papers stuck in or on the desk blotter. A marble-based gold pen-and-pencil set was centered on the desk above the blotter. An etched United States Supreme Court building and the slogan JUSTICE FOR ALL adorned a glass mug filled with sharpened pencils and a few pens that sat to the far side of the blotter. Two manila folders were stacked next to the blotter.

She pulled the handle of the middle desk drawer, but it didn't give. A quick check revealed all the drawers were locked, so she turned her attention to the file folders. Sarah opened the first one and skimmed the pages in it. One was Bill's codicil to the animal trust naming Jane RahRah's trustee, and the other documents were the ones relating to Bill's estate that Harlan previously showed her—only these were stamped "draft." She flipped through the other pages in the file quickly but slowed when she came to a group of deeds she hadn't seen before.

All of them conveyed property to B&E, Inc., a

corporation Sarah wasn't familiar with, but none were signed. Several of the sellers' names sounded familiar, but she couldn't place them until she examined the fourth deed. It purported to sell the property of George Rogers to B&E, Inc.

Sarah went back to the first deed and looked more closely at the address of the property being sold. It was on Bill's street. She went through the other deeds quickly. Each of the unexecuted deeds was for the sale of one of the properties belonging to one of Bill's neighbors.

Behind the deeds was a paper headed "Buyouts," but buyouts of what? She glanced at the list of five names. Next to four were recent dates. The fifth name, which didn't have a date beside it, was Jane's. There were no other papers in the file, so she opened the second folder.

It contained title descriptions and maps of some of the properties included in the stack of deeds in the other folder. There also was an artist's schematic rendering of "Main Street." The diagram showed multifamily housing, restaurants, and shops. Notations on the drawing caught her eye. She held it closer to the light to read the words "Southwind Restaurant" with a question mark written on Bill's house.

Sarah studied the labeling on the rest of the diagram. The two houses to the right of Bill's weren't marked. Mr. Rogers's house and the one next to his were designated as a restaurant and store, respectively. Two smaller homes, farther down the street, read "gallery" and "craft center." There was nothing written on the homes she knew already were subdivided into apartments.

She thought about the house that had been torn

down. Sarah checked to see if anything had been written in its space. It had. It read "park."

Unsure of what she was looking at, but wanting to be able to study it in more detail, she started to take the pages to the copy machine. As she approached the door, a creaking sound made her jump. She stopped and listened. Nothing. She inched to the door and pressed her ear to it. Could someone be out there? But how could they have gotten in? She looked around for a weapon to defend herself. She heard another creak, this time behind her. She jumped around, her heart in her throat. No one was there. She felt foolish reacting so dramatically to the sounds of a settling house.

Still, in case Harlan came back, she didn't want to explain why she was at the copy machine with folders from his locked office. She whipped out her smartphone and quickly shot copies of the schematic, a sampling of the deeds, and the buyout list. She started to put the files and Harlan's chair back in their original positions but decided she'd also like copies of the documents supposedly giving Jane custody of RahRah.

The unmistakable crunch of tires in the alley behind the office made Sarah jump. Abandoning her task, she shoved the pages back into the files, straightened them to look like she had found them, and switched off the light. As Sarah pushed the lock button of the door while she pulled it closed behind her, she realized she no longer heard a car's motor.

She plopped into her own desk chair, grabbing the top document from her to-be-filed pile in her trembling right hand, while throwing the key to Harlan's office into her desk with her left.

The door from Harlan's office opened. "I didn't expect to still find you here."

"Just finishing up. I thought you were gone for the day."

"I forgot a few things, so I swung by to get them before I went to the contest." He looked at his watch. "You better hurry if you don't want to miss the beginning. The Civic Center parking lot was almost full when I passed it."

Sarah nodded. She didn't know if he was merely being helpful or wanted to get rid of her. It didn't matter. She grabbed her purse and fled, without enlightening him that she had walked to work.

Outside, Sarah let out a sigh of relief as she distanced herself from Harlan's building. One part of her wanted to go straight home and review what she'd just recorded with her phone, but the desire to bounce everything off Emily before the contest began made her quicken her steps toward the Civic Center. She was sure anyone she passed could see her knees shaking. She wished she'd never gone to the office today, but there was no turning back the clock.

Nothing made sense to her. It was apparent from the artist's rendering and the unsigned deeds that someone had major designs to develop Bill's street but that was all it was—drafts and plans. The renderings appeared to be final schematics, but none of the deeds were signed. Plus, Jane and RahRah setting up a permanent residence in the carriage house and Sarah's recent run-in with Mr. Rogers underscored that whoever was behind this project lacked the most important thing—ownership of the properties.

Was Harlan the one trying to buy up the properties or was he representing someone else? Could sweet, kind Harlan be part of something shady? She didn't want to jump to the conclusion he was a backstabber, but she had found the papers on his desk.

The deeds obviously were drafted by someone with legal knowledge.

Then again, perhaps things were more innocent than they appeared. Maybe Jane's call and the papers on his desk were because he was drawing up a new deed or will for her.

Sarah knew she'd never typed the deeds or seen them before today. That was strange because, with Harlan being a terrible typist, her job required her to type everything, including his personal correspondence. Of course, nothing could have stopped him from asking someone who didn't work for him to type the documents or having another lawyer prepare them for his review.

Sarah wondered whether he or a developer really thought they could convince the various owners to sell their properties. What would it take to have no holdouts? She couldn't imagine Mr. Rogers letting anyone push him from the house he loved. No, he wasn't going to move off the street until he was carried out of his home in a pine box.

At the idea of Mr. Rogers protecting his property to the end, another thought crossed her mind. Maybe Bill was dead because of his unwillingness to sell his property to the mysterious developer.

Up to now, Sarah and Emily had linked Bill's and Richard's murders to food or Southwind. The idea of economic development introduced completely different possibilities. From reading mysteries and what she'd learned living with Bill, Sarah knew a good detective always followed the money. There might be money in food, but there certainly were bigger profits to be made from being on the ground floor of a project of this magnitude.

Chapter Forty-One

Sarah entered the Civic Center's main room and glanced at the big clock on the wall. Because it was just after one, she debated whether corralling Emily for a brainstorming session before the contest would be productive.

The sizable crowd ringing the stage made the decision for her. Much as she wanted to get to the bottom of what was going on, she needed to find Emily to give her support rather than distract her. She spotted a cluster of Southwind jackets near the stage and made her way toward them. As she got closer, she saw her sister in the middle of the group. Sarah squeezed through the people milling around her sister. "Emily!"

Emily looked up and waved. "I was afraid you weren't going to be here."

"You know I wouldn't miss cheering you on for anything. Besides," she blurted out, despite her previous intentions, "you won't believe what I've got to tell you!" She reached out to give Emily a good luck pat on her shoulder, but Emily moved, resulting in her hand landing between Emily's shoulder and neck.

"Wow, you're tight. Relax." Sarah kneaded her sister's

neck but couldn't feel any of the tension dissipating. "Something wrong?"

"I'm set up and ready to go, but, and I know you're not going to believe this, I'm worried about Jane."

Sarah made a face.

"Stop that! It's just that most of the contestants are here, but no one has seen Jane." Emily darted a glance around the room, as if trying to manufacture a glimpse of Jane. Considering what had happened to the last person not to show up on time, Sarah understood Emily's fear. "Marcus said he'd look for her, but one of the other contestants waylaid him because he didn't think his oven was heating right."

"Marcus is back?"

"Straight from the hospital." Emily pointed at the stage.

Sarah looked in that direction and saw Marcus deep in conversation in front of one of the four stoves on-stage. She tried not to laugh at how Marcus dwarfed the man he was speaking to. His sling was almost longer than the other man's upper torso. Like Emily, his face had a sunburnt flush to it. They appeared to be discussing something attached to a tube in the smaller man's hand. Sarah couldn't tell what was on the other end of the tube because it was stuck in the oven, but neither man seemed particularly happy.

"That looks like it could be a bigger problem than Jane being late. I wouldn't worry about her. She'd be the first to tell you she's a big girl."

Emily's lips tightened in a grimace as she played with her scrunchie, redoing her ponytail. "Normally, I'd agree and wouldn't think anything else about her not being here early, but the way things have been going lately, her not being here creeps me out. Some-one needs to check on her. Will you?"

"You're kidding me, aren't you?"

Emily shook her head.

Sarah scoured the crowd, hoping Jane's face would jump out at her. Although she picked out Jacob and Grace standing with some of the other young people she'd noticed working at different booths during the past few days at the Expo, she didn't see Jane. One look back at Emily and she knew she had no choice. "Don't worry. I'll find her. She's probably fixing her makeup or thinking of a way to sabotage all of her competitors."

"I actually hope that's the case." Emily straightened her collar. "How do I look?"

"Like a champion chef." Sarah gave her sister a hug. "Good luck and don't worry, I'll find Jane. And after the competition, have I got things to share with you!" She knew from the smile Emily shot her as she walked away that Emily was going into the contest feeling a weight had been lifted from her shoulders. The only problem was, Sarah wasn't quite sure how she was going to honor her promise.

Mentally whispering a prayer, Sarah climbed on the first riser near the stage to get a better view of the room. She didn't see Jane anywhere and Jane wasn't among the people still coming in, but she spotted Peter by the doorway. What better person to turn a missing person search over to?

Peter's head jerked up at the sound of his name, but from the way he kept turning his head, he couldn't pinpoint who had called to him. Sarah shouted his name again. She knew he'd seen her when his face relaxed and he moved in her direction.

He sidestepped when a big woman barged between them. Watching the woman bodily force her way closer to the stage, Peter laughed. "I guess I'm going to need to do some crowd control. What's up?"

Her words tumbled out. "Jane's missing. The contest starts in a few minutes and the judges are all here, but no one's heard from Jane. Emily is worried."

"Jane's not here?"

Sarah swallowed. "No one has seen her and the contest is getting ready to start. I ran late, but Emily looked for Jane. Em has a lot of complaints about her, but she said Jane's not one to be late for something like this. She's afraid something may have happened to her."

"I agree. Jane wouldn't be late for this competition. Did Emily check both exhibition rooms and the restrooms?"

"I only did a cursory check of this room. I can't speak for Emily."

"Okay. Do you have your cell phone?"

Sarah bobbed her head.

"Did you keep my cell number?"

"Yes."

"Good. Let's split up. You take the ladies' lounges, while I get a few of the Civic Center security guards to help me check the main rooms, backstage, and the loading dock. If you find her, call me. I'll do the same. Otherwise, I'll meet you at the main entrance in ten minutes."

Without pausing for a reply, he strode toward the far room, already talking on his cell phone.

Sarah didn't wait to watch his back fully disappear. Instead, she began her assigned task with the nearest ladies' room. It didn't take her long to cover the restrooms and, for good measure, the nurse's station. There was no sign of Jane.

Genuinely concerned, Sarah made her way back to the main entrance to meet Peter. As she reached the door, it opened and Jane burst through it carrying the animal carrier and a chef's jacket. Jane thrust the carrier at her and Sarah instinctively grabbed its handle. She peeked down to see what she now held. RahRah's scared little face peered through the wired end.

Sarah found her tongue. "Jane, where have you been? We've been worried about you."

"I got delayed by this little monster. Will you be a dear and hold on to him for me until I'm done? It's only for an hour or so."

"But—"

"I've got to go. Unless we're moving, he goes berserk in his carrier and I couldn't leave him roaming the house. It isn't cat-proof."

Jane glared at the carrier with such a flinty cold stare, Sarah pulled RahRah's cage closer to her body.

"He was a bad boy. Not only did he make mincemeat of the pants I laid on my bed to wear today, but he shredded the living room curtains trying to perch on the curtain rod." Jane hurried away, throwing a "Thanks a bunch, dear" back over her shoulder.

Sarah hoped Jane didn't turn around and notice her Cheshire cat grin. She carried RahRah out of the traffic pattern, set his cage on the floor, and bent to his level.

"You are so good. You certainly listened to me this morning." She continued a low-voiced commentary to comfort RahRah as she opened his cage. Carefully, she lifted him out of the carrier. He curled his body against hers, his little heart pounding.

She held him close, still whispering to him, hoping the firm grasp of her hands would let him know she would protect him. It angered her that RahRah had only been with Jane for a few hours and already was so agitated.

"There you are."

Sarah and RahRah both stirred at the unexpected sound of Peter's voice.

"I see Jane was found." Peter pointed at the stage before gently running his fingers through RahRah's soft fur. "What's RahRah doing here?"

"I'm not quite sure." Sarah rearranged her features into a more serious mode before she raised her head to meet Peter's glance. "If I understood Jane right, RahRah has been making her life miserable in the few hours she's had him."

"That's a good boy. I'm so proud of you." Peter stroked the tender area behind RahRah's ears. "She doesn't deserve him."

Sarah took a step back, forcing Peter to dislodge his hand from RahRah. "Where did that come from? That's what I've told you all along, but you made me give him to her."

Peter rested his now-freed hand on the back of his neck. "I didn't have a choice. My job requires me to enforce the law. Jane had the documents to prove Bill wanted her to have possession of RahRah." He ran his hand through his neatly combed hair. "I looked for a loophole, but even your own attorney agreed that the bequests, codicil, and custodial transfers were valid."

Sarah stared at Peter. "What do you mean Harlan agreed they were valid?"

"The day you stomped out of my office, Harlan stayed behind. It gave us a chance to talk off the record about whether there was anything else we could do to prevent Jane from taking RahRah away from you. I showed him the documents she provided me and he assured me the animal trust was specific in its intent and operation."

Although Peter only moved his hand through his hair, his expression made her think of a little boy caught with his hand in the cookie jar. "I'm sorry we talked about you behind your back, but I hope your ears were burning because I said you were the right person to care for RahRah. Harlan said that might be the case, but he was adamant we had to honor the terms of the animal trust."

"I had no idea." Sarah relaxed her grip slightly as RahRah raised his head to peek toward Peter. "Looks like you've made a friend in RahRah."

Peter reached over and stroked RahRah again. "That's because he knows I was willing to go to the mat for him. I honestly wanted to keep the two of you together."

Sarah focused her eyes on his now-still hand. Hands intrigued her. His were strong and solid. She believed hands reflected the soul of a person.

"I'm no lawyer," Peter said, "but Harlan is one of the best. Once he looked at all the documents and explained the legal ramifications of the Alabama animal trust statutes, including Bill's right to designate his successor, I understood my hands were tied. There simply wasn't any other option, in the face of the law, except to give Jane possession of RahRah in accordance with Bill's instructions."

Sarah felt a tingle as he brushed his fingers against hers.

He let them linger. "I'm really sorry how everything turned out."

He resumed petting RahRah.

Sarah bent over RahRah and brought her face closer to Peter's. "What if we could prove Jane's papers are phony? Would I have a chance of getting RahRah back?"

"Do you have any reason to think the codicil is a fake?"

"Maybe." Sarah debated whether to tell Peter about

the documents she saw on Harlan's desk or if she should wait to hash them over with Emily first. "Or, at least I hope it is. If the documents are phony, would I get RahRah back?"

"Of course, but that's a big if. From what Harlan explained, I don't see any way for you to challenge the trust."

Sarah looked around. Most of the people were checking out the various booths or had moved closer to the stage, where Marcus was explaining the judging process and introducing the contestants. She listened to see where he was in his remarks so she could judge how much time Peter and she had. She knew from Emily that once Marcus finished his introductory remarks, the contestants would pop their already prepped dishes into the ovens. While their entries cooked, each would have the opportunity to explain his or her recipe before the judges tasted their food and voted.

Sarah wished there had been time to bounce what she'd seen off Emily before she involved anyone else. Then again, Peter was the local law enforcer.

"Peter . . ." Sarah spoke so quietly he needed to lean forward to catch each word. "I learned something today that I think might make a big difference for a lot of things."

"I told you to leave investigating to the professionals."

"You did, but when you didn't seem to be getting any further than zeroing in on Emily, I had to do something."

"And what did your sleuthing discover?"

"You've got to promise you'll keep me out of it if you talk to Harlan. I don't know if he's involved in this or what, but if he's not and he thinks I squealed on him, he'll never trust me again. My job will be on the line if it gets out I'm telling you about this. So, you need to promise." She stood up straight, holding RahRah as a barrier between Peter and her.

"I can't make you any promises until you tell me what this is all about." He rested his hand on the top of his gun.

The phrase "Macho Man" went through her mind but, for the good of Emily, she swallowed the retort she was ready to zing him with. She tried to focus on the reality that unless Peter found a reason to take a different approach to this case, winning the cooking competition wouldn't help Emily in the long run. No matter what the consequences, she couldn't bear risking Emily's future simply to maintain her own job. Sarah took a deep breath and looked around one last time to make sure no one except Peter was listening to what she said.

"I saw something today that led me to believe someone is trying to acquire properties to develop the old part of Main Street, near where Bill's house is. Maybe economic development instead of food is the reason Bill and Richard were murdered."

Peter rubbed his chin. "That isn't something that's been on my radar. But you might have a point. A few of those properties have changed hands recently. I knew Bill hoped the area would be developed, but I'm not familiar with any actual plans or proposed projects. What did you see?"

He peered at her, his dark eyes holding her gaze. Sarah hesitated before she consciously broke the link between them and darted her eyes around the room. She lowered her voice to a whisper, but Peter interrupted her after a few words because RahRah's raised head blocked her mouth. Shifting RahRah to a more comfortable position in the bend of her arm, but still holding him firmly, she began again. This time she made it through her narrative.

Peter let out a low whistle. "Interesting Harlan has all these documents. He never said anything about them."

"Maybe there was attorney-client confidentiality involved. I probably shouldn't have told you about any of this because the deeds, drawings, and draft papers were in Harlan's office and are probably confidential work products or something like that, but what if Bill was killed because of something to do with those papers? Other owners, like Mr. Rogers, might be in danger, too."

Peter frowned. "I can see your argument for Bill, but how do you tie in Richard? That seems a bit far-fetched."

"Maybe he was involved in something to do with scouting the properties or strong-arming people to sell? I never met him when I was married to Bill, but from what Jane and Emily have said, he did different odd jobs for Bill. Bill and he had enough of a relationship that Bill arranged for him to be hired at Southwind. We simply need to find out what their connection was."

"We? Investigating is my job."

"Technically true, but Emily is my sister and I'll do anything to prove she's innocent."

He stared at her. "I'm well aware Emily is your twin and you've been doing things out of your belief in her innocence. If I wasn't cognizant of that, I'd have arrested you for interfering with a police investigation or something else by now."

She took a step back from him, clutching RahRah a little more tightly.

Peter responded by stepping forward and waving

his hand in a stop motion. "Calm down. I'm sorry. I didn't mean that the way it came out. It's just that you get me so mad. I know you're trying to protect Emily, but someone out there has killed twice and tried to hurt RahRah and you once." He shook his head. When he spoke again, it was through tight lips. "I don't want them to get another chance."

Sarah gazed at him for a second and then focused her eyes on RahRah's collar. In the few hours since she took RahRah to the carriage house, Jane already had traded his collar for a jazzier one. The rhinestones in this one weren't nearly as nice as the ones in the collar Emily used as a tiara.

"I appreciate you care and are worried about us, but don't you think the Main Street documents in Harlan's possession could be the key behind Bill's murder?"

Peter didn't answer. Instead, he posed a question. "So, you think Harlan is involved?"

Harlan's sweet face jumped into Sarah's mind. It couldn't be him. There had to be a good explanation for Harlan's folder of documents. But if it wasn't him, who was behind the development plans? The only other suspect with a claim to property on Main Street was Jane. Was Jane guilty or did Sarah simply want her to be?

Peter interrupted Sarah's musings. "You seem to have someone else in mind. Care to share?"

Sarah shrugged. She opted not to mention Harlan. She'd already thrown him under the bus. "Possibly Jane. Look at her with RahRah. She's got her clutches into him and his money and it's obvious the money and carriage house are the only things about him she cares about. Think about the profit she could make as Bill's heir if something happened to RahRah and she could sell the land, carriage, and main house to a developer."

Even as the words came out of Sarah's mouth, she could see the sense in them. It all seemed suddenly clear. "Peter, we have to follow the money."

"'We' again. I don't have time to fight. If you're right then, for Emily's sake, I agree we need to work together."

"All the way?"

"Well, as much as I can." He laughed and then struck a serious pose. "Remember, you're not a policeman, so I have a responsibility to protect you, too."

Sarah jerked her head up, causing RahRah to strain against her arm. "I've got it. Deputize me. You'll get a lot more done with me on the case than relying on your present sergeant."

Peter slapped his head and rolled his hands upward as if praying for help from a higher source. "Run-of-the-mill deputizing a private citizen is only going to happen in a book or the movies."

"That's a shame because I think, especially being at a food expo, we could probably come out with a better dish if we pool our ingredients and preparation."

Shaking his head, Peter offered Sarah his hand. "Truce?"

"For the sake of Emily, I guess so." Sarah lowered her voice again. "How do you want us to proceed, Chief?"

Peter laughed and picked up the carrier.

"First, we find a spot from which RahRah and you can safely watch the rest of the food contest and cheer for Emily."

"And you?"

"Oh me, I've got a little legwork to do."

Sarah sputtered, "But . . ."

"Relax, I'm going to do some title searching. It's an interesting theory, but I need something to go on.

Hopefully, with a little luck, with what you've told me, I'll find enough information independently to be able to ask some questions without anyone attributing anything back to you."

He rubbed RahRah's head while staring at Sarah. "Sarah, I'm in this with you, but right now, one of us needs to stay at the Civic Center to support Emily and take care of this little guy."

Chapter Forty-Two

Cradling RahRah, Sarah pressed her way nearer to the stage. A chef, whose name Sarah had heard but whom Sarah had never met, held a dish at an angle so that the audience could see its golden-textured yellow top. From where she stood, it appeared his entry was either a soufflé or quiche. She guessed, because time constraints were the reason Emily explained she chose a vegetable-related dish, his was probably a quiche containing fresh seasonal vegetables. It looked picture-perfect. The audience apparently agreed because he walked off the stage to a healthy round of applause.

Chef Marcus introduced Emily and her rhubarb crisp as the next entrant. Sarah marveled at how calm and collected her sister seemed, especially as two men down front heckled her about knowing how to make a killer dish. Except for the dash of color obviously rising in Emily's cheeks, she seemed to keep her cool in the face of their continued comments. Other members of the crowd shushed the men as she pulled her rhubarb crisp from her oven and placed it on a cooling rack.

"How many of you have ever eaten rhubarb?" She

turned to the portion of the audience from where someone voiced a loud groan. "I heard that. I bet you've simply never had a good rhubarb dish."

"Never had the stuff and don't want to start now!"

"Ah, you don't know what you're missing. Rhubarb can be used to make some of the most delicious pies, puddings, crisps, cobblers, jams, and even cheesecakes. It's easy to grow both in and out of greenhouses, but it prefers cool weather to thrive. That's why we don't see as much of it in the South."

She put her rhubarb on a cutting board and, with strokes that reminded Sarah of how Grace had prepped the other day, separated the stalks from the leaves. "Make sure you only eat the stalks. The leaves are poisonous."

There was a low-pitched stir in the audience.

"A drop isn't going to kill anyone, but you want to be careful. You don't want to make anyone sick."

Sarah wanted to signal Emily to move on to another topic. She couldn't believe that, considering the circumstances of Bill's death, Emily was obliviously talking about the poisonous aspects of rhubarb.

"For this recipe, which will serve ten to twelve people, you're going to need to slice two pounds of rhubarb crosswise about three-quarters of an inch thick. You're also going to need sugar, flour, brown sugar, unsalted butter, oats, and ground cinnamon. But don't any of you worry about remembering the recipe. You can find it on Southwind's website." She flashed a smile at the crowd.

Emily kept a running patter going as she retrieved the crisp cooked during her demonstration, but Sarah tuned her out. Instead, she looked around the crowd, trying to see if anything seemed off. Nothing jumped out at her. Perhaps the weirdest thing was how subdued RahRah was being in her arms. He seemed absolutely content snuggled to her chest.

Out of the corner of her eye, Sarah noticed movement offstage near where Emily had placed her freshly made rhubarb crisp. While most of the audience oohed over its beautiful gold-brown crumb top and her closing words that the crisp could be finished off with a dab of vanilla ice cream, Sarah kept her gaze trained on Chef Marcus.

Just behind the steps to the stage, he was deep in conversation with Jane and Grace. Sarah didn't think he looked happy but, try as she might, Sarah couldn't read his flying lips. She could tell from his tight expression the few times he slowed to listen, he was displeased about something. There was no way she could easily get behind the stage to be closer to the three of them, especially without jostling RahRah.

Trying to ease her way through the crowd, she saw Grace nod and walk away. Chef Marcus said something else Sarah couldn't make out to Jane, who recoiled from him. Based upon her scowl, Sarah figured whatever he'd said had impacted her blood pressure.

Sarah didn't know which one of them to watch. Jane, who was poised offstage on the bottom step with her hands clenching the railing, or Chef Marcus, who was bounding onto the stage. She went with the latter.

As Marcus reached the stage, his conversion from angry to genial host reminded Sarah of the books she'd read about the transformation of a teenage boy to a werewolf. With each step, Chef Marcus gained more spring and the tense lines of his face softened. By the time he grabbed the microphone from its stand, he was jovial—thanking Emily, making bad food jokes, and introducing Jane.

Her emotional meltdown also seemingly under control, Jane took the stage. She made small talk to the audience, describing "Jane's Jubilant Spinach Pie." As her demonstration progressed, she laid her knives out on the table, displaying her ingredients.

"There are lots of ways to make spinach pie. Greek, Italian, or some people simply take shortcuts using frozen or creamed spinach and a deep-dish crust. Can you believe they have the gall to call their concoction spinach pie? Real cooks like you and me know the difference. Right?"

Sarah felt like Jane was looking straight at her, but she couldn't be. How could she know where Sarah stood? Still, she thought, Jane was unbelievable. Even with Sarah taking care of RahRah as a favor to her, Jane couldn't miss the chance to mock Sarah's way of cooking. She wondered if Jane knew Sarah's recipe for spinach pie used two Stouffer's spinach soufflés and a premade pie crust.

Different pockets of the audience rallied behind Jane's words about real cooks. Sarah hoped those who remained silent were Emily supporters, including any other secret cooks of convenience.

Sarah tried to concentrate as Jane droned on about her spinach filling, but she was more focused on finding Emily. She couldn't wait one more minute to tell her everything she knew.

Chapter Forty-Three

Sarah spotted Emily, partially hidden behind a support wall to the right of the stage, watching Jane's performance. Balancing RahRah, it took Sarah a minute to work her way over to Emily. She figured they had about fifteen minutes to talk before Jane's presentation ended.

"What are you doing with RahRah? Did Jane give him back to you?"

"Only for the contest, but that's not important now. I've got a lot to tell you about." Emily's eyes widened as Sarah summarized what she'd found in Harlan's office and her discussion with Peter.

"Harlan is two-timing us? Supposedly defending me from being convicted of two murders I didn't commit, while actually tightening the noose around my neck?"

"That's what Peter implied during our conversation."

"And Peter's letting him get away with that?"

"Of course not." Sarah flung her head backward, settling her long hair out of her face. "He doesn't want to make a move without developing some independent evidence. Besides, I think there may be an explanation for Harlan's behavior—that the real culprit is Jane. Think about it. She now has the majority share of Southwind, she controls RahRah's money, she owns both Blair properties, and she's soulless enough to be behind all of this."

"Well, whether it's Harlan or Jane, it sounds like Peter could have gotten some of the same information a lot faster by simply questioning Harlan. Harlan doesn't impress me as someone who would particularly like being on the other side in the metal questioning room."

"Probably not. Even as we talk, Peter is running a title search. Hopefully he can avoid implicating me as his source."

"Still, Harlan seems like the logical starting point. If he had all the deeds and drawings, where did he get them? And what is he doing with them?"

"I wish I knew."

"Well, we need to find out."

"I think Peter would tell you that's his job."

"But it's my neck. You heard that heckler. Some people in this room already think I'm guilty."

"Peter doesn't."

"He has a strange way of showing it. Look, Harlan is standing right over there by the wine bar. Peter's nowhere around. You can do what you want, but I'm not going to let Harlan wander freely around this expo and possibly cause me more harm. Are you with me?"

Sarah answered by following Emily's lead, RahRah in tow.

"Harlan!" Emily ran up to him, Sarah and RahRah in her wake.

He smiled when she reached him. "Your presentation was spot-on, far better than the little bit I caught of your predecessor or Jane's performances. If you don't win, someone has rigged the ballots."

"That's what we're afraid people might say if she does win," Sarah said.

"Huh?"

"Never mind about Sarah. She's just being her usual silly self."

Sarah glared at Emily. She didn't expect her sister to put her down in front of her boss. Emily wouldn't be pleased if she told Chef Marcus something disparaging about his favorite sous chef. Rather than discuss this further, she changed the subject. "They certainly have a great crowd out here today."

"They do," Harlan agreed. "You know, people don't realize how much Wheaton has to offer. With a little more development and marketing, we could easily entice folks from Birmingham and some of the other surrounding small communities to make us their destination for a day of shopping or evening of entertainment."

"Do you have anything special in mind?" Emily's tone was less than friendly.

Harlan's answer was drowned out by static from the large speaker they were standing next to. He started to repeat himself but was interrupted again by a shrill whistle emitted by the speaker.

The noise stopped as abruptly as it began. Chef Marcus's voice filled the silence. "Sorry about our technical difficulties. One thing the judges haven't had any difficulty agreeing on is how hard deciding the winner has been. After much deliberation, honorable mention goes to Fritz Handler."

Emily stared at the stage as Marcus named the third-place finisher. Sarah let out a hearty "Woohoo!!!" when Marcus called Emily and Jane to the stage.

"Gotta go," Emily said, and glanced from Harlan to Sarah. Her gaze met Sarah's. Sarah took the stare as being a "You can do it and you better do it" instruction.

Sarah nodded and took a deep breath before turning back to Harlan.

"Here's rooting for Emily," Harlan said.

"Not Jane?"

Harlan coughed. "Excuse me. I swallowed wrong."

"I thought you'd be pulling for Jane."

"What would give you that idea? I'm in the Emily and Sarah camp."

RahRah chose that moment to stretch in Sarah's arms. She shifted her hold and he pawed at the air in front of Harlan.

"Surely you're not holding it against me for telling you Jane had a legal right to RahRah?" Harlan peered over his glasses at RahRah and her. "By the way, what are you doing with him? You didn't steal him back, did you?"

"I only wish."

Harlan threw her a stern look.

"For some reason, Jane didn't want to leave him at the carriage house so she asked me to hold him for her during the competition." Sarah steeled herself to steer the conversation back to what she needed to know. "It seemed to me, you were awfully chummy at the Expo with Chef Marcus and Jane."

Harlan wrinkled his forehead. "I'm not sure what you're talking about."

"Yesterday—" she began, but Harlan cut her off. Marcus was announcing the winner. Sarah wanted to continue to press her point, but her moment had passed. She joined Harlan and the rest of the crowd facing the stage for the results.

Jane and Emily stood next to Chef Marcus, holding hands like the final moments of a beauty pageant. Unlike Jane's confident smug look, Emily's expression appeared anxious. She knew how important winning this competition was to Emily and Southwind.

"Let's hope Aunt Emily pulls this off," she whispered to RahRah. "And that Jane . . ." She let her negative prayer go unfinished, but she held RahRah a little tighter and gently crossed his front paws.

Harlan, noticing what she'd done, laughed. "Looks like RahRah and you got your wish."

Jane gave Emily a perfunctory hug, accepted her green runner-up ribbon and certificate from Marcus, and walked off the stage straight toward Harlan and Sarah. A sweet smile was pasted on her face, but its frozen position made Sarah pray Jane wasn't too upset at coming in second.

As Jane neared them, her gait became more determined. Sarah realized the anger part of her prayer had gone unanswered. She hoped Jane wouldn't take her disappointment out on RahRah.

Without any small talk, Jane held out her arms. "My cat."

Sarah looked for guidance from Harlan, but his attention was fixed on the stage, where Emily was receiving her first-place accolades. Even though he didn't seem to notice her interaction with Jane, Sarah felt certain she saw him nod slightly.

Not having a choice, she slowly held RahRah out to Jane.

The stiff-armed way Jane took him made Sarah want to scream. If Jane didn't show warmth to RahRah now, after having been away from him for such a long period of time, Sarah couldn't imagine how she treated him without an audience.

Jane twisted her lips into a snarl. "Where did you leave RahRah's carrier?"

Sarah pointed to the corner of the room "It's back there, out of the way."

"Wonderful." She held RahRah away from her body, as if he was a battling ram. "Hopefully, while you left the crate unattended, no little monster got the brilliant idea to crawl in and try it out."

"I think you're probably safe on that one."

Jane raised her eyebrows.

To Sarah, Jane's face transformed itself into an angry replica of Bill's when he would wordlessly chastise her with his piercing eyes and features stiffened in disapproval. Her legs turned to jelly. She willed them not to shake. Bill was dead. He could never hurt her with looks or words again. No matter how much of a bully Jane was, she was no Bill.

Harlan tapped her arm gently. "Are you okay?"

"I'm fine." She swallowed. "Harlan . . ."

"Yes?" His hand stayed on her arm.

With difficulty, she pushed the swirling thoughts overtaking her mind about his gentle touch away and concentrated on what she'd seen in his office. She didn't want to tell him she'd snooped. She needed another way to broach the subject. Maybe a small white lie would work. "You started telling me about an idea for Southwind you discussed with Chef Marcus and Jane on Saturday."

He took his hand off Sarah's arm and placed it on his cheek. "I don't seem to recall that."

"It probably was right after you talked to me when I was under the table."

"Oh yeah, when everyone was a little hot under the collar. I tried to calm things down. You must have misunderstood me, though. I told them I had an idea for

Southwind, but believe me, as touchy as everyone was, I didn't go into any details then."

"Did you later?"

"No, why?"

Sarah decided to try another tactic. "How soon do you think Chef Marcus will be able to reopen Southwind?"

"I'm not sure Southwind will ever reopen."

"What?"

"Well, Marcus was struggling before the fire. I don't know what the state of his finances and insurance are."

"Surely he had insurance."

"Probably, but even if he is fully insured, he may not be able to sustain himself and his employees through the time necessary to bring Southwind back online. In addition, being a tenant in the shopping center, he doesn't control the timing for fixing his space."

Sarah realized this was her opening to work Main Street into their conversation. "Maybe he can open right away in a new location? Emily told me Chef Marcus's ultimate dream was to move Southwind from the strip center into one of the grand old houses on Main Street. Any possibility of that happening?"

"Not that I'm aware of."

Sarah clenched her fist at Harlan's obvious lie and struggled to keep any sign of anger off her face and out of her voice. "In Peter's office, you mentioned Bill had come to see you about zoning regulations for his house. Wouldn't that be a perfect place for Southwind to move?"

Harlan cocked his head and weighed his words. "It might be, but again, it would take money and time to bring Bill's house up to code for a restaurant. Besides, Marcus would either have to buy it or work out a rental deal with the new owner, once that's established."

Now it was Sarah's turn to shoot Harlan a quizzical look. "What do you mean?"

"Exactly what I said. I'm not sure who owns the house."

"What are you talking about? Jane's his heir and owns the house. You showed me Bill's will." She puckered her lips in a pout. "I seem to remember Peter and you had no problems with the terms of any of her documents when we were in his office."

"Well, call it the lawyer in me. I'm still researching it a bit. For all I know, everything might belong to you." He continued talking before the shocked look she knew was on her face faded and she could formulate a question. "Even if Jane is the lawful owner of all of Bill's properties, I can't imagine she'll want to pay the taxes and upkeep on the big house when the animal trust only covers the carriage house."

Sarah frowned. "I can't either. I would think she'd sell it for a bundle and live in the carriage house for free. Without Bill, she's on easy street in her own right." Which played right back into what she hoped Peter was investigating: follow the money = Jane. Then again, maybe she was wrong. What if the documents weren't what they purported to be? The consequences of Harlan's research offered different possibilities than hers suggested. Hopefully, she could keep an open mind to conceive of every alternative.

Chapter Forty-Four

Emily ran up to Harlan and Sarah, clutching a white business card and her blue ribbon.

"Congratulations!" Harlan said.

Sarah gave her sister a hug and raised the arm holding the blue ribbon over Emily's head. "The champion! You brought it home for you, Mom, Southwind, and the tradition of apple pie. Oops, I mean rhubarb."

Emily giggled and pulled her arm back down. "You're being silly." She leaned her head forward so only Sarah could hear her. "But it does feel pretty good."

"Winning or beating Jane?"

"Sarah Blair, you're too much." Emily swatted at Sarah with the business card, letting it cut through the air without touching her sister. "Truth be told—both."

"That sounds like it calls for a celebratory drink," Harlan suggested.

"So does this." Emily brandished the business card again. "Thomas Howell gave me his card."

"Who is Thomas Howell?"

"He owns that new luxury hotel that opened in Birmingham, the Howellian."

"So?" Sarah had heard about the new hotel that

featured cat and dog motifs, but she wasn't familiar with Thomas Howell.

"Mr. Howell came to the Expo to learn about some of the new young chefs exhibiting here. Apparently, he's been quietly going around and tasting our food this weekend. After I won, he congratulated me on my win and invited me to participate in a competition he wants to hold at his hotel in February. It's going to be the climax of his year of kickoff events."

"What did you tell him?" Harlan asked.

Sarah noticed his smile had disappeared. From the way Emily was bubbling over, it was obvious to Sarah that she was oblivious to the change in his expression.

"I told him, 'Of course. I'd love to.'"

"Harlan? Is there any reason Emily won't be able to participate? Anything else you haven't told us?"

"To paraphrase Emily, of course not." He smiled, but Sarah couldn't help but notice that, other than relaxing his lips to force the grin, his neck and jaw remained tensed.

As someone stepped up to congratulate Emily, Sarah turned to quietly ask Harlan, "Is there something wrong with Howell?"

"Not that I personally know of."

Sarah waited. It seemed to her Harlan was weighing whether to elaborate on his statement.

"He's known around Birmingham for being a ruthless developer and he apparently has some aggressive plans for Wheaton, too."

A bloodcurdling scream erupted from the far corner of the room. Sarah's heart skipped a beat. She jerked her head in the direction from which the shriek emanated. A crowd was gathering around someone.

"That monster! I'm going to kill him! Grab him! No, not him—my cat!"

At the clarification that it was a cat at the heart of the melee, the circle of responders splintered. Some drifted away while others bent and bumped into one another in their haste to locate the errant cat.

Sarah knew, even before she could confirm through a break in the group of bystanders, the screaming woman was Jane and the cat, RahRah. What had the witch done to poor RahRah now? Leaving Harlan and Emily behind, Sarah ran toward Jane's end of the room using the outside aisle, her eyes pinned to the floor. "RahRah, where are you?"

She figured if no one in the more clogged part of the room had spotted RahRah by now, RahRah probably had taken refuge as far away from Jane as he could. Sarah barely missed colliding with a pocket of Expo attendees as she glanced up to see if there was a place or ledge RahRah could have jumped to. There wasn't.

Dodging other attendees, Sarah concentrated her search efforts on peeking under the tables lining the aisle and checking behind a stack of boxes piled on the wall near the main door. For RahRah's sake, she prayed she found him before Jane or someone else did. This time, she'd never give him back.

Almost reaching the double glass front doors, Sarah saw Peter push one open. "Watch out!" Sarah waved her hands to catch Peter's attention.

He waved back. As he did, Sarah caught a glimpse of tan flash by his leg.

"No! Catch him!"

Peter whirled around and shot a questioning glance at Sarah as she raced past him. She had no time to explain.

Outside, she stopped to get her bearings. There was no sign of RahRah, but she felt certain he was hiding nearby. She called his name and waited. Despite her repeatedly saying his name, no cat appeared as she searched the parking area. She checked one row and then another, peeking under cars and around corners.

Giving up, she returned to the front of the building. Peter, Harlan, and Emily stood outside the main door.

"I didn't find him. Did RahRah come back this way?"

Peter shook his head. She wasn't sure if the way he squinted and twisted his face was an involuntary response to the sun being in his eyes or her statement.

"We need to find him before he gets hurt."

Sarah was surprised by the gentle tone of Peter's voice.

"Each of us can look in a different direction," Emily suggested. "He can't be hiding too far away."

Harlan nodded. "Why don't you two go around the building toward the loading dock while Emily and I scour this side of the building?"

"Let's meet back here in ten minutes," Peter said. "If we haven't found RahRah by then, I'll call in reinforcements to help us search."

The four separated. Peter and Sarah stayed together at the front door. "Sarah, if you go straight toward the loading dock, I'll check out these overgrown bushes and parked cars."

Peter started to slide behind the bushes planted next to the door, but Sarah remained rooted. This was the second time today he'd mentioned the loading dock. Had he forgotten she'd tripped over Richard's dead body there? She'd never be able to forget.

Glancing back at her, Peter hit his forehead with his hand. "I'm sorry. I wasn't thinking. I'll check out the loading dock and the parking area the chief of security and I blocked off for our use during the Expo. You can look around this area."

"Thanks." Sarah slipped into the space between the

building and the entryway beds while Peter made his way toward the loading dock. She tried to make herself think like a cat.

"RahRah, if I had nine lives," she said aloud, "I wouldn't want to chance wasting one in this parking lot. No, I'd try to find a space I could crawl into and hide."

Moving around the plants, Sarah noticed a drainpipe coming down from the gutter at the corner of the building. Its bottom was hidden by the edge of a large bush but she felt sure, if it was like the ones on a house, it curved into a drainage pan that might be holding rainwater. Sarah approached the pipe cautiously, keeping her eyes pointed down.

When she saw RahRah curled against the pipe, his back arched, she was too far away to reach him. She forced herself to move slowly, lest she scare him more. "It's okay, RahRah. No one is going to hurt you. I'm going to take care of you."

He didn't budge, but Sarah imagined RahRah was watching her every movement.

It felt like an eternity until she closed the gap between them, bent, and picked him up. RahRah didn't fight her. Rather than yell for the others, she simply stood in the flower bed and nuzzled him until everyone straggled back.

Emily was first. She reached out to pet RahRah but clearly thought better of it.

Smart. After being with Jane, RahRah probably was in no mood for company, even Emily. Sarah was happy to note that RahRah clearly considered her as family.

"Are you going to take him back to Jane or do you want me to go get her for you?"

"Neither."

"But Jane's looking all over for him."

"I'm not giving him back," Sarah said, as Harlan

and Peter joined them. "Jane doesn't know how to take care of RahRah."

As Sarah hugged RahRah closer to her body, Peter cleared his throat. Before he could say anything, she again declared, "I'm not giving him back to Jane. Surely, under the circumstances we can find a way to thwart the trust?"

Peter ran his hand through his hair. He exchanged a look with Harlan. "It seems pretty clear that Jane is entitled to—"

"But," Harlan interrupted. "If we all think there is a problem with the care RahRah's been getting, I don't see why you can't put him in some type of temporary protective custody while we try to persuade a court that RahRah deserves a different trustee."

If she hadn't been cuddling RahRah, Sarah would have thrown her arms up in joy. This was what she'd been saying for days. Unfortunately, from Peter's furrowed eyebrows, she could see he wasn't convinced.

"Peter, you'd be the first one to come up with something creative if we suspected a problem caring for a child," Harlan observed. "Why should RahRah be treated differently because he's a cat? If anything, he's even more helpless because he can't speak for himself. Remember, Judge Larsen is out of town this week. Do you want to leave RahRah in Jane's care for a week? Think about what could happen in seven days."

Peter swallowed. Sarah could almost see the wheels turning in his head. "Well, I don't see a tag on him, so I'm not really sure this is RahRah. I'll have to do some checking around as to which cats are missing and who might need to be brought in to identify him. It might take me a few hours or a few days. My jailhouse isn't the place for him. Any of you have a car here?"

The twins shook their heads.

"I do," Harlan said.

"Well, until a positive identification can be made of this cat, I think the three of you should get out of here and set up a temporary cat shelter for this little fellow." He reached out and petted RahRah. "Looking at him, I can see he's been an indoor cat. I'd hate to see him get hit by a car or be without food while I search for his rightful owner."

Still holding RahRah close to her, Sarah leaned over and gave Peter a kiss. "Our hero."

Peter blinked.

"Get out of here, you three." Harlan and Sarah didn't wait to be told again. As she followed Harlan, Sarah glanced back at Peter and wondered if he'd shooed them away so quickly to avoid Jane seeing them or so they wouldn't tease him about the pink tinge on his cheeks and neck.

Chapter Forty-Five

Emily loosened the clipped front seat belt of Harlan's SUV so she could watch him drive and maintain eye contact with Sarah and RahRah huddled in the backseat. "Now that we've effectively kidnapped RahRah with the chief of police's blessing, where should we go?"

Harlan braked to let a car out of the parking lot. "Someplace Jane won't think about right away."

"That rules out Sarah's apartment or your office. What's left? One of the extra rooms in Jane's house?" Only Emily laughed at her joke.

Sarah had no idea where they should go, but it wasn't the carriage house. She stared at RahRah. If a cat could trust a human to be his mother hen, she knew RahRah trusted her. That was it. "We can go to Mom's place in Birmingham."

Emily's eyes widened. "Perfect. Jane will never think to look for you there. I doubt she knows our mother lives in Birmingham, but if she does, she doesn't know where." She smiled at Harlan. "It's a good thing Mom is at the spa. She hates cats. Growing up, Mom claimed she was allergic to cats. We had dogs and goldfish, but cats weren't allowed to cross our doorstep."

"Maybe that's not the best place to go then."

Sarah laughed. "Oh no, it's perfect. RahRah's been there plenty of times when I've picked up something when Mom wasn't home. Besides, Mom's out of town. What she doesn't know won't hurt her."

"Won't she have a problem with RahRah's stuff having been there when she gets back?"

"We'll clean the house by then. We won't leave a trace and she'll never know."

Emily giggled. "I love it. What about food and the other things you need to take care of RahRah?"

"Jane didn't take the box of food and toys I put together for her. It's under my kitchen sink. Do we have time to get it?"

"I think it would be better if we go straight to your mom's. I can always run to the store and pick up some food." Harlan stopped for a red light two blocks from the Civic Center.

"Do you have the key to Mom's place with you?" Emily asked.

"Yes. I keep it on my key ring."

"Good. Use it." Emily opened the car door and got out.

"What are you doing?" Sarah said. She looked at the light. It still was red.

"The three of us need to split up. That will make it more difficult for Jane to find out we have RahRah. I'll go back to the Civic Center and get a feel of what she's doing while Harlan drops RahRah and you at Mom's. He can then go back to his office to figure out our next legal maneuver. Should Jane run into one of us, she'll never realize the three of us are colluding against her. Once things settle down, one of us can bring you stuff from your apartment."

"How will I know what's going on?"

"Keep your phone on." She slammed the door as the light changed to green.

Harlan pulled forward through the intersection.

"What's the best way to get to your mother's house?"

"I-65."

For the first few minutes after Harlan got on the highway, Sarah stared at the back of his head. She let him drive in silence, like a chauffeur, while she gathered her thoughts. "Harlan, why are you doing this? Can you get in trouble for helping me?"

He shrugged. "Maybe."

She looked at the partial reflection of his face in the mirror. "So why are you taking this chance?"

"Because it's the right thing to do."

Sarah leaned back against the leather seat of Harlan's SUV. Considering what she'd seen earlier in his office, everything about him at this moment confused her. She couldn't match the Harlan who was so driven to follow the letter of the law and care for his clients, including Emily and her, against a Harlan who possibly engaged in criminal behavior.

There wasn't much time left for her to decide whether she should let sleeping dogs lie or confront him about the papers she'd seen in his office. At the Civic Center, he'd kept a straight face while denying any knowledge of a Main Street development or the possibility of Southwind being moved into one of the old houses. And what about the discussion between Jane, Chef Marcus, and him? Whatever Harlan had said had diffused the tension of the moment. She sighed out loud.

Glancing at the rearview mirror, Sarah realized Harlan was watching her. She turned her head toward the window. What else had he fibbed to her about during the past few months? Maybe even her job had been a big lie. Perhaps Harlan hired her when no one else would simply to keep tabs on what happened with Bill's property during the divorce? Considering she wasn't secretary of the year, would he have kept her on after her divorce settled if he only hired her for ulterior reasons? She had a hard time believing that.

"Sarah? Earth to Sarah."

"What?"

"Hey, you seem a million miles away. Which highway exit do I take for your mom's house?"

Sarah looked through the window, trying to figure out exactly where she was. A flashing billboard alternating ads for an attorney, a jewelry store, and a local sporting event caught her eye. "It's the exit after the one we're about to pass. Go to the second light and take a right. It will be the fifth house on the left."

She swallowed hard. She wanted and needed to confront Harlan before they reached her mother's house. Still, what if the knowledge of Harlan's involvement in the development project was what had gotten Bill and Richard killed? If it was, and she revealed what she suspected, would she be his third victim?

Seated in the back of the car, she weighed the consequences of the confrontation going badly. Harlan could easily turn in any direction other than the way to her mother's house and she'd be stuck. Jumping out of a moving car with RahRah wasn't a viable option. No, there was no question Harlan could do something horrible to her and no one would be the wiser.

Well, that wasn't quite true. Emily would be able to tell Peter that the last time she saw Sarah, Harlan was taking her to their mother's house. Of course, Emily wouldn't be able to refute Harlan if he told Peter, "I dropped Sarah off and went for cat food. When I got back to the house, no one answered. I saw RahRah through a window, but no one else appeared to be there. I figured Sarah went out for air or to run some other errand, so I left the food on the doorstep. I had no idea where she went."

Sarah shuddered. If she pushed him too far, he might kill her in her mother's house and then tell Peter, "Through the window by the door, I saw RahRah lying peacefully on the hallway rug. I knocked several times and rang the bell, but no one answered. I never thought to look in any of the other windows. Maybe if I had, I would have seen her lying on the floor and been able to help her."

Neither scenario was particularly pleasing.

"We're here," Harlan said. "Street parking or the driveway?"

"Your car will be less obvious to the neighbors if you go down the driveway." After the words left her mouth, Sarah could have kicked herself.

Harlan pulled down the driveway and put the car in park, but he didn't turn the ignition off. "What kind of food should I get?"

"Excuse me?"

"Cat food." Harlan drummed his fingers on the steering wheel. "I'll run over to the grocery store before I go back to my office. Just tell me what kind of food you want and whatever else you need."

"That would be great." Sarah leaned over the seat and rattled off a quick list of items for Harlan to pick up. When she finished, she grabbed RahRah and her purse, slid across the seat, and exited the car.

As she started for the door to the kitchen, Harlan rolled his window down. "Sarah?"

With her foot on the first step, she turned back to face him. "Yes?"

"Is something wrong? Something besides RahRah."

She stared at him, weighing her words. "Have you forgotten Bill and Richard are dead and Peter doesn't seem to have any suspect except my sister?" Granted, Peter had admitted to her last night that he thought Emily was being framed, but he still had no idea by whom. And, as of this moment, Emily was the only one who'd been arrested.

Harlan grimaced. "No, I haven't forgotten. Believe me, I've been racking my brain why Peter has been so hung up on Emily as his primary suspect."

"Have you gotten anywhere in your figuring?"

"Maybe. What do you really know about Chef Marcus?"

Sarah thought about what she knew about Marcus. The things that came to mind were his size, balloon pants, and quick temper. "Only whatever Emily has told me about him and I like his food."

"Me too. When I realized things weren't adding up between what I was finding and Emily was saying, I did a bit of digging. According to Emily, he's an expert chef, but not so good with numbers. Well, that doesn't seem to be quite true. Apparently, he owned and sold a piece of the restaurant they worked at in California for a profit."

"Maybe that's what he invested and was losing in Southwind?"

"It would make sense based upon what Emily told us about him begging her to come home and help him salvage Southwind and his need to sell Bill a controlling interest, but from the incorporation and license filings I found, Chef Marcus didn't put a penny of his own money into Southwind. He had an equal ownership interest for being the working partner. From day one, Bill and a few others put up the collateral to get a line of credit at the bank. That means they were original partners and if the restaurant failed, Chef Marcus walked away debt-free."

"Are you sure?"

"Pretty sure. I've checked the incorporation papers and Alabama Department of Revenue records. During the period Emily thought they were losing money, Bill and Marcus bought out all of their partners except Jane."

"Jane? Jane was an original investor?" Sarah shifted her weight and changed her grasp of RahRah. Less restricted, RahRah stretched in her arms. She looked at him and an idea formed in her head. "Between her shares and what she inherited from Bill, is Jane the controlling partner rather than Marcus?"

"It would appear so."

"I can't believe Emily knows. She swears she didn't find out Bill was involved until after she already was working at Southwind."

"I'm inclined to agree with you. Which brings me back to wondering what other things Marcus lied to Emily about."

"But why? Why lie to Emily?"

"Maybe Marcus knew how she felt about Bill and for some reason it was so important to him that she take the job, he shaded the truth. Once Emily found out about Bill's involvement, Marcus was boxed into a corner. He invented a new lie to justify his first one. I don't think Marcus was lying about the business not making money, but part of the loss may have been money being siphoned off cash flow for the Southwind buyouts."

"What about moving the restaurant to Bill's house

and maybe doing some further development of the Main Street area?"

"Other than Bill coming to me with his zoning question, I never handled his legal work. People have talked about converting Main Street into an entertainment district for years, but I'm not aware of anyone actually going forward with their plans."

Sarah stepped back from the car. Up to now, everything he'd said was plausible and explained much of what she'd seen in the folders on his desk, but how could he deny someone was trying to develop the area around Bill's house or that he knew about it? The proof was in the papers on his desk. What possible reason could he have for not admitting his knowledge of someone's development plan to her? Suddenly, she felt a sinking sensation in the pit of her stomach. "Harlan, were you at the Civic Center the night Bill died?"

"Earlier in the evening. I was supposed to meet a client, but the client was delayed. I left long before Emily and Bill were there."

"Why were you meeting your client there? After all, wasn't the Civic Center closed?"

"It was a convenient location for us."

Sarah wrinkled her forehead. Just when she thought things were making sense, she was more confused than ever. "I don't understand."

"Most of the Expo committee and those cooking or setting up were down there at some point the night Bill was killed. My client and I both had to be there so it was an easy meeting place for us. The last time I saw Bill, well before he must have died, he was talking to Marcus. I have no idea if Emily was in the building or already had left. Anything else?"

He sounded annoyed. Sarah didn't care. Although

she didn't want to ask him about what she'd seen in his office, she needed to be alone to sort out what he'd said against the papers he had. If it still didn't make sense, she'd ask him to explain the deeds and diagrams—when they weren't alone. "Nothing else. I think while I settle RahRah in, you better go get the food and cat litter so you can get back to your office."

Chapter Forty-Six

"RahRah, it's a good thing Mom is on vacation. For it only being an hour, you seem right at home." Sarah leaned against her mother's granite kitchen island. "Mom wouldn't be too pleased to see you drinking water from one of her cereal bowls."

As RahRah lapped away, Sarah went to work on making a makeshift cat litter box out of a pink plastic hospital washbasin she'd found in a closet and the bag of cat litter Harlan had dropped off. "This won't be perfect, but it will have to do until we get you back to my house."

Finished, Sarah washed her hands at the kitchen sink. She peeked into her mother's pantry and was struck to see it was almost as empty as her own. Picking out a single-serving can of tuna, she opened the refrigerator. It, too, was sorely lacking in the food department, but Sarah found a full carton of eggs. "Perfect, there's enough tuna to give you a treat with your cat food and enough eggs for me to practice what Emily taught me when I make myself scrambled eggs."

RahRah stretched out next to his makeshift water and feeding bowls. "Guess you're waiting for that tuna, aren't you?" She opened the white meat tuna and drained the water it was packed in. Using a fork, she took a pinch of the tuna and put it on top of the cat food she'd already put in the feeding bowl. She wrapped and refrigerated the unused tuna before cracking a couple of eggs into a frying pan.

Sarah poured a glass of iced tea and sat at the table with her scrambled eggs, tea, and smartphone. As she thumbed through the pictures she'd taken in Harlan's office, the buyout list caught her eye. All the names on the sheet had recent dates next to them, except Jane's. There was no date associated with her name. The other dates fit the story Harlan had told her about the recent Southwind partner buyouts, but she didn't know if these were the partners he'd referenced.

Using her phone, she ran a search on the first name listed. A picture of a handsome man about twenty years older than Bill popped open. There were numerous citations referencing his name. Ralph Hightower. She clicked on one and saw him listed as a donor for the hospital's new cancer wing. Another click brought up contributors to the "Campaign to Elect Ralph Hightower." Apparently, he'd run for a local state senate seat a few years ago.

Luck was with her on her third try. She devoured a detailed article about him being a self-made entrepreneur, but nothing connected him to Southwind. Of course, that didn't mean he wasn't or hadn't had some type of connection to Bill. She couldn't imagine Bill not wanting to be in the good graces of someone who might be a state senator.

Finished with the article, she glanced at the second name on the buyout list and had a fuzzy memory of having just seen it. She went back to the hospital fund-raiser article, but that wasn't it. She brought the political donor list back up and scanned it against the names on the buyout list. She found the original name she'd searched and read the next group of contributor names: Anne Hightower, Peter Mueller, and a third name from the buyout list. As she read further, she realized the political fund-raiser for Ralph Hightower must have been some event. Not only was every name on the transaction sheet a donor, but Harlan and Bill also made sizable contributions.

Interested in finding out why everyone donated to Hightower's campaign, she ignored her eggs and began a more specific search of his name. She read several similar articles and then opened one that was only a large picture of a man and a younger man she immediately recognized. According to the caption, it was a photo taken when Ralph Hightower conceded his political race. It showed Hightower, the principal owner of RJH Realty, with his arm around his handsome son.

Staring at the picture, she heard a key turning in her mother's front door. Unsettled, she grabbed RahRah.

Chapter Forty-Seven

"What are you doing here?"

"Is that the kind of cordial welcome you give all of your guests?" Emily teased as Marcus, carrying a picnic basket, stepped around Sarah.

He acknowledged her presence with a quick "Hi."

"We brought you dinner. It needs heating, though." She pointed Marcus toward the kitchen. Emily started to follow him down the hallway, but Sarah grabbed the sleeve of her blouse.

"I thought we were going to keep my being at Mom's quiet."

"Don't worry. Marcus is safe."

Sarah glowered at Emily.

"Look, I didn't think Mom left any food in the house while she was away, so I whipped up a meatless lasagna and salad for you for today and tomorrow. Marcus noticed what I was making and asked me what I was doing. I couldn't lie to him, could I?" She peered down the hall in the direction Marcus had gone and then back at Sarah. "Well, could I?"

Considering the lies he'd apparently fed Emily, Sarah thought Emily could have done the same, but with Marcus in the next room, this wasn't the time to tell Emily what Harlan had learned. "That's debatable. What happened to the two of you not being an item anymore?"

When Emily beamed, Sarah groaned.

Marcus stuck his head out of the kitchen. "Hey, are you two hungry? I've got the oven preheated, but one hand won't do it. You're going to need to pop the lasagna in."

"Of course!" Emily started for the kitchen, Sarah three steps behind her. "I was just telling Sarah how we decided to take our break and bring her something to eat."

Sarah looked at her watch. "I'm confused. What break are you on? Isn't your booth still open?"

"Jacob, Jane, and Grace are staffing the booth until seven. We decided they could manage for an hour or two without Emily and me hanging around or getting underfoot."

"We'll be back in plenty of time to handle the final shift and to break the booth down. In the meantime, especially since we won't have any other time for dinner, we thought we'd eat with you." She reached into the picnic basket and brought out a bottle of wine. "Marcus thought we should have something to wash the lasagna down with."

"And to celebrate Emily's blue ribbon win."

Sarah took the bottle from Emily and checked its label as she opened the drawer nearest to her. She rummaged in it for a corkscrew. "Happily, there are some things we can count on Mom never moving." She popped the cork out of the bottle and handed the bottle to Marcus, while she went to the cupboard for glasses.

He put the bottle down to breathe. "Does your mother move things a lot?"

Sarah and Emily exchanged a look and both burst out laughing.

"What's so funny?"

"Everything except her kitchen is fair game for her to redecorate. I went abroad for the year before we graduated high school, but Sarah was still living at home."

Bringing the glasses back to the table, Sarah poured wine for everyone. "I'd always coveted Emily's night table."

"I came home for the Christmas holiday break and found Sarah and Mom had moved the night table to Sarah's room and replaced it with a small bookcase."

"Well, you weren't living there."

"True, but when I came home again for our graduation and Sarah's wedding, the bookcase was missing. Mom had put a hassock next to the bed . . ."

"And moved the bookcase into my room."

"Admittedly, she did put a lamp on the hassock. Unfortunately, if I bumped the footrest, no matter how slightly, the lamp went flying. For safety, I had to put it on the floor."

"That really doesn't sound so bad."

"It wouldn't have been if Mom had stopped there. Instead, she decided once I left for CIA and Sarah was married that with both of us out of the house, she only needed one guest bedroom. The next time I came home and went to go to bed, I discovered the bed was gone."

"What?"

"Mom put both beds in Sarah's room and made my room into her own personal den. She painted it mint green and outfitted the room with a comfortable chair, stereo, and a floor-to-ceiling rack of records."

Marcus laughed.

"You think it's funny that my mother completely erased my existence?" Emily said with a straight face.

At that, all three of them lost it so badly that RahRah raised his head from where he lay.

"It's okay, RahRah." Sarah threw out her uneaten eggs to make room for Emily to set the table.

RahRah cocked his ears. He assumed a resting but ready position under Sarah's chair. Sarah was amused. It was doubtful RahRah would see a crumb from the three of them, but she admired RahRah's scouting sense of preparedness.

Marcus stood by the table with the salad while Emily made room for the food. She picked up Sarah's phone and glanced at it as the screen lit up. Emily showed the screen to Sarah as she handed her the phone. "What are you doing with a picture of Jacob?"

"I found it by accident." Sarah took her phone and clicked off the screen, not about to discuss her discovery with Marcus in the house.

"Everything smells delicious. Marcus, what did you bring besides lasagna, salad, and wine?"

"Emily made garlic bread and I grabbed one of her rhubarb crisps to top off the meal."

"Sounds good." Sarah speared a tomato slice in her salad. "What do you two plan to do after the Expo wraps tonight?"

Emily tore off a piece of garlic bread. "Clean up and keep providing top-notch service at the Civic Center until the contract is rebid."

"What about Southwind? Marcus, when will you be able to reopen it?"

"Let's not talk about that now," Emily said. "Marcus, would you please pour me some more wine?"

Marcus complied.

Emily held her glass up. "I'd like to propose a toast to our futures."

"To our futures," Marcus replied with a tap of his wineglass.

Sarah followed suit.

After taking a sip, Sarah put down her glass. "So, what is the future for Southwind? Will you be reopening it in the strip center or moving it to one of the old houses off Main?"

Marcus ignored the guttural noises coming from Emily. "I'm not going to reopen Southwind in the strip center. Insurance will fix up the kitchen, but we'll probably do a neighborhood pub in that location. Our goal is to find an old house to reopen a white tablecloth Southwind in."

"Do you have a line on a property on Main Street yet?"

Emily held her hand up to stop her sister. "I think that's enough interrogation for one day."

Marcus waved her off. "It's okay, Emily. To be honest, I'm hoping when things settle down and the insurance money comes in I can buy or rent Bill's house from Jane. If not, I'll approach some of the other neighbors. I really think that area has the potential to become a true entertainment district. I'd love getting in on it from the beginning."

"Do you think you can get a good price from Jane?"

"Considering our relationship, I certainly hope so."

Our relationship? He *was* involved with Jane. "So, you're openly taking Bill's place with Jane? His body is barely cold."

Marcus's eyes flew wide. "Sarah, my relationship with Jane is strictly business. We're professional colleagues."

Emily glared at Sarah. "You're out of line. Are you trying to start a fight with us?"

"No, I'm only trying to find out the truth." She put down her fork and stared across the table at Marcus. "Marcus, why don't you tell Emily and me what the truth is? You're not exactly Jane's boss, are you?"

Emily turned toward Marcus. "What is Sarah talking about, Marcus?"

Ignoring her, he walked over to the sink and filled his glass with water. Marcus peered out the kitchen window at Emily and Sarah's mother's garden.

"Marcus, is something wrong? You're scaring me."

Rather than responding, he gripped the edge of the sink so tightly with his right hand that the knuckle on his hand whitened.

"Well, Marcus? Going to tell Emily the unvarnished truth? Even if you don't, it's going to come out, you know."

RahRah sidled over and rubbed his body against Marcus's leg. Marcus knelt, his face averted from Emily and Sarah. He stroked RahRah behind his ears. "I didn't think you'd ever have to know, Emily, but I guess the cat is out of the bag in more ways than one." He sighed. "Em, you knew I made some money selling my share of the California restaurant?"

"Yes."

"Well, when I asked you to come here, I wasn't exactly losing money like I led you to believe."

"What?"

"I told you the truth about Bill being a silent partner, but I never told you that Bill and Jane were my partners from the beginning. My interest came from being the working partner, but all the actual money came from Bill and four other people. Bill, three of them, and I had an equal interest partnership—nineteen percent each. Bill also put in a small amount of capital to buy a five percent interest for Jane so she could have a management say."

"Jane has been an owner?"

"Yes."

"Typical Bill," Sarah said. "Because he controlled Jane, he effectively had majority ownership of Southwind from day one."

Marcus nodded but kept his attention focused solely on Emily's face. "During the past few months, a third party convinced Bill that not only could we have a successful restaurant, but there was an opportunity to position Southwind as a hub in a planned entertainment district. Bill brought the proposition to the partners. I was as excited at the prospect as Bill, but some of our partners weren't. When they wouldn't go along with our plans, Bill and I worked out deals for us to buy them out. When Bill died, we were equal partners, but Jane still had her minority five percent interest."

"So, what you told Emily about Southwind losing money was a lie?"

"Not exactly. No restaurant is profitable at first, but we were on target to break even during our first year. Things changed in the last few months."

"While you were doing the buyouts?"

"That's right. As we negotiated with our partners, profits dipped enough to make them more than willing to sell their interests."

"Were you manipulating the numbers?" Emily stared at him.

His face took on a pained look. "Never. You know I wouldn't do that. It seemed like food and profits suddenly were walking out the door, but I couldn't figure out where. That's when I asked you to come back to watch over the daily management to help me stop whatever had changed." He smiled at her. "And just like I knew you would, you put your finger right on where the problem was."

"But why didn't you tell me about Bill?"

"Because you wouldn't have come. The way you felt about how he treated your sister, I knew you'd never willingly work for him."

"You were right about that."

Marcus spoke to Emily, seemingly oblivious to Sarah's presence. "But I wasn't right about how I handled things once you got here. It was a mistake to break off our relationship. You're a great chef and you command respect in the kitchen. I know I've screwed things up but, even with all this, I hope you'll give Southwind and me a second chance."

"I'm not sure. This is a lot to digest."

"Oh, my," Sarah interrupted as it hit her like a two-ton truck why Harlan hadn't shared what he knew about the plans for Main Street with her. "Marcus, if you weren't actually developing the entertainment district with Bill, who was?" She held her breath as she waited for his reply.

"Bill was partnering with Jacob on that project. Since Bill's death, Jacob has continued working behind the scenes with a group of other developers."

"Jacob?" Emily asked.

"Yes. You remember when he worked with me in California?"

Emily nodded.

"He quit the restaurant to come home to Alabama and go into his dad's real estate business. Apparently, they didn't see eye to eye, so things didn't work out.

He tried another venture that also failed and decided his best option was to return to cooking. He's the one who introduced me to his partner, Bill, and enticed me to open Southwind here in Wheaton."

Sarah got up and brought the rhubarb crisp to the table. She cut each of them a piece. "If you wanted to be on Main Street, why didn't Bill and you simply open it in one of Bill's houses?"

"That would have been a lot easier, but the zoning laws hadn't been changed yet, plus the big house requires a major renovation before it can be a restaurant or a bed-and-breakfast."

Emily glanced toward Sarah's phone again. "If Jacob was working with Bill to develop Main Street, why did he let you buy his share of Southwind out? Wouldn't it have made sense for him to own a piece of the new entertainment district?"

"Jacob never was a Southwind owner. He wanted to be involved in more than just Southwind. Jacob is part of a group quietly buying up land on or around Main Street."

Sarah reached for her phone. She opened the search screen. The picture of Jacob and his father popped up. She held the phone out to Marcus. "What about Jacob's father? Wouldn't he have been able to help finance the restaurant and the other aspects of Jacob and Bill's project?"

Marcus glanced at the picture and handed the phone back to Sarah. "When he came home, Jacob originally thought his dad's realty company would be a natural fit for developing Main Street into an entertainment district. He didn't count on his dad's loyalty to preserving historical Main Street. You can imagine his shock when his dad ran for the Alabama State Senate on a 'revive downtown and preserve Main Street' platform.

Mr. Hightower lost the election, but a lot of people supported his viewpoint."

"But not his son?"

"Definitely not. Jacob and his dad never have seen eye to eye on anything. That's why Jacob and his ex-brother-in-law are keeping a low profile while they move forward with developing the entertainment district."

Emily shook her head. She took a bite of the rhubarb crisp and put her fork down. "This isn't my crisp. Where did you get this one, Marcus?"

"From the big refrigerator at the Civic Center."

"Well, it's not mine." She pulled the serving dish closer to her and scrutinized the topping on it. "This one doesn't have a nut topping. I think it's one of Jane's."

"It shouldn't be, I got it off a shelf with your name taped to it."

"Oh, that's the problem. When we were setting up on Wednesday afternoon, she complained I had the big top shelf plus two more while she only was assigned three small shelves. Rather than listen to her complain all weekend, I gave her the name tape and told her to assign the shelves any way she wanted. Oh no, I wonder—"

"—if she didn't move your crisps when she relabeled the top shelf and Bill made the same mistake Marcus did," Sarah said, finishing her sister's sentence.

The twins stared at each other.

"It still doesn't explain why he'd have willingly eaten anything with rhubarb, though."

"Love sometimes makes you do things you wouldn't normally do," Marcus said.

"We should call Peter about this right away." Emily

glanced at the clock on the stove. "I didn't realize it was so late. We need to get back to the Civic Center." She started clearing the table.

Sarah took the plate from Emily. "I'll take care of this. Don't worry, I'll clean up and call Peter."

"Are you sure?"

Sarah nodded.

Emily handed Marcus the empty picnic basket. With a quick good-bye, he hurried out the kitchen door to the car while Emily hesitated by the table and picked up another dish.

Sarah took it from her and loaded it into the dishwasher. She shooed a still-talking Emily toward the door.

"I'll be back when my shift is over. Lock up behind me. I've got my key in case you go to bed before I get here." Emily stopped in the doorway and came back into the middle of the room. "I know I don't always say it, but I love you."

"It's mutual. Now, get going."

"Okay, but thanks again for everything."

"No problem." Sarah gathered the used paper napkins from the table. "Go. Cleaning up is the perfect busy work for me to do while I'm trying to connect the dots. After all, if Bill's death was an accident, maybe Richard's murder had nothing to do with Southwind."

Emily nodded and gave her sister a hug.

Chapter Forty-Eight

Alone, except for RahRah, Sarah rinsed the dishes and loaded them into the dishwasher. She tried to piece together the information she'd acquired but felt like a juggler throwing balls into the air. Keeping everything balanced in her head wasn't working. She decided to outline what she'd learned and then call Peter.

She grabbed a pad and pencil off her mother's desk and sat at the kitchen table. RahRah came and curled up with his head on her foot. She enjoyed the warmth of his little body.

Pencil in hand, she said, "Okay, RahRah, we're going to figure this out."

At the top of the page, she wrote Bill's name and attached her name to his via a line that went to the far right of the paper. Above his name, she wrote "Mother Blair." She connected "Mother Blair" to Bill with a solid line and to her with a dotted line. Using separate solid lines, she linked Bill to Jacob, Marcus, and Jane, and then used a dotted line to Harlan. She joined Emily to her through a thick line and tied Harlan to Emily and her with stars. Finally, Sarah marked the connections between Jane, Marcus, Emily, and the other Southwind chefs with squiggles.

She held up her paper. "No wonder I can't figure out anything. It's a spiderweb!" Frustrated, she added the cat to the bottom of the page. "Now, let's see how everyone fits in with you." When she finished, she chuckled. "Well, that pretty much makes the page unreadable. I don't think this cleared anything up for me. Maybe I'd do better diagrams if I did the relationships for one question at a time."

Sarah put her pencil on the line between Harlan and Jacob. "Okay, RahRah, listen carefully. Unless Harlan is involved in the development scheme, the only reason Harlan wouldn't have shared the folder materials and development plans with me must be attorney-client privilege. It makes sense because I know Jacob is Harlan's client."

She leaned back, trying to figure out why Harlan told her and everyone else about Bill raising zoning questions with him. Just like he wouldn't say anything about his dealings with Jacob, either through council confidentiality or attorney-client privilege, Harlan shouldn't have mentioned the discussion with Bill, either.

"RahRah, the only thing I can come up with is that, in Harlan's mind, with Bill dead, the random zoning question didn't outweigh Peter's need to know anything that might solve Bill's murder."

RahRah stirred. He strolled across the kitchen and pushed his nose into his dish but didn't eat.

"You still have cat food."

RahRah hit his dish with his nose again.

"Don't look for more tuna. You ate all of it. Unless you find a bit mixed in with your food, that's it for now. I'm not giving you any more." She stared at the

dish and RahRah and then jumped up and gave
RahRah as much of a big hug as she knew he would
tolerate. With Sarah holding RahRah's right paw with
one hand and the other bracing him around his mid-
section, they did a few "dance steps" around the
kitchen.

"You're a genius, RahRah! Harlan couldn't tell me
anything about Jacob and the entertainment district,
but he purposely provided Peter and me enough of a
tidbit to entice us to poke around until we found out
the details ourselves."

Sarah set RahRah back on the floor. He immediately tucked his paws beneath his body and assumed
a relaxed sphinxlike pose, ignoring his food bowl as
if he had never intended to imply he wanted more
tuna fish.

"Don't pull a Peter on me. That's what he's been
doing. Not digging in to find the facts."

With his head erect, RahRah meowed at Sarah as
she sat at the table again.

"Do you want to dance more? No? Are you telling
me I should keep investigating and trying to figure this
out instead of dancing?" She rested her face on her
hand and bit her lip.

When RahRah let out another string of sounds,
Sarah saluted him and turned to the task of clearing
her phone back to the first screen of the search engine.

She was about to hit go when she heard a text
coming in and saw it flash at the top of the screen. It
faded so fast she barely saw the message was from
Emily. More interested in continuing her investigative
efforts on this screen rather than backing out of it immediately to read Emily's message, she ignored the
text. This time, she typed "William Blair and Jacob

Hightower" into the search engine and concentrated on reading the different results.

Thirty minutes later, Sarah pushed back from the table. RahRah, who had curled back up on her, rolled a few inches off her foot, turned on his side, and struck at the air with a paw. "I haven't found anything new, RahRah. We're stuck here at Mom's until Peter or Harlan come up with a solution. You've been so good. Do you want to play?"

She picked up the corkscrew that she'd left on the counter and then rummaged in her mother's kitchen catch-all drawer. "This will do." She took a ball of string and a six-inch ruler from the drawer.

Sarah dangled the makeshift toy, the ruler hanging by a long piece of string from the corkscrew, in front of RahRah. When he swatted at it, she inched the ruler just out of his reach. He turned over and positioned himself to pounce when the ruler was dragged in front of him. For a few tries, Sarah kept the ruler away from him, but then she let him catch it. "Very good." She waited a few seconds before beginning the game again.

After a few more rounds, RahRah figured out that he could maintain possession of the ruler by keeping a paw on it.

Sarah laughed. "Guess we've had enough of this game for a while." She eased the makeshift toy away from him and undid the string from the ruler and corkscrew. "We'll play again later." She dropped the game pieces into the drawer.

Behind her, RahRah hissed. Turning, she saw he stood with his back arched, his body pointed in the direction of the kitchen's back door.

Chapter Forty-Nine

"RahRah, what's wrong?"

"I don't think he appreciates there won't be time for the two of you to play again," Jane said from the doorway.

Sarah whipped around to face her. "How did you get in here?"

"You left the door unlocked."

Sarah groaned inwardly. Emily's reminder today and in the past to make sure she locked her door came to mind. Harlan's, too. She promised herself, if things ended well today, she'd always lock and double-lock her doors in the future.

"Did you think you could hide my cat from me for long?"

"This isn't your cat." Sarah swallowed, thinking of how to add to her bluff. "It's a stray I picked up."

Jane walked nearer to the hissing cat. She stared at him. "A stray that just happens to be named RahRah?"

"I told you, this isn't RahRah." She blurted out the first cat name that came to her, which belonged to a friend's Siamese cat. "It's Siri."

"Siri? I don't think so."

"I know they're both Siamese cats, but anyone can see the difference between the two."

Jane kept her distance but scrutinized the agitated cat. "You're lying. I heard you call this cat RahRah."

Sarah moved closer to RahRah to put a hand on his back in the hope of calming him before he pounced at Jane. "I'm so used to talking to RahRah, I may have accidentally used his name, but you're a cat person. Surely the differences are obvious to you."

While Jane stared at RahRah, Sarah warmed to her argument.

"This cat is a tortie point. RahRah is a chocolate point. As you know, a chocolate point is far lighter in color than a tortie point. From the time RahRah lived with you, I'm sure you can easily see this cat is darker than RahRah. More importantly, look at the behavior of this cat. RahRah was warm, friendly, and playful."

Jane frowned and dropped her purse into the chair across from where Sarah had left her cell phone on the kitchen table. "You were playing with this cat."

"That's my point. Unlike RahRah, Siri needs to be entertained. RahRah loved to play with me, but he could play by himself. Think how he jumped on your curtain rods, played hide-and-seek, and made nice to you. Look at Siri's body posture. He's defensive. If you come anywhere near him, I wouldn't be surprised if he doesn't leap at you and grab that hideous green scarf off your neck."

Jane's hand went to the thin scarf loosely looped around her neck. She pursed her lips into a pout. "Enough of your games already. I overheard Marcus explaining to Jacob that Emily and he were late for their shift because they'd had dinner with RahRah and you at Emily's mom's house. That reminded me Emily lived with your mother, not you. One quick search of our employee records yielded her address."

Sarah tried to keep her features calm. She didn't know who to kill first—Marcus for his loose lips or Emily for bringing him with her to RahRah's safe house.

Jane planted her feet solidly on the floor in front of Sarah and RahRah, her hands on her hips. Her red hair and the color of her face blended together. RahRah growled from deep within his throat.

"If you're going to be like this," Jane said, "I'm going to have to call Chief Mueller."

"Why don't we do that?" Hoping RahRah would only stay on alert, instead of pouncing, Sarah stepped in front of him and retrieved her cell phone from the table. She tapped her recents icon and speed-dialed Peter's personal cell phone number by hitting the number she hadn't deleted since their last phone discussion. His voice mail picked up.

Crap. Sarah waited for the beep but talked into the phone as if Peter had answered. She wrapped up with a "Thanks. Please come as quickly as you can. Jane is trespassing on my mother's property and making crazy allegations about catnapping. She doesn't seem to realize she's the only catnapper here."

Sarah slipped her cell phone into her pocket. "He'll be here soon. Don't you think it would be better if you left now, before Peter gets here? You can make your false accusations that I've got your cat wherever he interviews you, but if you stay here, you'll be the one charged with breaking the law."

"Are you crazy?"

"No, I work in a law office. You're trespassing. You also came in here uninvited and you've threatened and frightened me so you've committed assault. I bet you're the one who broke into my apartment the other day to steal RahRah. You're the crazy one."

Jane stepped closer to Sarah. She raised her arm.

Sarah held her hands up in front of her body, while staying close to RahRah. "Don't touch me." Her voice was low and measured, without an inkling of the fear she was feeling.

Jane blinked and put her hand down. She didn't move. Slowly, Sarah lowered her hands so her palms faced Jane in a more open fashion. "If you leave now, all of this can be worked out. Surely you don't want to serve jail time because of a misunderstanding about a cat. Go now, before something else happens." She held her breath.

For a moment, Jane did nothing. Then, the tight lines of her face crumbled and tears welled from her eyes. "I don't know what to do. Before he died, Bill swore that cat was our golden ticket."

"How?"

"I don't know, but since the day Bill died, I haven't wanted to live in that house or take care of your darn cat, but he said the only way I could keep cooking at Southwind was to follow through with the plan Bill and he had."

The only plan Sarah could think of that linked Bill and Southwind together was Jacob and Bill's Main Street redevelopment project. "I don't understand. Has Jacob been making you live in the carriage house with RahRah in order for Bill's property to be the linchpin of the new entertainment district?"

"No, Jacob's one of the good guys. He even offered to help me move, if that's what I wanted."

Then who . . . "You said you had to stay in the house to keep cooking at Southwind. Marcus controls the kitchen at Southwind. Is he behind the redevelopment project?"

"No. How did I end up in this mess? All I've ever wanted to do is cook. He told me that if I stayed in the carriage house and took care of RahRah, there'd be legal documents that made certain no one could force me out of Southwind."

Clearly, Jane didn't understand that once Bill's will was probated, she'd own Southwind, no matter where she lived. Whoever was the mastermind apparently was more familiar with the legalities and the documents than Jane was. This wasn't the time to explain everything to her.

"So, who is *he*? This person telling you what to do?"

Jane pursed her lips tightly together, as if afraid to say more.

Sarah tried coaxing the answer out of her in another way. "Why are you so determined to work at Southwind? There are plenty of more established restaurants in the Birmingham area."

"Not willing to hire me." She sat at the kitchen table. "I don't have any formal training, but I've improved, thanks to Chef Marcus. Look at me, I'm no kid. For me, Southwind is my last chance to dance this dance."

Sarah slid onto the end of the other chair, avoiding Jane's pocketbook. "You're underestimating yourself. You've got me beat by a mile in the kitchen."

A faint smile crossed Jane's features. "No offense, but that doesn't take much."

"True." Sarah pointed at Jane's face. "But the idea made you smile."

As if understanding the tension between the women had changed, RahRah sauntered away from them toward the laundry room.

Jane used her fingers to wipe her tear-stained face. She swallowed. "I know Bill wasn't perfect."

Sarah refrained from nodding in agreement.

"But I miss him. Everything is so different without him."

"I understand." And she did. A part of Sarah wanted to comfort Jane, but there wasn't time for that. She needed to refocus Jane, whose gaze had wandered beyond Sarah, back to talking about the house, RahRah, and Main Street. "If it's not Jacob and it's not Marcus, who is involved with Bill and you on the development plan?"

"It's . . . Jacob's former brother-in-law." Jane averted her eyes as if she wanted to come clean but was too afraid to say the man's name.

Sarah quickly thought through everything Emily had told her about Jacob. She had no idea if he'd been married or if he had a divorced sister. "Jane, you have to tell me. Who is Jacob's ex-brother-in-law?"

Chapter Fifty

"Peter!"

Sarah gasped. "Who?"

Jane stared over Sarah's shoulder and jumped up. "P-Peter," she stuttered. "I was just leaving."

Sarah flipped her head around. Peter stood inside the kitchen doorway. This time she was glad the door had been unlocked. Considering he was off duty, she was surprised he was in full uniform. "You came." She knew from the shake of his head he'd heard her, but he kept his attention on Jane.

Peter crossed his arms across his chest. "Jane, it would have been smarter if you'd never come here."

Jane thrust herself near Sarah, her temper blazing as vividly as her fiery red hair. She poked a finger toward Sarah, who marveled at this Dr. Jekyll and Mr. Hyde transformation. "She kidnapped my cat. I want you to arrest her."

Peter gave the room a cursory examination. "I don't see any cat here." He moved toe-to-toe to Jane. "Even if RahRah is here, it seems there may be some question as to whether RahRah belongs to you. In fact, it appears the claims you've made about RahRah, Bill's homes, the jewelry, and Southwind may not be credible."

The color drained from Jane's face. "What are you saying? You, of all people, knew Bill's plans for me. You have copies of all the documents Bill prepared."

He shrugged. "They've been challenged. It looks like you may have falsified them."

"What?"

"I'm considering the accusations. In the meantime, you'd do well to go home and stay away from Sarah and RahRah." He reached behind Sarah for Jane's pocketbook.

Jane grabbed the purse from his hand. "We'll talk about this!" Head high, she left the kitchen.

The door panes shook as Sarah watched her best chance of finding out who was behind the Main Street development march out.

"Don't let the door hit you on the way out," Peter called to Jane's retreating figure.

Sarah smiled. The image of Jane being slammed by the door as she sashayed out of the kitchen amused her.

"Are you okay?" he asked.

"Yes." She stood and pointed to his uniform. "I didn't think you were on duty today."

He winked. "I was earlier, but I ducked out to watch my son's Magic City Invitational ball game."

"In Birmingham?"

"Hi is on the traveling soccer team."

"I didn't mean to take you away from his game."

"You didn't. They washed out of the tournament two to one because of a penalty kick."

"I'm sorry."

"Don't be. Like most of the parents, I was praying for a loss."

"What?"

"It's the end of a so-so season. We've been to so many games that the prospect of having to sit through another game tonight seemed like a fate worse than death. Better to feed them pizza and take our players home."

"But didn't you want to go to the pizza party?"

"Not particularly." Peter grinned. "My ex-wife is the team mother. Anne is in her element at team parties. As long as Hi saw me at his game today, Anne and a team party were more than I wanted to deal with to-night." He moved closer to her. "I decided I'd rather check on you."

She felt a tingle and didn't know if she should scold herself or go with it. "I'm glad you did."

"The minute I saw Jane's car in front of your house, I smelled trouble."

Sarah was confused. It sounded like coming to her mother's house was his idea. "You didn't get my mes-sage?"

Peter pulled his cell phone out of his pocket and punched a button. Sarah heard her voice coming from his phone.

He stopped the message. "I guess I didn't hear it at the game."

"So how did you know where I was?"

Peter lifted his head back and ran his hand through his hair. "I don't recollect. Harlan must have told me when we were talking about RahRah."

She knew from his body language he was lying. Why? Then again, maybe he was a detective and figured it out, like Jane did, but, in his case, it was because he cared about RahRah and her.

"Speaking of RahRah, where is he?"

"In the laundry room. Want to be his hero and rescue him again?"

Peter laughed. While he went into the laundry room, Sarah checked her cell phone messages. She read the text from Emily warning her Jane had overheard Marcus talking and was on the way. Sarah immediately texted her back: *Jane has come & gone. Peter here now! Other than Mom, is there anyone who doesn't know where I am?*

"Look who I found snuggled between the washer and the wall." Peter carried RahRah into the kitchen.

When RahRah strained to get away from Peter, he put him on the floor.

RahRah shook himself and then walked over to nuzzle Sarah's leg with his nose. She bent and rubbed him behind his ears.

Raising her head to look at Peter, she continued petting RahRah. "You told Jane her documents were being questioned. Did Harlan or you find something?"

"Yeah." He leaned against a kitchen counter. "Apparently, Jane's been scamming us."

"Really? On what?" Maybe she was wrong, but call it woman's intuition—once Jane started to cry, Sarah finally believed she was telling the truth. She hadn't stayed in the carriage house because she wanted to.

"On almost everything. A lot of questions have come up."

"I hope they include the jewelry she accused me of taking."

He made a check mark in the air. "We'll question her credibility on that, too."

"Thank you. What did Harlan find that clears Emily?"

"I didn't exactly say Harlan voluntarily brought any information that benefits Emily to our attention." He pushed a falling lock of hair out of his eyes. "I wasn't going to say anything yet, and I'll deny it if you repeat this, but it might be a good thing for you to hire someone else to represent Emily." He ignored her sharp intake of breath and the question she began. "Sarah, let's talk about something else. I've already said more than I should about an ongoing investigation." He mocked clamping his mouth shut.

She stood and took a moment to straighten her shirt while she processed what he had said. RahRah curled himself into a ball at her feet. She was so confused. Only minutes ago, she'd been convinced by no other than Jane that Harlan was on her side.

She needed time alone to think this through, but she got the feeling Peter planned to stay for a while. "Okay, new topic. Tell me about your sons."

"They're good boys. The pride of my life."

"You must enjoy spending time with them."

"As much as I can now that they're living with their mother. Anne prefers to have Pete and Hi spend time with the almighty Hightowers."

Hightower. Sarah racked her brain to remember where she'd seen the name Anne Hightower before. The contribution list. "That's it!"

Peter cocked his head in her direction.

"I saw your wife's name on a contribution list, but I didn't connect her to Jacob."

"My ex-wife. They're brother and sister."

She hesitated before slowly stating the obvious. "So that means you're Jacob's brother-in-law?"

"Officially was. Why?"

"No reason." Her eyes tracked his fingers picking at the butt of his holstered gun. "I've always been fascinated by how people here connect to each other. There's a lot of overlap between families in Birmingham and Wheaton. I'm sure you find that all the time in your police work."

He nodded.

"I saw a picture of Jacob and his father. The caption mentioned Anne Hightower as a donor to his father's campaign. Based upon her name, I figured she was related somehow. I didn't put her together with you or the rest of her family."

"You mean her father? Mr. Anti-Development?" Peter snorted as Sarah nodded.

"He almost won on that platform of his. Anne decided to take her maiden name back after the divorce. I guess she thought she'd politically do better as a 'Hightower' than a 'Mueller.'"

"Politically?"

"She's gearing up for a run for mayor."

"You mean we might have a mayor and a police chief whose family pictures share the same kids?"

"I doubt that. Anne and I can't stand to be in the same room together. We disagree on everything. She's her father's child. She wants to run on the same platform he ran on."

"So she was against Bill and you in trying to develop Main Street into an entertainment district."

The words were barely out of her mouth when she realized what she'd said.

Peter's hand was now sitting solidly on his gun and the vein in the center of his forehead was suddenly protruding. She tried to make eye contact with him to backpedal her comment, but from his flinty stare, she knew the warmth they'd shared was permanently gone. Or maybe it had never been there. Whichever was true, it didn't matter. She needed to get RahRah and herself out of the kitchen, now, somehow.

Sarah gently nudged RahRah off her foot in the direction she was walking. She bent over to the garbage can and noisily removed its top. She pulled the ends of the garbage bag up and tied the red closure loops of the bag together. RahRah sidled up to her. Using the side of her leg, she guided him toward the kitchen door.

"What are you doing?"

"I just remembered I opened a can of tuna for RahRah's dinner tonight." She reached for the door. "You know how fish can reek? Mom will kill me if I smell up her kitchen."

"Leave the bag and sit at the table."

She put her hand on the doorknob. RahRah was still by her foot. "Come on. It will just take me a second to run the bag out to Mom's can."

"I said sit down. Now!"

Sarah took a deep breath, flung the door open, and prayed RahRah would behave as he had at the Civic Center. She was relieved when her cat barely brushed against her leg as he ran from the house past Peter's parked police cruiser. Sarah tried to follow him, but she couldn't control her feet. She felt the muscles of her face contort. Her arms flailed, and she fell to the ground curled in a fetal position.

Chapter Fifty-One

When Sarah became aware of light around her, she made a futile effort to get her bearings. She had no idea how long her Swiss cheese brain refused to listen to her commands. Eventually, she moved her head and watched her legs twitch. Another attempt produced the same result.

She waited a few minutes more before she ordered her hand to touch her legs. At first, she thought her inability to move her hand was tied to whatever was going on with her head, but then it dawned on her she was cuffed to one of her mother's kitchen chairs. Peter sat across the table shifting a Taser from hand to hand.

"Peter." Her voice was barely a whisper. She licked her lips before using them to haltingly formulate more words. "What are you doing?"

He banged the hand not holding the Taser on the table. "Shut up. I need to think. You couldn't leave well enough alone."

She wasn't sure what he was talking about, but she obeyed him while she tried to retrieve her memories. The names Jacob and Anne floated through her mind.

She moaned.

He glared at her. "I told you, be quiet."

Sarah had no choice but to do as he asked. She wasn't responding fast enough to pull her ideas together. Suddenly, one thought no longer was clouded—he had to be thinking about what he was going to do with her.

"Peter, I won't say anything. We can stop this now."

"Not for you, we can't. Just like Richard, you had to stick your nose where it didn't belong. If you'd just let Jane have that darn cat, we'd never have gotten to this point."

"Because you were going to pin Bill's murder on Emily?"

He stood, leaving the Taser on the table just beyond her reach. As he paced the kitchen, she stared at the Taser.

"Bill's death happened by chance. We planned to meet to talk about another buyout. Emily wasn't supposed to be there, but I guess when he got to the Civic Center, something displeased him and he flew off the handle and called her to meet him. It doesn't matter. If you'd kept your nose out of things, this would have been over without our ever proving a case against her. Bill died from his nut allergy. The tox reports will confirm that and the medical examiner won't be able to say if Bill ingested the nuts by accident or it was a homicide."

"But people would still have thought her guilty—after all, she was there."

"Maybe, but she could say he called her to be there and note she gave him CPR. I would have said something, too, when I dropped the investigation, saying I accepted the conclusion that it was an accident, not a murder." He leaned over the table, resting on his hands. The Taser was only a few inches away from her.

"An accident?" Sarah shifted in her chair, hoping to get closer to the Taser. With her hand cuffed to the chair, she couldn't reach it without scooching forward. If she did that, her chair would scrape the floor and Peter would hear it.

A wave of nausea hit her. Sarah gagged. She grabbed for the edge of the table, hoping she could stop the room from moving in circles. As the sensation passed, she focused on listening to Peter rather than watching him again pace the room.

"When I got there Wednesday night, I didn't know he'd called Emily. I wanted to discuss our business, but Bill only wanted to talk about Jane."

"Jane?"

"She was upset, so he was upset. I don't know why, but he had a thing for her."

"She's a firebrand." Sarah's mind wandered to her marriage to Bill. "I guess I wasn't his type after all." She forced herself to concentrate on what Peter was saying rather than her random thoughts. "Why were they upset?"

"Bill was concerned because Jane was nervous about the Expo and competition. He refused to talk business until I tasted Jane's rhubarb crisp."

"What?"

"She begged him to give her his honest opinion of her dish and he promised he would; but, as he explained to me, he hated rhubarb so he didn't think he could swallow it, let alone be impartial. He wouldn't talk business until we tasted and discussed the rhubarb crisp he'd pulled from the refrigerator. We both took a forkful and Bill started having trouble breathing."

"You didn't call for help?" Sarah blinked a few times. Her head felt fuzzy.

"I was going to when I heard someone shout his name. At that moment, he gasped and was gone. I lay him on the floor to give him CPR, but I could tell he was beyond hope. I panicked and decided I better leave and let the other person find him."

"Emily?"

"That's who it turned out to be. I slipped into the shadows with my fork still in my hand—the only evidence I'd been there—and went out the back door. I didn't know who found him until nine-one-one was called."

"Surely you could have explained everything."

"If I'd called nine-one-one immediately, but not once I left. Not if I wanted to keep my job." Peter pounded his fist on the table. The Taser gun bounced slightly closer to her from the force of his hit.

She tried to figure out how she could reach it.

"I honestly don't know how I let things get so out of control." He surveyed the room. "If I'd called an ambulance for Bill immediately, none of this would have happened. Sarah, I never wanted anyone to get hurt, especially you, but you've backed me into a corner."

Peter stared at her with pleading eyes, as if asking for her forgiveness. She certainly couldn't give it, but she could pretend.

"I understand." Sarah wanted to say something else, but she suddenly felt very tired. She struggled to keep her head erect so Peter would keep talking. "What happened next?"

"Bill and I had been talking about him either selling his property or using the main house to move Southwind into, but if he sold, the carriage house needed to be unencumbered. For all intents and purposes, he already had control of Southwind through adding his shares to Jane's, but he figured that he could also get control of the carriage house back if he installed her as the trustee. In anticipation of their getting married and his changing her to the trustee, he had an attorney in Birmingham draft a new will and trustee form."

"Draft?" Sarah wrinkled her brow. "The unsigned ones in Harlan's office were marked 'Draft,' but the ones you showed us in your office were signed."

"And those signatures would have sufficed with Judge Larsen if Harlan hadn't started poking around on Emily's behalf. He complicated everything when he brought me evidence Bill had pulled a fast one on you with the carriage house and animal trust."

"Animal trust," Sarah repeated. She fought to keep her head from falling to her chest but couldn't do it.

"Harlan didn't tell you?"

"Tell me what?" Her words slurred.

Peter picked up the Taser and went behind her. He removed the handcuff and, pulling on her arm, yanked Sarah to her feet. "It seems Mrs. Blair named you as RahRah's caretaker."

"Mother Blair and RahRah." Sarah raised her head and smiled.

"Yeah." Peter steadied her. "I'll find him later. Now I've got to get you out of here."

"Where are we going?"

Peter rubbed his hand over her cheek. "I'm so sorry. I never wanted this." He push-dragged her toward the door. The police cruiser was parked in the driveway.

She dug her heels into the floor. If she allowed Peter to wrestle her into its handleless backseat, she'd be stuck until they reached his final destination for her. She needed to stay within the safe walls of her mother's house.

"Please, Peter," she grabbed her stomach, "I'm going to be sick."

He ignored her and shoved her forward.

She grabbed the kitchen counter by the sink. As she grasped the counter, a slight movement outside the window caught her eye. She looked away for fear Peter would see it, too. She clutched the counter as tightly as she could, but the hard end of Peter's Taser stuck in her back made her let go.

Sarah took a few steps, then deliberately stumbled. She tucked her head to her chest as she fell to the floor, rolling her body away from the window. Peter tripped over her but managed to stay on his feet. He seized the end of her blouse, but the material gave. He reached for her again.

Before he could get a firm hold, the kitchen door opened. Marcus, head down, hurled himself football player–style across the open space to head-butt Peter. Peter sidestepped, allowing an off-balance Marcus to ram the kitchen table, bad arm first. Harlan, who had followed Marcus into the kitchen, tried to rush Peter. Peter raised his arm with the Taser.

Sarah screamed. Harlan ducked, forcing Peter to adjust his aim. As Peter steadied the Taser, a tan shadow leapt across the room and sunk its claws into Peter's outstretched arm. Peter jerked his arm up but couldn't shake RahRah off. He swatted at him with his free hand, but RahRah held on as Marcus shoved Peter from behind.

The Taser fell.

Both Sarah and Peter dove for it, but Sarah reached it first. As she gripped the Taser, Peter slipped his arm around her neck and pulled her back toward him. She struggled to catch her breath against his tightening hold. Except for a few flashes and spots of light, the room darkened. With one final effort, she swung her arm backward and pulled the Taser's trigger before everything went black.

Chapter Fifty-Two

"Guess you didn't need the cavalry. Though I wouldn't try playing football if I were you. Two concussions in one week are a bit much." Harlan sat in a chair next to her hospital gurney. He put a hand on her shoulder to keep her from sitting up, but she pulled away from him.

She searched the triage room until her eyes landed on Emily. "RahRah? Peter?"

"RahRah is happily lying in the sun in your kitchen and Peter is a resident in his own jail." Emily leaned over the edge of the stretcher and took Sarah's hand. "He confessed to murdering Richard and zapping you. He apparently feels quite guilty. We've been waiting for you to stay awake long enough for the doctors to let us take you home. RahRah misses his mother."

Sarah ran her hand over her face. "How long have I been here? I don't seem to remember everything."

"That's because you did the almost impossible. You Tased Peter, managed to shoot yourself, too, and bumped your head again when you passed out."

Sarah stared at Emily.

"It's very simple," Harlan said. "Tasers have a stun

field between two electrodes. When Peter shot you the first time, both electrodes apparently hit you in the back. If you'd hit him with two electrodes when you pulled the trigger, even if you were touching, nothing would have happened to you, but you managed to be touching and to hit each of you with one of the electrodes. Consequently, you were both in the stun field." Harlan glanced at Emily. "Too much information?"

Both sisters looked at each other and then at Harlan. In unison, they said, "Yes."

Emily patted Sarah's hand. "Relax. It's only been a little while. It just seems like hours to you. The main thing is you're fine. The aftermath of everything should fade quickly."

"And you're off the hook, too," Sarah said excitedly, her memory returning. "Harlan, you need to get the tox reports. Peter told me Bill really died from an unintentional allergic reaction. You've got to—"

Harlan motioned for her to calm down. "Peter told the authorities everything about Bill and Richard."

"Richard? Peter said he put his nose where it didn't belong. And that I had, too." Sarah lay back on her pillows.

"Peter probably isn't the only one who ever accused the two of you of poking your noses where they don't belong."

"That's not fair. Sarah and I simply have a healthy level of curiosity."

Harlan glanced around the triage room. "I don't think this qualifies as healthy."

Sarah ignored Harlan's remark. Instead, she followed up on the question still bothering her. "What did Richard do that pushed Peter over the edge?"

"He attacked you on the stairs of your apartment. You surprised him by coming home from the Expo early when he'd gone to your place on Jane's behalf to get RahRah. When Peter confronted him on the loading dock about it, Richard threatened to publicize Peter's knowledge of and acquiescence to Bill's shady activities with his deals and the Southwind buyouts. Apparently, Richard did enough odd jobs for Bill, he knew where the skeletons were buried."

"But wouldn't that have implicated Richard, too?"

"Peter claims he wasn't thinking straight. Apparently, when he found Richard on the loading dock having a smoke and sharpening his knife, Peter's police chief hat went on. He accused Richard of breaking into your apartment and sabotaging the Southwind refrigerator. Richard didn't deny doing these things, but he suggested Peter look the other way, as he'd done with Bill. Things got edgy and Richard crossed the final line, according to Peter, when he pointed out neither Peter's ex-wife nor Ralph Hightower would look kindly on letting the 'Hightower' children associate with a dirty cop. Threatened with losing access to his sons, Peter lost it and grabbed Richard's knife."

Emily squeezed onto the stretcher next to Sarah. "Until Peter confessed, I completely forgot Richard took his knife roll with him when he left Jane's booth."

"But I don't understand. There was so much blood, but when we saw him, Peter and his uniform were clean."

"He got lucky there. His car was behind the loading dock. Remember, that's where the security chief and Peter blocked off spaces for themselves? Everyone was so busy with the Expo opening, no one saw him run to his car or go directly into his office and private shower from his reserved underground office parking spot."

"And the knife roll?"

"Could have been out of a TV show. The murder weapon was already in the evidence room, so he hid the knife roll in plain sight there, too."

Sarah shook her head, but the cobwebs remained. "But what made Richard take on Peter? Surely, if he knew Peter was involved, he would have wanted to keep him on his side?"

Emily fielded the question. "When Bill died, Richard weighed what would be best for him. He knew Peter and Jacob didn't own any land, yet, so their plan was still a pipe dream, but both Bill and Jane had boasted they controlled Southwind's future. That's why he allied himself with her against me. He cut the refrigerator cord and put out the Ex-Lax brownies to sabotage my management efforts and my participation in the Expo. To keep her happy, Richard even took a break from prepping spices and broke into your apartment to get RahRah when Jane was afraid Peter's stalling meant he was reneging on her having possession of RahRah. She feared he'd also take away the houses and restaurant."

The smell on the stairs came back to Sarah. "That's it. It was cinnamon and vanilla, not cologne. It still doesn't make total sense to me. Harlan, Peter and you were making me give RahRah to her. Why take the chance of breaking into my apartment?"

"Jane was afraid to wait in case someone realized all the signatures on the documents Peter had were fake. You should thank her for meddling. If Jane hadn't stirred everything up, I probably wouldn't have gone looking for the original documents and discovered the ones Peter showed us had never been formally signed, witnessed, and notarized."

"So, who?"

"Probably Peter on the copy he showed us or maybe Bill on some. It doesn't matter now as they were never signed in accordance with Alabama law. I got lucky when I recognized the name of an attorney on one of the documents and could trace the real will executed by Mrs. Blair. It left the carriage house and a funded animal trust for you to care for RahRah. The big house and her remaining assets went to Bill."

Sarah lay quiet, stunned. "Harlan, when you knew the documents Peter showed us were fake, why didn't you tell me? Were you going to tell me when you fired me?"

"Your job has nothing to do with anything. It's yours as long as you want it, but don't expect a raise soon." He laughed and then got quiet. "Sarah, I wanted to protect you, so I thought it best not to say anything until I put this to rest once and for all with Peter. Unfortunately, my desire for you to see me as your white knight backfired."

Sarah exchanged a glance with Emily. She'd been so busy fantasizing about Peter, she'd never considered that all the extras he had done for Emily and her might have been from an interest in her rather than their employer-employee relationship.

"I shudder to think what might have happened because I didn't realize Peter was involved. I not only shared what I found with him, but told him I was waiting for confirmation Bill never executed a new will after your divorce."

"Is that important?"

"Yup, the way I look at it, after we probate Mrs. Blair's and Bill's original wills and the animal trust, you'll be

RahRah's trustee, part owner of Southwind, and you'll own both houses, plus whatever assets there are."

"Does that include the bracelet I'm accused of taking?"

"Yes, but it's pretty apparent that was another fib designed to undermine your credibility. It's moot now, anyway. Whether you find it or not, all of the jewelry is yours."

Sarah swallowed, but Emily let out a "woohoo" whoop. "Just think, Bill's given you the chance to finally try to follow in Perry Mason's footsteps. You can do whatever you want. Maybe you should thank Bill for putting RahRah and you on Easy Street instead of Main Street."

Sarah rolled her eyes upward. "I think I need to thank Mother Blair for that."

RECIPES

Sarah's Spinach Pie

A family friend makes this with an honest to goodness thinly sliced onion and diced mushrooms that she browns in oil, drains, and uses in the layers, but Sarah's recipe is one of convenience.

   1 c. shredded cheddar cheese
   1 pie crust (deep dish)
   1 package Durkee's French Fried Onions
   1 can or jar of diced or sliced mushrooms,
      drained
   2 pkgs. Stouffer's frozen spinach soufflé

Spread a layer of cheese in the bottom of the raw pie crust. Spread onions and mushrooms next. Repeat. Retain some cheese and onions to top off the pie. Place thawed soufflé in pie crust and mush it around to cover the layer below. Bake 50 minutes at 350 degrees and then sprinkle remaining cheese and onions on top and finish for 7–10 minutes. For best results, let stand for 10 minutes before cutting. Delicious as a leftover.

Jell-O in a Can

In the 1950s, Jell-O and Dole Pineapple joined forces to create the Jell-O in the Pineapple Can recipe.

> 1 20 oz. can of sliced pineapple
> 1 3 oz. pkg. of Jell-O gelatin, any flavor choice
> 1 cup boiling water
> Optional: 1 banana or other type of fruit

Open the can and pour off the pineapple juice but leave the pineapple in the can. Dissolve the Jell-O in boiling water and permit it to cool slightly before pouring the Jell-O and water mixture into the can, over the pineapple. If desired, place the banana or other fruit in the center of the rings of pineapple.

Chill until set.

To serve, run a knife around the inside of the can and tip it out. (Before rimmed flip-top cans, one pushed the jelled mixture through and out using the bottom of the can.) Slice between the pineapple rings and serve.

Connect with
U s

Visit us online at
KensingtonBooks.com
to read more from your favorite authors, see books
by series, view reading group guides, and more.

Join us on social media
for sneak peeks, chances to win books and prize packs,
and to share your thoughts with other readers.

facebook.com/kensingtonpublishing
twitter.com/kensingtonbooks

Tell us what you think!

To share your thoughts, submit a review,
or sign up for our eNewsletters, please visit:
KensingtonBooks.com/TellUs.

Grab These Cozy Mysteries
from
Kensington Books